The Detective Joanna Best Mysteries
Book 8

The Covid Killer

Cenarth Fox

The Detective Joanna Best Mysteries
Book 8
The Covid Killer

First published in 2020 by Fox Plays
www.foxplays.com
www.cenfoxbooks.com

Cover design by Oliviaprodesign

ISBN 978-0-949175-65-6

Dictionary of Australian words

Here are some of the mainly Australian words/sayings in this novel.

ABC – Australian Born Chinese
AFL – Australian Football League
AFP – Australian Federal Police
Bendigo – regional Victorian city, 160 kilometres north of Melbourne
biscuits – cookies
blower – phone
codger – an old man
cooee – a shout to find or announce a location
DHHS – Department of Health and Human Services (a government body)
G'day – hi, hello
good-oh – expression of happiness
Harold Holt – Australian Prime Minister who drowned near the Heads of Port Phillip Bay
Heinz 57 varieties – a dog of mixed breed
ICU – Intensive Care Unit in a hospital
in like Flynn – based on Errol Flynn's life as a ladies' man, be enthusiastically romantic
kays – kilometres
loo – toilet, lavatory
Mallee – rural region of North-western Victoria
Melbourne Cup – famous horse race with 24 starters
mollydooker – left-handed person
Mummy/Mum – Mommy/Mom
red rover – rhyming slang for over
Ron Barassi – famous Australian footballer and coach
rozzers – the police
SIO – Senior Investigating Officer
Spark – an electric train
stir the possum – start a controversy
takeaway - takeout
the flick – the sack
Triple O – emergency number as in 999 and 911

For
Dr Cheryl Threadgold OAM
Writer, Broadcaster, Historian, Tap Dancer

Chapter 1

Peg panicked. 'I'll ring you straight back,' she said. Her incapacitated husband, Hugo, stared at his wife.

'What's wrong?'

'Jo hasn't collected Grace.' Peg hit Jo's number.

'Could be a simple flat tyre. We're talking Detective Senior Constable Joanna Best here, the safest, most reliable person in the universe.'

Peg stared at Hugo. 'It's Voicemail. What'll I do?'

His heart pumped faster. This was definitely not like Jo Best. If delayed, she would call.

As the grandparents worried, Jo was being held captive by a crazed gunman in a warehouse with grandson Harry in the adjacent office.

Peg left a message. 'Hi Jo, it's Peg. Hope everything's okay. Grace's therapist rang to say you haven't arrived yet. Give us a call. Bye.' She studied her husband's face. 'Did I sound rude?'

'Of course not.'

'If there's a problem, surely she'd let us know. Something's wrong.'

'Perhaps but we don't know for sure. Try and stay calm.'

'I'll ring, Jack.' She did and her son answered immediately.

'Yes, Mum?'

'Jack, Jo Best popped in and because your father's twisted his ankle again, she offered to pick up Harry and then Grace. The therapist called to say Grace is still waiting and I can't raise Jo. It goes to Voicemail. What should I do?'

'Give me a couple of minutes. I'll call you back.'

He was between patients and now conflicted. He knew the young detective was super responsible and would be the ideal person to care for his kids. He also fancied her something rotten. But something didn't feel right. He rang her number, got Voicemail and left a casual message.

Then he went to a colleague, explained the situation, and asked if she could take his patients. He didn't finish the request as she agreed without hesitation and ordered him gone.

In his car, he rang his mother, told her he was going to the therapist to collect Grace and would keep in touch. The tension kept rising.

He knew a great deal about cases solved by Jo, and how she clashed with violent and dangerous criminals. If anyone wanted to hurt her, it could mean his children might be in the firing line.

Jo's tasks were to stay alive, disarm the madman, and keep Harry's involvement to an absolute minimum. Cain Reid, the kidnapper blew it. He thought Jo was DCI Robertson's daughter and Harry was Jo's son; wrong on both counts.

Decades ago, Robbo went to arrest Cain's father, Nipper Reid, who in trying to escape, accidentally ran over and killed Cain's little boy, Nipper's adored grandson.

Now it was payback time; an eye for an eye, a little kid for a little kid. Jo hoped explaining Cain's mistakes would end the terror. She lost her temper hoping to frighten him into surrendering.

The gunman lost it. His planned, well-rehearsed scheme failed. He didn't want to kill the kid, any kid, and now when it came to the crunch, he grabbed the wrong one. The kid was no relation to the cop.

Not wanting to involve or frighten young Harry, Jo screamed with control. 'I'm not DCI Robertson's daughter and the kid's not my son.'

Cain absorbed the facts, put his hands to his head with the gun pointing to the roof and pulled the trigger. Jo sprang. They landed on the concrete floor and fought. Slaps, punches and kicks were exchanged.

Jo lost her grip on his right wrist and the gun was jerked around to face her. She kicked and the gun jerked up and discharged again. The echo of the gun went on and on. Then silence took over until broken by the voice of the child.

'Detective Jo? Can I come out now?'

The child was genuinely scared until he heard a reply.

'Hang on, Harry. I'll be right with you.'

The second shot grazed Cain's head. He died inside. Jo grabbed the gun, flipped the sobbing failed criminal on his front and cuffed him.

'Hang on, Harry,' she called grabbing her phone. She rang her favourite colleague, Acting Detective Senior Sergeant Deborah "Billy" Hughes.

'I don't want to hear from you,' said Hughes.

'Sarge, shut up and listen.'

Billy knew something was seriously wrong for Jo to speak like that.

'What's happened?' Jo explained. 'Leave it with me. And the boy's okay?'

'Yes but I need to get him away.'

'Understood. Help is coming.'

Jo rang the Carr household. Glancing at her phone, Peg screamed. 'It's Jo.' She went to answer.

'Stay calm,' said Hugh hoping for good news.

'Hi Jo.'

'Peg, I'm so sorry. I haven't been able to collect Grace.'

'Don't worry, Jack's picking her up. Is everything okay?'

'Fine. Harry and I were helping someone but we're all good and should be home soon. Please tell Jack I'm so sorry.'

Peg was thrown. She wanted to ask questions but her husband's face told her not to. 'Okay, see you soon. Oh, and you'll stay to tea?'

'Lovely,' said Jo not wanting to stay anywhere. 'Bye.'

Hugh was all ears. 'And?'

'She said she was helping someone, whatever that means.'

'And Harry's fine?'

Peg struggled. 'Yes but I know that girl, and she's either lying or definitely not telling the whole truth.'

'Ring Jack,' said Hugh.

Peg rang her son. He was near the therapist and about to collect his daughter. When told Jo and his boy were okay, the GP whacked the steering wheel with joy.

'She's staying for tea,' said Peg and Jack's heart skipped.

Relief washed over Jo but now she needed a way to handle the situation without the child in her care being upset or more upset. He must have heard the shouting, and the shots were deafening.

How can I keep his fear factor as low as possible?

She felt guilt and fear. *I've taken responsibility for this child and caused him to suffer possible lasting mental harm.*

Making sure the gun was secure; she examined the man who felt pressured to kill a child. He lay on his stomach, moaning softly with his hands cuffed behind his back. He hated doing what he did but years of pent-up emotion drove him mad. Jo knelt beside him.

'The police will be here soon, and an ambulance. You're under arrest for multiple charges including kidnap, and I suggest you say nothing until you've spoken with a solicitor. Do you understand?'

'Go away,' he babbled through tears and saliva, his misery obvious.

'Don't move,' said Jo and quietly approached the office while watching her prisoner. She stopped by the door and spoke in a playful voice.

'Hello, I'm trying to find Master Harry Carr. Is he here?'

The lad joined in the game feeling much safer and the sound of the woman he admired and loved gave his heart a boost.

'He's in here,' called Harry.

Jo opened the door and poked her head around the corner. 'There you are. How's it going, mate?'

He grinned and moved to her, stood to attention and saluted. 'Have you finished your special work, Detective Jo?'

She slipped into a serious mode. 'Yes, Harry; another few minutes and we'll be off. Gran's invited me to stay for tea.'

'Oh brill,' he said clapping his hands.

'First I need you to do me one more favour. I want you to sit in the big chair, Harry. I have a couple of jobs to do. Please.' He moved to the chair, sat and found his feet were a long way from the floor. She heard vehicles approaching and pointed at him. 'Stay there, Harry, and I'll be back in a minute. Okay?'

'Okay,' he said and smiled when she winked at him.

Two uniformed constables came through the wicket gate in the roller door with guns drawn. Jo raised her hands.

'Whoa, no weapons,' she said and produced her ID. 'Detective Senior Constable Jo Best, Homicide,' she said and the officers settled. She pointed at the prostrate gunman and all three cops moved to Cain.

'I've arrested and cautioned him. There will be multiple charges.' She patted her jacket. 'I've confiscated his weapon. I'm hoping my phone call will bring detectives and forensics.' The two uniforms were impressed with Jo's calm and thorough demeanour.

'Shall we take him?' asked a constable.

'Let's wait and see who turns up. But please, keep an eye on him.' She pointed to the office. 'There's a small boy in there and I want him to see as little of this as possible.'

Then the cavalry arrived. Jo explained everything to a DS, handed Cain's gun to a Forensics' officer, answered questions and then was excused. She collected Harry, shielded and distracted him and they both hitched a ride back to her car outside Harry's school. The ride in the squad car was a highlight for the boy. He was given a short blues and twos, and his eyes became like saucers.

In the car, Jo rang Peg and confirmed their ETA. The Carrs were relieved, and Jo was relieved but worried about how she would explain the last couple of hours.

As Jo drove Harry home, she tried to figure out a way of handling him. If he spoke of the strange van, the loud explosions and the shouted voices, his family would be horrified. But the idea she would ask him to not discuss it, frightened the detective even more.

It's like I've abused the child and told him it's our little secret.

'They pulled up and Jo wanted to ask Harry to let her explain their adventure but couldn't. Father and grandmother came to greet them. Harry was bursting. The adults turned to Jo who apologised.

'I'm so sorry, Jack and Peg.'

'Dad,' said Harry jumping with excitement, 'I went for a ride in a real police car.'

'Wow! You lucky boy,' said his father.

'Have you thanked Detective Jo?' asked his grandmother.

The lad turned to Jo, hugged her, his face looking up to the sky. 'Thank you so much, Detective Jo. It was a brill time.' Everyone smiled although Jo worried she might vomit. 'Can we do it again, please?'

They went inside to be greeted by Grace and Hugh, and the mood was relaxed and friendly. Jo never fancied herself as an actor but did everything she could to lie with conviction, make a joke of anything Harry said, and kept her explanation as normal as possible.

The adults sensed something was wrong but as Harry was bubbling, they asked no questions and talked about anything else.

The meal was fabulous with Peg apologising for her cooking. She was worried sick about her grandkids and favourite detective.

The kids went to bed and the four adults took coffee in the lounge. The Carrs were reluctant to ask Jo about her recent bereavement, and when she began to cry, they assumed it was the death of her fiancé.

Jack and Peg went to her which wasn't easy because she shared a two-seater with Hugh who couldn't move thanks to his twisted ankle.

Jack declared Hugh's death was not imminent but he couldn't or wouldn't hop up allowing his wife and son to attend to their visitor.

Jo recovered and despite the others saying she didn't have to say anything, she wanted to. What she said stunned and shocked them, leaving the Carrs speechless. Jo wasn't crying because of Pierre's death but because she nearly caused the death of little Harry.

It took the wind out of everyone's sails. Jo's tears refused to stop flowing. Peg squeezed in beside her. 'Move you great lummox,' she snapped at her husband.' He did a little. She concentrated on Jo.

'Now listen to me, girlie, what happened today was nothing to do with you, nothing.'

'She's right,' said Hugh.

'And what you did in saving Harry was brilliant, and what you then did in making him think it was all a big game was even more brilliant.'

'Hear, hear,' said Hugh.

'So dry those eyes, Jo Best, and know we think you are not only a fantastic copper but an absolutely wonderful person.'

The males agreed but Jo disobeyed Peg's instruction and cried even more. The praise was terrific but her emotional investment in little Harry was so great, the dam wall burst.

It took a while for everyone to find their own chair and for Jo to become less teary.

'More coffee,' said Hugh then realised he couldn't move.

'You idiot,' said Peg heading for the kitchen.

Jack wanted to give Jo a hug for friendship and romance but was wary of Jo's recent bereavement. He didn't know if her feelings for him were as strong as his for her and besides, his dear old Dad hogged the two-seater.

'What's the latest with this Coronavirus thing?' asked Hugh.

The others were glad to discuss a new topic. 'Not good,' said Jack. 'And especially not for an old codger like you.'

'Is this Project Fear, son?' he asked half-jokingly.

'Those with chronic conditions can ill afford to get a new infection, and many older citizens don't have a strong immunity which is why ventilators are needed with Covid 19. So I want you and Mum to stay here as much as possible.'

His father saluted. 'Yes, Doctor. Now, how much do I owe you?'

Peg arrived with a fresh pot of coffee. 'What's the latest with this Coronavirus thing?' she asked mimicking her husband and causing the others to laugh. She frowned. 'What's funny about a serious disease?'

Hugh explained. 'And Jack told us to stay locked in our bedroom.'

More laughter from the others as Peg poured the coffee. 'I'd rather have Covid,' she said, which helped lighten the mood even more.

'So what's happening at work, Jo?' asked Jack.

'Not a lot for me. With Pierre's passing, they've told me to take a break and attend to his estate and remembrance service.'

Silence. The others didn't know what to say. They sent a condolence card when they heard about the DI's death, and were reluctant to mention the matter until now.

'And what about your grandfather?' asked Hugh. 'How's he going?'

Jo's sadness increased. 'I'm worried about him. He's on his own and while my Gran had dementia, at least he could visit her every day.'

The mood darkened. 'If I can help,' said Jack, 'please ask.'

They chatted about Grace and her recovery, and Jo called it a day. Jack walked out with her.

'As Mum said, Jo, you did a brilliant job today and we're all super glad you were with him. Harry loves you and knows you protected him. He'll remember that.'

They stopped at her vehicle. The scene was on replay. She unlocked her car wanting to get going, mainly because she didn't want to embarrass herself. He opened the door for her.

'Drive safely,' he said.

She turned to face him, kissed him quickly and hopped in her seat. 'Good night,' she said and started the engine.

'Goodnight,' he said and closed the door.

She drove away and he stood there for so long, his parents peered out the window to see where he was.

Chapter 2

Early morning jogging worked best for Holly. It kick started her day. Take Bessie the Border Collie for her run, come home and feed the pooch, shower then breakfast for herself before heading to work. This morning was different. Same route and good weather but as she whistled to Bessie and ran across the foot bridge at the end of Avoca Crescent, the Moonee Ponds Creek displayed a new selection of rubbish. Shopping trolleys and stolen goods were occasionally found but this was different. The water flow was hindered by a body.

Holly stopped and peered into the concrete-lined creek. Bessie stopped, confused. Holly grabbed her phone, took a couple of photos and rang Triple O. She explained the situation, gave her details and was told to wait. Bessie barked.

'Come on, I want my breakfast,' she complained. Holly always carried treats for an emergency although dead bodies were new.

The cops were quick. Uniformed officers parked on the grass beside Pascoe Vale Road and hurried to the footbridge. Holly pointed. The male constable clambered down the bank, slid into the water and determined life was extinct. He yelled to his colleague on the bridge and she made the call. The constable with wet feet realised the amount and speed of water in this part of the creek would not push the corpse to the Yarra River and thence to Port Phillip Bay. He waited by the deceased.

Holly was keen to go and Bessie desperate. Having given her details, the jogger and pooch skedaddled. The police cordoned off the area awaiting the heavies.

More uniforms arrived—a dead body is not your normal shout—followed by DI Elly Rose and Acting Detective Senior Sergeant Billy Hughes. A team from Forensics turned up plus more Homicide detectives. Last to show was Pathologist Dr Petr "Rowdy" Laudi.

With the discovery of a body, the first job is to establish if the person is deceased. Then it becomes a juggling act. Can the victim be examined in situ? If not, how can the body be retrieved with as little disruption as possible?

The pathologist made the death official, and the decision was made to remove the corpse from the creek. It was examined on the grass not far from the busy road. Elly Rose wanted a simple confirmation.

'Foul play, Doctor?' she asked.

Rowdy, so named because of his taciturn nature, lived up to his nickname. His Belgian roots gave his few words a hint of an accent. 'This head wound could have been caused falling into the creek but there are no obvious signs, Inspector.'

'Great,' sighed Rose wishing her preferred pathologist, Dr Gabrielle Strange was the officer on duty.

Billy Hughes whispered. 'You're missing Doc Strange.' Rose nodded. 'But she could never have climbed down that steep bank.'

Rose continued nodding. 'Good point and we'd have needed a forklift to fish her out.' She turned to Rowdy. 'We'll await your report, Doctor.'

He raised a wallet. 'There is ID, Inspector.'

Billy Hughes collected it. The DI ordered the immediate area searched, and chatted with Forensics as Billy Hughes studied the ID. It was the ideal find with credit cards and best of all, a driver's licence.

DS Justin Fletcher and Detective Senior Constable Charley Baldwin were shown the licence with the name John Banks of 12 Leighton Crescent, South Yarra. There were three identical business cards in the wallet with the name *Advanced Security* of Greville Street, Prahran.

'Home and business, gentlemen,' said Rose. 'We'll take the home and remember, say nothing till they say plenty.'

'Ma'am,' said Fletcher and Baldwin, and the males departed.

Driving to the address on the driver's licence, Rose and Hughes chatted about a certain detective currently on compassionate leave.

'What's happening with Jo Best?' asked Billy.

'Have you spoken to her?' responded Rose.

'No. You?'

'No. I heard she went bush for a few days.

'How long is her leave?'

Rose made a face. 'As long as needed. But if she's inherited Pierre's estate, why would she ever come back to Homicide, to any job? The girl's as rich as Croesus.'

'Do we know she inherited his estate?'

Rose wasn't sure. 'We know his mother's dead, his wife and half-sibling are both on murder and conspiracy charges, and unless he's kept it quiet, he has no kids. Don't forget Jo's a lawyer so would know all about Wills.'

Billy took offence. 'You're not saying she agreed to marry a sick man to get her hands on his money?'

'I don't believe that for a minute but now we have fake news, your truth, my truth and *the* truth.' She turned the corner. 'I know nothing.'

Fletcher and Baldwin arrived at a building in Prahran. The sign *Advanced Security* was the one on the business cards. It was early and the door locked. They pressed the bell, waited then turned to leave when a middle-aged gent came up the stairs.

'Can I help you, gentlemen?'

The detectives showed their ID. 'Police,' said DS Fletcher.

Most people react in this situation. Owen Jones was most people. 'What's happened?' His guts began to rumble.

'And you are?' asked Fletcher.'

'Owen Jones. I own the business.'

'Can we speak inside, Mr Jones?'

All three sat in the boss's office. He was dead keen to know the reason for their visit.

Fletcher led the charge. 'Do you know a John Banks?'

'He's my partner. What's happened?'

'Do you know Mr Banks' home address and phone number?'

Owen did and rattled it off. 'Is he in trouble?'

'Why, should he be?'

Owen tried to stall. Before he said anything else, he wanted to know why the cops were in his office.

'Okay, you guys aren't here for a parking fine. He's my business partner and a mate. Why won't you tell me what's happened?'

Fletcher and Baldwin exchanged looks. They knew it was time.

'We found a body this morning with a wallet and driver's licence belonging to a John Banks. Can you describe his appearance please?'

'A body? Was he killed?'

'Describe your partner, please.'

Jones was thrown. He blurted. 'My height, mid 50s, short dark hair, bald patch, well built.' To the detectives, that description sounded like their man.

'When did you last see Mr Banks?' asked Baldwin.

'Yesterday, about 6, before he left work.'

'And where was he going?' asked Fletcher.

'Home, as far as I know. Look, was he murdered?'

'Why do you think he might have been murdered?'

Fletcher asked the question and Baldwin liked his technique. The dead man can't speak so put pressure on someone who can.

'I don't know. Look, you're cops in suits. This is not a mugging in Chapel Street.' Owen lost it. 'Oh for God's sake, tell me.'

'We don't know what happened, sir. The post mortem will reveal cause of death. Now can you help us with details?'

'Where was he found?'

'In the Moonee Ponds Creek in Strathmore.'

'Strathmore? What was he doing there?'

''We were hoping you might tell us.'

Jones shook his head. He appeared shocked. If this was a show to cover his involvement, he convinced the cops.

Baldwin took over. 'What did Mr Banks do here?'

Jones surrended. 'The same as me. We advise, quote and install security systems in homes and businesses.'

'And what was Mr Banks' role?'

'I told you, we do everything; the lot.'

'Any problems of late? Any customers upset with Mr Banks?'

'What, so they killed him? That's crazy.' The police waited. 'Okay, a few customers reckon the alarm doesn't work as well outside as inside, or we left a mark on their precious wall or whatever but we've been in business for years. None of our customers want to kill us. We get far more wine and chocolates than complaints.'

'Tell us about Mr Banks' family.'

'I only know his girlfriend, Liz. His other relatives live overseas in Serbia. He came here years ago, changed his name and started a business with me. We're doing well.'

'He changed his name?'

'Yes, it's a mouthful; Branko Bankowitz. People couldn't pronounce or spell it. Everyone calls him John.'

'*Called* him, sir,' said Fletcher. 'He's dead.'

DI Rose and Billy Hughes parked and walked to a single-fronted terrace house. Pot plants on the verandah, with pastel colours on the weatherboards, window shutters and frames. Neat as a pin it was.

'You lead,' said the DI, and Billy sarcastically muttered "Thanks".

Cops dislike, even hate delivering a death notice.

A striking blonde female in a black leotard and tights opened the door. The tears attacking her make-up suggested the cops were too late with their news.

Billy led. 'Is this the home of John Banks?'

'I know,' cried the woman who turned and went inside. The detectives exchanged glances and followed. The woman grabbed a tissue and wiped her eyes. She sat on the settee. The detectives identified themselves and asked if they might sit. A brief nod was the woman's reply.

DI Rose took over. 'Please accept our condolences, Ms ...?'

'Liz Delahunty,' she said and went back to her grief.

'We know this is a terrible time but it would help us if you could answer a few questions.'

'I knew something was wrong. He wasn't home when I went to bed and when I woke I thought he'd gone for a run. I went to the gym and when I came home he wasn't here. I rang his phone; no answer. Then Owen rang and said John's been murdered.'

That grabbed the detectives' attention. 'Sorry, who said he was murdered?' asked Rose.

'His business partner, Owen, said two detectives came to their office and said John was murdered in a creek in Strathmore.'

The female detectives doubted their male colleagues would ever say such a thing and knew if they did, their homework would be doubled.

DI Rose tried to calm the mood. 'Can you tell us about your relationship with Mr Banks?'

Liz exploded. A stranger, two strangers was bad enough but referring to her beloved as Mr Banks turned her shock into anger. Rose switched to the personal, the softer approach.

'Is John your partner, Liz?'

She nodded with a mix of tears and a runny nose.

'We're not sure how John died which is why we carry out tests. Did John have any medical conditions you know of?'

'No, we're both fitness fanatics. He was super healthy. He wouldn't drop dead.'

Rose added the odd pause between questions trying to keep the situation calm. 'And did he have any reason to be in Strathmore?'

'Unless it was for work, no. But they work on this side of town.'

Rose paused knowing her next question might send Liz off again. 'Did John have any enemies, someone he clashed with at work?'

The woman didn't react. She appeared concerned. 'I know he changed his name because there were people back in his homeland who didn't like him.' The visitors were fascinated.

'What was his former name?' asked Rose.

'Branko Bankowitz. He told me there were people back in Serbia who threatened him; nasty, dangerous people. The detectives took notes, thanked Liz and stood to leave.

'Can I see him?' she asked.

'Of course,' said Billy. 'Once we've finished the medical tests we'll let you know.'

Without warning, she exploded. 'You're not going to cut him up! No!' She screamed. The detectives both tried to calm the hysterical woman. 'His body was a work of art. He will never forgive me if I let you destroy him.'

It took a while and heavy persuading but eventually the cops were able to leave.

John or Branko's back story sounded as if it contained dark matter. This suburban murder, if it was a homicide, had overtones of a shady past in a foreign country. The term, "a nice, juicy murder" seemed apt.

Chapter 3

Jo woke and checked her clock radio. Ever since Pierre's death, she suffered mood swings resulting in restless nights. For a change, she slept well. She knew her planning for Pierre's memorial service didn't exist. She knew his Will could change her life forever. She checked her phone and wondered if it would ever ring again with a call from anyone in Homicide. Life right now seemed strange, was strange.

Last night she watched the news and saw the story about a body found in the Moonee Ponds Creek. TV footage showed people she knew including colleagues Elly Rose and Billy Hughes.

Will I ever work with them again?

She slipped into her running gear, tied her hair and hit the road. Living in Clifton Hill meant access to parks with the daddy of them all, Yarra Bend Park. Fitness was her drug, her religion. Not only did she feel good physically, her emotional and mental health improved.

Not going to work didn't sit well with her. She liked being showered, suited and booted, and wanted out of her flat. As she ran, she made a list of tasks to perform. Then it was into her car and away.

Her first port of call, the Victoria Police Academy, brought back memories. She trained here as a new uniformed constable and then returned for additional training as a detective. She made an appointment to discuss a remembrance service for DI Pierre Richelieu but didn't realise there were two possibilities; a memorial service in the main chapel, and a dedication service in the small chapel.

The building was built decades ago for seminarians. Victoria Police bought the entire complex from the Catholic Church which included its impressive basilica. To one side stood the much smaller Chapel of St Michael which housed plaques with the names of serving Victoria

Police officers who were killed in the line of duty. DI Pierre Richelieu's name was eligible to be placed in this small chapel.

On foot, he was en route to investigate a possible homicide in the Fitzroy Gardens when he became the victim of a deliberate hit and run. A car owned by his true love, Detective Senior Constable Joanna Best became the suspect vehicle in the investigation. The memory of the nightmare lingered for Jo.

The chapel could seat 500 and Jo wondered how many officers and friends would attend. She'd asked a few people if they would speak and everyone agreed. What was needed now was a date and a time.

Jo needed reminding of the side chapel, St Michael's.

'Would you like a plaque for DI Richelieu in the small chapel?' asked the administrator.

Jo was thrown. 'I would but can I let you know?'

'Of course. Now let's go back to the office and choose a date for the service.' Once done, Jo set off for a family reunion.

Being in Glen Waverley, it was a short trip to see her grandfather. She rang but he didn't answer. Worried, she tested the road rules, pulled up and knocked on his door. Nothing.

He could be out but I thought his neighbour did the shopping.

She went along the drive and opened the gate to the back yard. 'Pop,' she called, you there?'

'Over here,' he replied and Jo sighed with relief. But when she reached the vege patch behind the garage she panicked. The former detective was slumped with his legs on the lawn and his torso flattening the lettuce.

'Pop,' she shouted and rushed to his side. 'What's happened?'

Was it a heart attack or stroke? It was neither as he spoke.

'Old age, Officer. I admit everything and promise to come quietly.'

'Shut up, you silly old bugger,' she said, trying to help him back on his feet. He helped as best he could and once upright, they managed to "stroll" to the back door and into the kitchen. He sat and appreciated the hardness of the chair.

'I'm fine when upright,' he said. 'But once I kneel, it's a bloody struggle to get back up.' He grinned with a twinkle in his eyes. 'I don't suppose you have that problem.'

She made tea while watching him like a hawk. He waffled as if nothing serious had happened.

'Lovely to see you, Jo. I've been thinking about you a lot. Come on, tell me, how have you been? All that trouble with your Inspector must have been horrible.'

'There are no biscuits, Pop,' she said.

'Yes, I'm cutting down.'

'What about meals?' She explored cupboards, the fridge and freezer. 'Pop, what are you eating?'

'You sound like your mother; same words, same tone of voice.'

She sat beside him. 'We need a serious chat, DCI Robertson.'

'Your mother's a bully too.'

Jo came straight out with it. 'How about you move, Pop?'

'Move?' he snapped then became a knob of butter in a hot pan. His hands went to his head. He needed help. While his late wife lived in care because of Alzheimer's, at least he could get out and visit her. Sure her response frustrated him, made him weep. But now alone, he dropped his bundle. He needed help and now. Like many adult males, he was too proud to ask. "I'm all right, Jack" thrived all over the Great South Land, and the tougher the bloke, the more likely it was he wouldn't say boo.

Jo dragged her chair in close, grasped his hand, leant in and kissed him. 'I'm on leave, Pop. How about we do the rounds of a few places and find you the ideal spot.'

He nodded. No way would he cry. 'Thanks, Love, I'd like that.'

They talked about what he would and wouldn't like, and where he'd like to live. Jo would make the appointments then drive him. She asked if he was happy to have his estate agent ex-son-in-law, Jo's father, handle the sale of his home.

'Will he do mate's rates?' asked Pop.

'My father has no mates.'

They both laughed. She rang a local Chinese restaurant, ordered dishes she knew he liked and paid to have them delivered.

He came close to shedding a tear when told what to expect. 'I'll be back in the morning, Pop, and we'll find your new forever home.'

'You haven't told me about your cases.'

'Tomorrow,' she said, kissed him and he followed her to the front door. At the gate she waved; he waved, and finally managed to cry. He moved into this house 51 years ago.

Jo headed home. She made a slight detour and drove to East Melbourne and to a block of apartments, one of which she would soon own. Probate on Pierre's Will still needed attention and she wondered if objections would be raised from France. But if not, here was an apartment worth millions and yes, she would soon be the owner.

She parked and walked. It was an expensive area. She stopped in different places and gazed across the roads at the building. It exuded age, class and inside, the quality shone.

Do I want to live here?

Back in her car, she prepared to head home when her phone rang.

'Sarge,' she said checking her caller ID. 'I was about to ring you.'

'Oh,' said Billy Hughes, 'and why?'

'Pierre's memorial service is at the Academy, two weeks on Friday.'

'Great.'

'Can you spread the word, please?'

'Of course.'

'So what's happening at Homicide? Did I see you found a body in the Moonee Ponds Creek?'

'Yes and it's tricky. Victim came from war-torn Eastern Europe with history in drugs and war crimes. If his enemies in the old country found him, we could have a revenge hitman slip Down Under, or even a local assassin complete the payback in downtown Strathmore.'

'I could solve it in ten minutes.'

'Ten? Wow, once you would have said five.' They laughed. 'I rang to see how you're going. What are you doing? Where are you?'

'Sitting in my car outside Pierre's apartment in East Melbourne.' Billy went quiet. 'Sarge, you still there?'

'Still here. How have you been?'

'Okay thanks but I'm still not sure what I'm going to do.'

'Why don't you come in and have a chat?'

'Did DI Rose put you up to this?'

'No, but we all miss you. If anyone knows about you being a suspect in Pierre's hit run and his death, we do. You've been through the mill.'

'Not to mention those responsible trying to knock me off.'

Billy stirred. 'God, you've always been a drama queen.'

Jo purred inside. She needed a friendly voice, and the flicker of hope about resuming her career at Homicide made her smile.

Jo paused. 'I'll think about it, Sarge. DI Rose's old boss, DCI Robertson is in a spot of trouble, and I'm helping him move to a retirement village. I'll give you a ring next week.'

'Don't leave it too long. A good detective never loses their instinct but they can lose their desire. Ciao.'

Jo thought about that. So much was new in her life. She headed home then made a third detour. She hadn't seen or heard from Michael Chan in a while and wanted to catch up. Theirs was a unique relationship. Great partners in solving crime. Good friends but non-existent lovers. *What's he doing?*

She thought about ringing first then decided against it. As usual with all his whiz-bang IT equipment, he knew she was on the property, and opened the door smiling.

'Detective Best; long time no see, how the heck are you?'

They did the cheek kiss routine then sat in Michael's intimate barn. Big, yes, but with nooks and crannies and one friendly cat, it was cosy.

They chatted over coffee and both wanted to know what the other was doing. Jo had nothing police wise to report so it was Michael's turn. His news grabbed Jo's attention, even worried her.

'I bumped into a fellow ABC, a girl I knew from uni. Cathy Feng's a nurse and super busy now with this Covid thing. We went for coffee and she told me a fascinating tale. Her mother recently died, and on her death bed told Cathy she was adopted as a baby.'

'Wow,' said Jo, 'that's scary.'

'Cathy's mother was single. When Cathy was a teen, her mother said she was in a relationship with a man who left before Cathy was born.'

'So she never knew her father?'

'Never. Then last year, Cathy's mother got a bad cancer diagnosis. The doctors told Cathy the end was nigh. That night her mother confessed. What she said all those years ago about the relationship with a man wasn't true. "I am not your mother," she said.'

Jo whistled. 'Did she name the birth mother?'

'No and being stunned, Cathy let her mother sleep.'

'Don't tell me, she died that night.'

Michael nodded. 'So Cathy discovers her single Mum isn't a blood relative, and dies without naming the birth mother. Cathy is flattened and now, weeks later, has decided to search for her real mother.'

'And father?'

'Sure but she's got next to nothing to go on. Her birth certificate tells her little. Her mother's name, Gloria Feng, is there but no father's name. And wait for it, Cathy's date of birth is February 29, 1992.'

'She's a Leap Year baby and still a little kid.'

'No relatives she knows about, so the poor girl is up against it.'

'Which is where ace investigator, Michael Chan, steps in?'

'I wish. Cathy went online searching for private investigators. She struggled as most were not interested or charged a mint. One PI gave her a name and this is where the story gets interesting.'

'You mean it's not already?'

'The PI Cathy found is an absolute gem.' Michael paused. He could hardly wait to continue his tale.

'I'm expecting something impressive, Michael.'

Out came his half grin. 'The PI's name is Starlight Freeman.'

'Starlight? That's his given name?'

'That's *her* given name.'

'You're kidding?'

'It gets better. Cathy has a phone interview, thinks the woman is the best PI in town, and is about to meet her and sign a contract. Out of the blue we bump into one another and she asks me to go with her.'

'To meet the PI?'

'Being an old friend and all-round nice guy, I think, why not, and so off we go to meet Starlight at *All Round Investigations*.'

He paused and grinned. 'Come on,' complained Jo, 'tell me.'

'She's Methuselah's niece, about to retire, with an office borrowed from a Dickens' novel. Can you believe there are filing cabinets?'

Jo noted Michael's enthusiasm. *Is it because of the time-machine madam or has he found a more interesting partner?*

He bubbled away. 'She's still using Manilla folders, *paper* notepads, and a telephone she bought from a car boot sale under Noah's ark.' Jo laughed. Michael told interesting tales and always with humour. 'I thought our Uber driver was H. G. Wells.'

'I hope you didn't make derogatory comments.'

'Starlight owned this Amstrad PC which is probably worth a fortune today as an antique. I asked her about it and she said it was useless. She pointed at a manual typewriter and told me it never breaks down, doesn't need electricity, and can "shoe up" in an instant.'

'Shoe up?' He nodded. 'As in boot up?' He nodded and his half grin opened up to three-quarters. 'As usual, Michael, your tales are fascinating, but what about your friend's birth mother?'

He pointed a finger at her. 'Good point, Holmes. I could see Starlight might need a helping hand checking records, reports, et cetera and then thought; I've been trained by the Best detective. I've watched her up close and personal as she's cracked all sorts of cases. It's time I stepped out of Watson's shoes and stepped into Sherlock's.'

'You're kidding,' said Jo and it sounded like she didn't believe he could succeed. He reacted.

'What, you don't think a nerd like me can solve a mystery?'

Jo backpedalled. 'No, Michael, you know I worship your brain.'

Yeah but not my body, he thought.

'No, I'm just surprised you've gone from homicide to missing persons. Surely your career move would be to international espionage or virtual reality in the stratosphere. NASA needs you, Michael.'

He became shirty. 'Detective, I do believe you're taking the piss.'

She wasn't but it sounded like it. She became defensive. 'I'm not. Michael, I'm pleased for you and your friend.'

'You're jealous I've branched out on my own. The office boy has stepped up and doesn't need big sister's approval.'

Silence. Both said things they didn't mean leaving the atmosphere simmering with a soupcon of anger and a sprinkling of confusion.

Jo stood. 'I wish you well, Michael and particularly your friend.'

'Cathy,' he said and stood, annoyed she hadn't used her name.

'Cathy.' She patted Alan then headed for the door. 'Let me know how you get on.'

She left with troubled emotions. He suffered the same malady. It was their first disagreement with feeling.

Chapter 4

Homicide detectives gathered in the Incident Room with DI Rose calling them to order. DI Callum Blunt sat at the back still smarting from his latest failure. Far worse was the fact that the bitch Best got the bloody chocolates. Losing was bad enough but not to her; shit and double shit.

Rose announced Billy Hughes as the SIO for the Strathmore homicide, and Blunt felt okay not having the spotlight on him after his concrete shoes episode.

Billy addressed the group. 'Our victim was known as John Banks who was once Branko Bankowitz. Apparently, yet to be confirmed, John as Branko fell foul of the law or fellow crims or both back in his homeland of Serbia.'

Charley Baldwin interrupted. 'I speak the language fluently, Sarge, and my passport is up to date.'

A reaction of ridicule and mockery began and Baldwin enjoyed the interest to his attempt at humour.

'We're getting ahead of ourselves,' said Billy Hughes. 'This may not be a homicide. Until Dr Laudi completes the PM and we know the cause of death, we may not be required.'

DS Justin Fletcher was careful in asking his question. 'Will Doctor Strange be involved in the PM?'

Everyone knew this was a loaded question. Rowdy Laudi was yet to convince detectives he was up to the mark, whereas Gabrielle Strange's reputation for finding clues and giving investigators the lead or even leads was what they needed and appreciated.

Hughes was on the ball. 'You can tell us, DS Fletcher, as you and Senior Constable Baldwin are off to interview the pathologist. Oh and Charley, you won't need your passport for this trip.'

Everyone laughed.

'Assuming Mr Banks was murdered, we have several leads one of which includes allegations about his shady past in Serbia. So, what do we know?'

DS Fletcher explained. 'Charley and I went to *Advanced Security* where we met the boss, Owen Jones.' Fletcher clicked a handheld device and a screenshot of the landing page from the web site of *Advanced Security* appeared on the screen.

'It's a two-man operation, Jones and our Mr Banks. They install security systems in homes and businesses. Seem to be doing all right. Jones appeared genuinely shocked at his mate's demise, and he volunteered details about Banks' shady past.'

'Anything else?' She stared at Baldwin. 'Charley?'

'Jones said there was no security work in Strathmore.'

Billy sniffed. 'DI Rose and I interviewed his partner. Ma'am?'

'Her name is Liz Delahunty and Jones rang her so she knew Banks was dead before we arrived. She didn't know why he was in Strathmore. Most of their work is on the other side of town. She too mentioned his name change and the problems with locals back home.'

Billy Hughes continued. 'The girlfriend's a fit woman and so is Banks. With no outward signs of a fight on his body, the cause of death as Alice would say is curiouser and curiouser.'

That remark didn't register with many detectives. A quote from Ron Barassi might have gained a greater recognition.

'So,' said Billy, 'we want cause of death from the pathologist, and if it's a homicide, the fun starts. Then workmates, clients, friends, family, and girlfriend are all worth a look but so too is his fascinating history in Serbia. Questions or comments?'

DI Blunt decided to come out of his hidey hole. 'What are we doing about this Covid thing?'

It was a good question. The Coronavirus headlines were big and constant. First found in China, the virus spread rapidly across the globe. The fact that Callum Blunt raised the matter was even more remarkable.

'Thank you, DI Blunt,' said Rose. 'The top brass are concerned, wanting us to take precautions like hand washing, keeping apart in what is called social distancing, and even wearing masks.'

That stirred the squad. 'Masks?' scoffed several.

'You want us to join the Bank Robbers Union?' asked Baldwin.

'I'm only reporting what's come down from on high. Now let's get the results of the PM and, if it's a homicide, we start work.'

Fletcher and Baldwin arrived as Dr Laudi was tapping on his keyboard.

'G'day Doctor,' said Fletcher not comfortable using any first or nickname for the quietly spoken pathologist.

'Gentlemen, I have no smoking-gun.'

'Okay,' said Fletcher, 'but do you have cause of death?'

'A couple of theories, the first of which is a heart attack.'

Both detectives frowned. 'But he was relatively young and super fit,' countered Fletcher.

Laudi shrugged. 'There is considerable damage to his heart although what caused it, I cannot say. He has bruising to the side of his head which I suggest was caused by falling in the concrete based creek. Heart attack, stumble, hit head, die,' he explained.

'Did he drown?' asked Baldwin.

'No. When found his face was under water but I think he might have struggled, died of the heart attack, and then slumped with his face falling under the water. But his lungs were water free.'

'Nothing else?' asked Fletcher thinking Dr Strange would never offer so little or such unhelpful information.

'There are no cuts or bruises, no broken bones and until there's a full toxicology report, we're all none the wiser.'

This was not the answer the detectives wanted—homicide or accident, please Mr Pathologist.

'When will you know?' asked Baldwin.

Rowdy shrugged. 'These matters take time, gentlemen.'

'So apart from his heart, all his organs are fine, no sign of disease?' asked Fletcher.

'He was fit, a man who ate well, didn't smoke, and who attended a gym on a regular basis. He could be described as a bodybuilder. Whatever has killed him I cannot say but I doubt it was an accident.'

'You mean he was murdered?'

'So it seems but if so, how may only be revealed through an analysis of his blood.'

The detectives said nothing more. They were about to leave when Fletcher stopped.

'You don't suppose he was killed by this Covid virus?'

Laudi frowned. 'Highly unlikely.'

'How do you test for Covid 19?' asked Baldwin.

Laudi came under pressure and explained. 'A swab is collected via the nose or throat avoiding the tongue. A test can involve phlegm or blood. The lab examines the sample checking for the virus.'

'Did you test for Covid, Doctor?' asked Fletcher.

'No. The lab technicians would do that.'

'Did you ask the lab to add the test to the list you sent?'

Laudi looked embarrassed. He checked an email. 'Ah, no, I didn't.' He typed. 'I'll ask them now.'

The detectives exchanged glances. 'Thanks,' said Fletcher and they left. Rowdy's reputation remained in the average category.

Jack Carr had a regular gig attending an aged care facility in Surrey Hills. His patients were well enough not to be in hospital but unwell enough not to visit his surgery. The average age of his patients was nudging 90, and having been their GP for many moons, he didn't expect much of a change between visits.

That was until the Coronavirus situation hit town. Jack found the resident nurse, Marion.

''Afternoon, Marion,' he smiled.

''Ah, the very man I want to see.'

'Not so loud, Sister, people will talk.'

She liked his banter. 'I'm worried about this new virus, Jack. Tell me there's a vaccine in your little black bag.'

'I wish,' said Jack. 'If it starts spreading, the elderly are the ones who must never catch it. You can forget pneumonia and heart failure. Covid will take them and quickly.'

'So what should we do?'

'Anyone with a cold, high temperature, flu-like symptoms and such is to be isolated.'

'What, keep them away from others?'

'If they have Covid, they're infectious for their families, staff and other residents. Make sure all staff wear protective gear; gloves, masks, even those plastic shields.'

'The shields? Why them?'

'Marion, how many of your carers work elsewhere in aged-care?'

Many did. 'Quite a few.'

'If only one picks up the virus elsewhere, they'll bring it here and you'll have the staff killing the patients.'

Behind her mask, she wore a glum face. 'This is serious.'

'Who's the nurse handling the night shifts, Grantley?'

'Bradley.'

'You'll be sent a ton of bumpf from the DHHS, so make sure he knows the drill. Both of you may have to pull up the drawbridge and only let healthy approved visitors across the threshold.'

She changed to more glum. 'What's the threshold?'

'It's what your husband carried you over when you entered your first home.'

She pondered that historical event. 'He couldn't do it today.'

The GP nodded at Marion's waistline. 'More's the pity. What's happened to your latest diet?'

She became crestfallen. 'It's rude to make personal remarks.' She didn't mean it and knew his gentle prodding was solely to help her adopt a healthier lifestyle.

'I'll make a move. Anything to report?'

'Tommy's back being a jockey so he might be good for a tip.'

Dr Carr made his rounds and when he called in on Tommy, the old codger was watching replays of races a family member brought in for him. Tommy had seen these races time and again but never complained. Did he know? Who cares? He loved it and that's all that counts.

He wore a jockey's helmet in bed but left his whip in the stable.

Chapter 5

Jo arrived home to find a letter from Pierre's solicitor. Once Pierre's mother died and his new family consisted of Joanna Claire Best, the former DI moved his legal services from Paris to Melbourne.

The letter was simple yet powerful. Jo, as she knew, was the main beneficiary of Pierre's Will. He'd left money to two of his mother's favourite charities but the real estate both in Melbourne and Paris, and the shares and cash were all bequeathed to his wife to be, Ms Best.

Seeing the facts in print jolted and shocked. The lump in her throat grew bigger. Cold shivers came out to play. There it was in black and white—I am a wealthy, a *seriously* wealthy woman. The business of probate was explained but to a trained lawyer it was familiar stuff and the rest of the text blurred.

She collected a smorgasbord of emotions. Grief because the man she loved died; guilt because she has acquired vast wealth having done nothing to deserve it, and giddiness because it all seemed so unreal.

She filed the letter, opened her laptop and searched for Retirement Villages in Melbourne. There were plenty. She made judgements on Pop's behalf.

He doesn't want to join hobby groups and has no interest in gyms. He fancies gardening. He detests a happy hour and prefers a small group of people to a large one. In fact, the more privacy, the better.

She knew his tastes and the places she liked were listed. Then from her list made calls seeking extra information. Any venue with a rude or boring person answering the phone dropped off the list.

With her top 3 clearly marked, she rang the retired detective.

'Hello?' was his standard greeting and heaven help you if you were a cold caller flogging something.

'I'd like to speak with DCI Robertson in Homicide, please.'

He laughed. 'How are you, Love?'

'So you're not sunbathing inbetween your tomatoes then?'

He laughed again. 'No and what's the nature of your complaint, Officer?'

'You and I have a date tomorrow morning with three upmarket retirement establishments.'

He was thrilled, his heart fired up but his inbred reluctance kicked in. His daughter, Jo's mother, inherited that trait from Pop.

'Are you trying to get rid of me?'

'I'll pick you up at 10 and be prepared for a call from your former son-in-law.'

'I knew there'd be a catch. And thanks a million, Jo. I needed a push, and you've made an old copper very happy.'

'See you tomorrow, Pop.'

She rang her real-estate agent father. The two operated an on again off again relationship. 'Malcolm Best,' he said with his usual professional sincerity. He bought a truckload of it when on special years ago.

'Hi Dad, it's Jo.'

Her voice rocked him. He was pleased, surprised and worried all at once. 'Not *the* Jo Best, the superstar cop?'

Jo inherited one trait from her old man, an inbuilt bullshit meter and right now it was ticking. 'How are Natalie and the kids?'

'We're all good and when are you coming to see us? We keep seeing reports of your famous cases and the kids ask when is Jo coming to our house? They call you Big Sis.'

'I've been extra busy lately, Dad, what with Pierre dying and being suspected of a serious crime.'

'Yeah, Caitlyn said you were engaged to the guy who died. I never knew you were engaged.'

'It wasn't what you'd call a long engagement, Dad, about 48 hours.'

'But you should have told us. We would have thrown a party and then we could have discussed how I was going to walk my little girl down the aisle.'

Jo noted her father managed to get almost everything wrong. Nothing was ever his fault. Sensitivity was a foreign language, and every event was described in terms of how he could be involved and preferably downstage centre.

'Dad, I may have some business for you.' He purred.

'Oh, my daughter wants a spotter's fee?'

'Robbo wants to sell his house and I suggested you as agent.'

'Of course, of course. When does he want to sell?'

'ASAP.'

'And where does he want to move to? I know I can find him another place he'll love.'

God he's good. Never miss an opportunity is my father's motto.

'No need, I'm taking him to look at some retirement villages.'

Jo thought she heard her father swear. 'Good on you. I'll give him a call. Leave it with me.'

'Thanks but leave it for a couple of days,' she said, 'and remember he's an old man, a widower and my grandfather. To me, he's family. Okay?'

Malcolm knew a threat when he heard one, and knew his little girl, the detective who tracked and tackled murderers, was as smart or smarter than him, and would only accept the best possible deal for the former cop.

'I'll do you and him proud, Jo. And thanks for the business.'

'Thanks Dad. Bye.'

His 'Bye Love,' never made it as Jo hit the Off button in record time.

Helping Pop gave her pleasure. Selling the house he and Gran lived in forever would be tough for the old boy. The thought of getting him settled in a new place he liked gave her a warm glow. He played a huge part in her childhood and steered her towards becoming a cop. He never suggested it, but challenged her to think about solving puzzles. When she was older, he reminded her about how she helped him solve a murder when she was all of six.

On one of her many visits to Pop and Gran's house, little Joanna with big sister Caitlyn, were each given a chocolate frog. Robbo was stuck on cracking a case when little Jo, staring at a photo of a motorcyclist, asked a question making the perfect observation.

'But how do you know it's him, Pop? You can't see his face.'

Out of the mouth of babes and little granddaughters, her observation helped Robbo crack the case.

Years later when he told Jo about the incident, she thought he was teasing but no, he would never lie to her.

Now she could help him when he most needed it. So selling his home and finding a new one were ticked off the list. Then she checked her Contacts and rang two of Robbo's now retired former colleagues.

She met them recently. DS Raymond "Tucky" Tuck and Detective Senior Constable Colin Melk were unofficially recruited to help Jo on a cold case. Pop roped them in and all three loved it.

The Three Amigos were more like the Keystone Cops but in the end they helped bring home the bacon.

She wanted Tucky and Colin to know about their old DCI selling up and moving. She reckoned Pop would appreciate a call or visit from these old mates.

Both ex-detectives were thrilled to hear from her. Both promised to contact their old DCI but both, and this is what surprised Jo, wanted to know when the next cold case was being investigated and how they could be involved. Her answers left them flat. She offered no cold case.

During the afternoon and into the evening she thought about their reaction. *If jumping straight back into Homicide is not a good idea, why not hop back in the saddle via a cold case?*

Billy Hughes saw Jo's name on her phone. 'Don't tell me you know who killed that bloke in Strathmore?'

'Good evening, Sarge. Have I rung at a bad time?'

'Okay, I'll bite. Who did it?'

'No idea, Sarge, not a clue but I've been thinking.'

'Here's trouble.'

'What do you reckon to me coming back to work on an old homicide?'

'Old? You mean a cold case?'

'I did it before. It'd give me a challenge and I won't have to be around where Pierre worked.' She paused as Billy pondered the request.

'It's possible. I'll have a word with DI Rose.'

'Would you?'

'Leave it with me. There's a retired mate of mine, DS Ronnie Bumstead, beavering away on a cold case at present. You'd like him. He thinks outside the box.'

'You've made my day, Sarge.'

'Well it hasn't happened yet. I'll let you know. Oh, and what have you heard about Gabrielle Strange?'

Jo's heart hit a brick wall. 'Nothing, why?'

'There's a rumour she's caught this Covid 19 thing.'

'What?'

Jo rang Gabrielle's number with heart racing and hands shaking. The phone kept ringing then switched to Voicemail. The awful so-called joke in her answer message had her using a creepy Gothic voice saying, 'I'm Strange. Speak up, it's your sixpence.'

The message said a lot about the good doctor and even more about her late father's sense of humour.

Jo left a message. 'Good evening Pathetic Pathologist. This is the Deranged Detective. How are you, Madam? Call me. Soon. Bye.'

Jo's day and night were full of good events. Her grief about Pierre lingered but little things like helping Pop and getting back to work on a cold case massaged her emotions. Then, before retiring, a possible bummer arrived. *Gabrielle is crook. She has Covid? Will she die?*

Chapter 6

Jack Carr was in bed when his phone rang. Being a GP was a bit like being a priest. People die at all hours and ambulance crews, medicos and clergy are always on call.

'It's Marion from Cedar Avenue, Dr Carr.' He knew from her voice something serious had happened. Tommy thinking he was a jockey would not be cause for a phone call.

'Good Morning, Sister. What's happened?'

'We had a death overnight. Mrs Beasley passed away although we're not exactly sure when. Bradley said he checked on her at 5.30 and she was sleeping soundly. One of the carers went in not long after and found her unresponsive.'

'I think she was 92,' said Jack.

'Turned '93 last week.'

'Okay, I'll be there as soon as I can.'

'Before you go, Jack. I'm worried a few residents seem poorly.'

'Oh?'

'They all have a bit of a fever, cough, and runny nose.' Jack said "Shit" under his breath. 'Are they the symptoms for this Covid 19.'

'Some of them, yes. Are you all wearing the full PPE?'

'We are and I've contacted the DHSS.'

'Well done. I'll be there as soon as. Pull up the drawbridge, Marion. Isolate.'

Peg was in the kitchen organising the household. Jack sipped his coffee. 'Gotta go, Mum. Say bye to the kids.'

'You can't work on an empty stomach.'

'I'll grab a bite from the café.' He stopped. 'And I don't want you and Dad going outside without wearing a mask.' He gave her a look. 'Okay?'

She nodded. 'Okay.' He wouldn't make such a request unless something troubled him; something did.

As Jack headed to the nursing home, Jo worked her phone. She rang Gabrielle's phone again with the same recorded message. She rang the pathologist's office and Petr Laudi answered.

'Oh good morning, Doctor, it's Senior Constable Jo Best from Homicide.'

'Good morning.'

'I've been trying to contact Dr Strange without success. Do you ...'

'She's in hospital; took herself to outpatients at Epworth last night complaining of shortness of breath.'

'And what's the latest?'

'I've heard nothing this morning.'

'Okay, thanks. Bye.' She rang the hospital and was put through to the ward. 'Hi, I'm ringing about a patient, Dr Gabrielle Strange.'

'Are you family?'

'No I'm a friend, well, work colleague and friend.'

'She's receiving the best possible care.'

Jo gasped. She wanted to be blunt but held back. 'When can I visit?'

'I'm sorry, absolutely no visitors and that includes family members.'

'Can I telephone her?'

'I'm sorry; Dr Strange is in Intensive Care.' There was a pause with Jo struck dumb. 'Call back later this afternoon.'

'Please tell her the deranged detective has the drugs.'

The nurse was used to unusual messages but that took the biscuit.

The pain in Jo's chest matched the pain in her head. Pierre was in ICU last month, recovered, proposed marriage and within 48 hours was dead. Now her beloved mentor, the woman with more brains and heart than anyone she knew was in ICU. You wait ages for a bus and then two arrive together. She couldn't handle the loss of Gabrielle so soon after Pierre.

Her tear ducts started a petition about overwork and she cried with ease. While planning the remembrance service for Pierre, she now faced the possible death of her best mate.

Jack Carr arrived at the nursing home and was pleased to see a large sign on the glass front door. NO VISITORS was the heading with details below about how to contact the office.

He slipped on a face mask and gloves and entered. Marion, the registered nurse, came to greet him wearing mask, gloves, plastic gown and a shield.

'Good morning, Doctor. I think we have a problem.'

'It doesn't sound like a good morning, Marion. Have you contacted the DHHS?'

'They're sending someone and told us to close the home to everyone other than essential staff.'

'Okay, let me attend to Mrs Beasley and then we'll check on the others.' Marion followed him along the corridor, and Jack was pleased to see carers all wearing plastic gowns, masks and gloves. 'How many residents have the symptoms?'

'When I arrived it was three, now it's five.'

The GP didn't like the stats, opened Mrs Beasley's door, examined her then completed and signed the death certificate. Marion replaced the sheet over the deceased patient and led the doctor to the first of the symptomatic patients. As they were about to enter the room, the nursing home manager, Noelene Gray, arrived in a hurry.

'Good morning Doctor,' she said, puffing. 'The phone's ringing non-stop and there are journalists outside wanting answers. Can you come and talk to them? Please?'

Jack didn't hesitate. 'I have patients who might be seriously ill, Mrs G. If your elderly mother or father was in need of medical care, would you like me to chat to the press or attend to your loved ones?'

'I'm sorry,' she muttered and left. Dealing with people holding TV cameras and microphones on long poles wasn't covered in her training. She headed to the front door and a bunfight. As well as the media throng, she recognised some of the adult children of her residents. They wanted in. They waved, beckoned and called. The manager approached the glass front door.

She spoke softly sounding like a person using sign language and pointed to the sign. Family members didn't understand or didn't accept the ban. Mrs Gray stressed and didn't know how to leave without appearing rude. She was saved by two suited individuals who reached the front door and held up ID cards. The manager saw the words *Department of Health and Human Services* and unlocked the door. The officials entered and the voices outside were loud and clear.

She announced. 'I'm so sorry. I've been ordered to restrict entry to essential staff. I'll post further details as soon as we have more news. Thank you.'

As she went to close and lock the door, a foot jammed it open.

'I demand to see my Dad,' shouted a middle-aged woman.

'Have you got a Covid outbreak?' yelled a journalist.

Mrs Gray performed a first. She kicked, albeit gently, the protruding foot and managed to shut the door. Once locked, she led the DHHS staff to find Dr Carr.

He went from patient to patient and was examining an octogenarian when the two health officials knocked. Jack turned.

'Please wait,' he said.

The bureaucrats did as ordered. 'We're from the DHHS,' said one.

'Congratulations and I'll be with you once I've seen my patient.'

Jack returned to his examination, finished, spoke intimately to the elderly resident then headed to the corridor. The officials stood back, looking sheepish under their face masks.

'Is it Covid, Doctor?' asked the woman.

'Symptoms yes, but the testing is your department.'

The GP kept moving. 'Where else?' Jack asked the nursing sister.

'It's Tommy,' she said and the party of four headed to the would-be jockey's room.

Jack and Marion entered and chatted to the resident who wanted the GP to know about a certainty in the last at Caulfield because he, Tommy, was on board. Because of his cheerful and normal behaviour, Jack reckoned Tommy was the least infected resident.

In the corridor he addressed the bureaucrats. 'There are five elderly residents all with multiple symptoms of Covid-19. Like most of us, I'm new to this virus but if my diagnosis is correct, they're highly infectious and at least two, because of chronic health problems, need hospital and ventilators sooner rather than later. What can you offer?'

Marion liked the GP. He was friendly and tactful but with a streak of steel, cutting through when needed. This was one such time.

The male bureaucrat stalled. 'We're here to assess the situation and report our findings to Head Office.'

'Tits on a bull,' said Jack in a calm voice. He turned to Marion. 'An ambulance, Marion, and don't let the ambos in without full protective equipment.' She left and Jack turned to the now silent officials. 'Are you able to get testing staff here and if so, when?'

More concern for the DHHS staff who bore the brunt of complaints. The woman made a call. Jack waited patiently, his insides churning.

'Within two hours,' said the woman hoping the expected reprimand would be less cutting.

'They need to test everyone, patients, staff, cleaners, cooks, the lot. And the media outside is waiting for your calm and detailed explanation. My tip; if you tell them nothing, you'll make the situation worse.

'Will you come with us, Doctor? Please?' They wanted an expert on their side. He spoke with his partly hidden face. It was a definite no.

Jo faced a full day. She'd lined up a number of retirement homes for her grandfather to inspect. With his reduced mobility and rattling around alone in his family home of 50 plus years, the sooner he moved the better. Being on leave, Jo was in the perfect position to help.

She needed to respond to the solicitor's letter about Pierre's Will. She needed to find out more about the retired DS Ronnie Bumstead, and the possibility of working with him on a cold case. And she needed to know the latest on the health of Dr Gabrielle Strange. The thought the pathologist might die without Jo having the opportunity to say goodbye drove Jo's depression with a vengeance.

Chapter 7

Dr Laudi rang DI Rose. 'Results are back on the Strathmore victim, Inspector. Unusual detail but they point to murder.'

'In a nutshell, please Doctor'

'There is a significant level of epinephrine in his system, causing a rapid acceleration of his heart rate. He would have experienced breathing difficulties, staggered from the bridge, fallen in the creek, struck his head on the concrete and died of a heart attack.'

'But he was a fit middle-aged man, he worked out.'

'You don't have to be old and overweight to have a heart attack.'

'What is epinephrine?'

'It's adrenaline which the body produces naturally. How he ingested it is the question. My guess is by injection but whether he did so voluntarily or by force I cannot say. I didn't see any bruising to suggest a rough syringe attack. But a sudden overdose of adrenaline could be the cause of death; his heart more or less imploded.'

DI Rose wanted more. 'How much of this can you prove?'

'The presence of the drug, certainly, but how, when or where he ingested it, will need more time and examination.'

More think music for Rose. 'So what's your next step?'

'Examine his organs again, particularly his heart, in the light of the presence of epinephrine. If I find anything new, I'll be in touch straight away.

'Thank you, and do you have any more news on Dr Strange?'

'No, condition unchanged.'

'Okay, thanks again.'

They disconnected and Rose despaired about Gabrielle Strange contracting the bloody Covid virus, and doubly so because her expertise was sorely missed at Homicide. Rose went to address the squad.

She chatted with Billy Hughes who called the meeting to order.

'No more news on Dr Strange. She remains in hospital in Intensive Care we think suffering from this Covid 19 virus. Jo Best has tried to see her but without success.'

'Hospitals and aged care homes are putting up the shutters, Sarge,' said Charley Baldwin.

'Well we can't stay at home, and the word from on high is we're to wear this PPE gear whenever we're dealing with the public.' Rumblings began. 'DI Rose has heard from the pathologist, and it appears our victim was murdered with the best explanation being his heart blew up due to an adrenaline rush.' Detectives reacted. Billy indicated DI Rose. 'Ma'am.'

'I was told John Banks' blood had a large amount of the drug epinephrine which is basically adrenaline. We think he may have been stabbed with a syringe. The drug caused his heart to go crazy, and mixed with shortness of breath, he staggered off the bridge, fell in the creek, whacked his head on the concrete base and died.'

'Did he drown?' asked DS Fletcher.

'No,' said Billy and DI Rose in unison. The boss moved away leaving the OIC to run the session.

Billy pointed to the photo of the deceased. 'We have enough to believe it's a homicide. His car was found parked about a kay from the body, locked and untouched. His keys were in his pocket. So, questions aplenty. If he died from this drug overdose, did he ingest it himself and if so, why? If he was given it by his killer, why and of course, who the hell is the killer?'

'Or killers,' said Baldwin.

'What about his life of crime back in Europe?' asked DS Melody.

Billy was a step ahead. 'We need to know what he did back in the old Yugoslavia. Did his behaviour warrant a revenge killing in Oz? And that's not enough; why the hell did he drive to Strathmore, park and then walk to a creek a kay away?' She stared at them. 'Anything else?'

'Yeah,' said Charley Baldwin, 'when is Jo Best coming back?'

The woman in question moved from detective to driver with her grandfather on board as she swung into a fancy retirement village in Burwood.

'Now remember, Pop, there's no pressure. We're having a stickybeak. Take your time, ask whatever questions you like and don't be afraid to tell me you want to go.'

'But isn't that a bit rude?'

'No, because you'll do it politely. If the place is not for you, let's move to one that is.'

'Can we have a code word for when it's time to go? You know like, *The moon is full tonight.*'

Jo laughed as they parked the car. She played along. 'Or what about, *Is there honey still for tea?*'

He laughed louder and they headed to the office.

Billy doled out tasks. 'We need details of Banks' criminal activities o/s. DI Blunt; you're a man with high-flying contacts. I'd like you to run the investigation on our victim's life overseas. Was he involved in drugs, prostitution? Did he commit war crimes? The whole kit and caboodle, please.'

Callum purred. He was being headhunted to tackle a serious part of the investigation. His mate, DI Steele, the former head of Homicide and now policing with the Feds in Canberra, would be the best contact to investigate overseas criminals.'

'Can do,' he said.

Charley Baldwin raised his hand like a kid in class. He spoke like a 10 year-old desperate to be picked. 'Miss, Miss, can I go too, Miss? I've got me passport and me sandwiches, Miss.'

His quip set off laughter and ribbing. Billy ignored him.

'DS Fletcher, I'd like you and the comedian to investigate Banks in Oz. Go over his work history, workmates, clients, family and any enemies. If he was a crim overseas, did he continue offending here in Oz? Okay?' Fletcher nodded. 'DS Melody, I want you and Senior Constable Payne to liaise with the pathologist and forensics. How did the victim ingest this drug? What was found at the scene by the creek? Did his car have any relevant DNA? Yes?'

'Yes Sarge.'

'I'll co-ordinate. Now please, none of this "reveal all at our next meeting" caper. Give me any results as soon as you have them. The best result is a quick result. Let's go.'

Blunt was back in town and on the blower. 'Gavin, it's Callum Blunt.'

'G'day mate. How's it going?'

'Good. Listen There's a homicide here where the victim is a bloke from Serbia.'

'Lovely place.'

'Word is he's changed his name since landing Down Under because he was a naughty boy back home.'

'What sort of a naughty boy?'

'We think drugs and possibly war crimes.'

'Then it's good he's dead. Those bastards are tough with a capital T.'

'So I need his track record. Are you the man?'

'Silly question. I'll ask around.'

'Thanks mate, I owe you.'

'Text me the details.'

'Will do.'

'So what's happening in my old squad?'

'Bugger all; we're still under petticoat government. When the Frog finally carked it, Billy Hughes got bumped up to Acting Detective Senior Sergeant and is SIO running this current case.'

'It's called positive discrimination, mate, which is Commissioner speak for bullshit.'

'And Superwoman Best is on compassionate leave.'

'What? Why?'

'Didn't you know? She was engaged to Maurice Chevalier for two whole days.'

'Engaged?'

'He's dead.'

'I heard but not that he was going to marry the bitch.'

'Word is she's inherited his estate worth a squillion bucks.'

Steele squirmed, his braces stretching. 'What ... a ... bitch.'

'Yeah well she won't be solving this homicide because she ain't around and probably won't come back.'

'What, ever?'

'Would you if you won First Division?'

Steele didn't answer. As soon as he met Jo Best, he developed a professional jealousy about the woman who was so much smarter than any other Homicide detective, including him, and he desperately wanted her to fail. Now she appeared to be so wealthy she could tell her employer, Victoria Police, where to stick it. Steele struggled with the news. His professional jealousy moved up a notch; *two* notches. His failed marriage meant he lost half his super in one hit, and he was paying the private school fees of his two kids, both of whom he rarely saw. And far, far worse was the fact his ex-wife's new boyfriend is an ex-AFL star and his kids think he's awesome. What a bitch!

He meant both the ex-wife and Jo Best.

Steele promised to get back to Blunt with whatever info he could find on the late Branko Bankowitz.

DS Fletcher and Charley Baldwin headed off to investigate Branko Down Under.

'Do we call him John or Branko?' asked Baldwin.

'Forget his European life. Everyone knows him as an Aussie. Besides, DI Blunt is the international sleuth.'

They chuckled and played a game thinking of who DI Blunt could be in this latest case. Baldwin spoke with a terrible French accent.

'DI Blunt, why, 'e is Inspector Clouseau,' then impersonated the French policeman. 'The pheun, the pheun!'

Fletcher went upper-class English. 'Oh no, old chap, DI Blunt's definitely Sherlock Holmes.' He used an upper-class English accent. 'I say, Watson, old bean, the damn thing is elementary.'

This banter carried on until they turned serious and discussed tactics. At *Advanced Security* they climbed the stairs. The front door was glass meaning they could see into the empty small reception area.

The detectives rang the bell. Nothing.

'Could be out installing a system,' said Baldwin.

'There's someone there,' said Fletcher craning to see. He pressed the doorbell again and Owen Jones, the boss appeared, looking strange, unlocked the door and walked away. The detectives made faces at one another, opened the door and followed Jones into his office. He sat behind a desk wearing a death mask. He trembled.

'Mr Jones? What's happened?' asked Fletcher.

He struggled to speak. 'They said unless they get their money next week, they'll kill me.'

Chapter 8

The retirement village inspections went well. The first offered beautiful rooms and excellent facilities, and Jo reckoned Pop could have as much privacy as he wanted. Big tick. They went to the second village which was huge. Pop worried about the number of residents but again the rooms were full of classy comforts. Another definite possibility.

They drove to their third and final inspection. This was in upmarket Brighton which put Pop on the back foot. 'What's a humble copper doing in a toffy place like this? I can't afford it.'

'Yes you can.'

'They'll think I'm corrupt.'

Jo's eyes widened at the luxury of the place. 'If you don't fancy this one, Pop, I might move in myself.'

They met the saleswoman and as they moved around, Pop kept making faces at his granddaughter, whispering, 'It's a palace.'

They finished in one of the rooms ready for the potential new resident, Mr Robertson. He struggled with the superb quality and Jo sensed he didn't want to be rushed. When the saleswoman put on the pressure, Jo wanted to intervene.

'I'll think about it,' said the prospect and with such emphasis, the saleswoman surrended.

She handed Robbo a brochure. 'My number's on the back, Mr Robertson. Give me a call if you want any further information.'

He smiled. Jo smiled feeling proud of the old man but worried he might procrastinate himself to inertia. He needed a shove. They headed down the corridor, wide enough for two B-Doubles, and reached the front reception area, the size of a small ballroom.

They headed to the main door but stopped when a voice was heard.

'Robbo? Is that you?'

A woman of senior years wearing a suitable and expensive ensemble with a fascinator, and oozing personality, smiled and walked towards them.

'Fanny?' said Robbo. 'What are you doing here?'

'I live here,' she said. 'But more to the point, what are *you* doing here?' Robbo hesitated. Meet the tongue-tied copper who watched the spotlight move from him to his fellow visitor. 'And this must be your brilliant granddaughter, the famous Jo Best.'

The women shook hands. 'Hello,' said Jo.

'I'm Fanny and I first met your grandfather long before you were even a twinkle in your father's eye.'

Robbo was toey and Jo intrigued. He knew an explanation was due. 'Fanny married a DS of mine back in the old Homicide days.'

Fanny was all over both of them. To Jo she waxed lyrical. 'I study all the murder cases, and when I heard you were Robbo's granddaughter, I've been watching your brilliant career like a hawk. You have your Pop's genius for cracking cases.' She turned to the former DCI. 'So who are you two visiting? I know everyone here.'

Robbo decided to confess. 'We're not visiting, Fanny. Jo's helping me find a new home.'

Bang, the fireworks exploded. Say no more. Life is just a bowl of Cherry Ripes. Fanny rejoiced and embraced the startled grandfather.

'Oh Robbo, how wonderful. You'll love it here. Now, have you seen the breakfast room, the garden and the cinema?'

Robbo tried to escape. Jo tried to help. 'It's kind of you, Fanny,' she said, 'but I need to drive Robbo home. I have an appointment.'

'You go,' said Fanny, 'I'll run Robbo home.' To Robbo she beamed. 'Stay for tea, be my guest. Enjoy the fine dining, meet the residents and staff. They have an excellent cellar.' She pointed at him. 'If I remember, you're a red man.' He was.

Jo saw her grandfather's eyes change as if by magic. The fear faded and a strange excitement washed over his face.

He wants to stay.

'You're very kind, Fanny,' said Jo. Then to her grandfather, 'But give me a call, Pop, if Fanny can't drive you home.'

Fanny guided Jo towards the front door. 'We'll be fine, Jo. You go and crack another case. Besides, the Merc needs a run. I look forward to seeing you soon.' She kissed Jo as if she were a member of the family. Jo turned to see the former Head of Homicide grinning.

Michael decided to accompany Cathy Feng to her second meeting with the remarkable PI, Starlight Freeman. He couldn't work out if Cathy was nervous because Starlight was unusual, or because she desperately wanted to find her Mum. It was a challenging time and having a backstop, a friend beside her, gave Cathy a boost. Secretly, Michael wanted to learn. He always fancied himself as a Jo Best type detective, and wanted to learn from a real Private Investigator.

They arrived and again Michael was in heaven gawping at vintage or rather prehistoric equipment. They sat and Starlight lit a cigarette.

'Here's what I know,' she rasped. 'The woman you thought was your mother, Gloria Feng, died six weeks ago. Her death certificate led me to find her mother's name, Alison Feng. We'll call her your step-grandmother, and she's still alive.'

Cathy gasped and Michael's pulse got busy.

'If Alison was close to her daughter Gloria, there's a good chance she'll know how Gloria adopted you. But if she *does* know, the question remains, is she willing and able to speak? If a baby swap was done under the counter, Grandma may say nothing for fear of prosecution; although at her age and with your adoptive mother's death, she may feel free to tell all.'

Michael was impressed by Starlight's brutal analysis. Her bedside manner was rough as guts, but the clients wanted more.

'Now finding Alison Feng proved tricky. All my usual channels turned up nothing. Some people don't want to be found. I used a contact in the Chinese community who found her and can confirm your step-Grandmother is old, and you might only have one chance at asking about your real mother. Not being Chinese, I may be no good taking this any further but you two might find her. People feel comfortable with those from their own culture. You know what I mean?'

'Yes,' said Cathy, her hands shaking.

'Here's the lady's name and address. It's a nursing home which is where some residents have dementia. If she's away with the fairies, you may get nothing. If she has a family, they may not want anything to do with you. "Leave my mother alone" could be their response, or "we have our own family, and you are not related, piss off". You follow?'

Cathy checked the details and nodded. 'And this woman is the mother of my mother?'

'No, she's the mother of the woman who adopted you.'

'Of course, I understand.' Cathy struggled to accept the fact a person was alive who might know the name of her real mother.

Michael found himself drawn into the search. 'Have you contacted this Alison Feng woman?'

'Keep up son. You'll never make a PI if you don't listen.' He froze. 'Now I've not made this public so there's no way the old lady could know about you and your interest—so far.'

Michael was fascinated with the progress of the case, and was keen to learn the secrets of being a PI. 'I don't understand. How can you make enquiries without tipping off people?'

Starlight observed him. 'Are you paying me to find her birth mother or to train you as a PI?'

Michael copped the well-aimed smack. His standard half-grin appeared. He looked at Cathy. 'I think we should go and talk to this lady, your step-grandmother,' he said. 'Thank you, Ms Freeman.'

'It's Starlight, and let me know what happens.'

Cathy needed help descending the stairs, her legs becoming like cooked spaghetti.

Charley Baldwin drove while Justin Fletcher phoned Billy Hughes. 'Men threatened him? Who?' she demanded. Fletcher knew nothing.

'No idea. He said two blokes burst in waving shooters and made the threat. Jones said he thought our Strathmore swimmer had a gambling problem but didn't know how bad.'

'Bugger,' said Hughes not pleased with the latest development. 'He could be in trouble from old comrades in Sarajevo or new comrades in Sunshine. What are you doing now?'

'We're about to interview sonny Jim's missus.'

'Let me know what she says.'

Fletcher rang off as they arrived outside the small South Yarra cottage. 'What do we know about her?' asked Baldwin.

'She cut up badly about her old man being killed. She's a fitness nut like her fella, and is good at crying.'

'Well I'm happy to let you lead, Sarge.'

They knocked using the small metal knocker. No answer. They knocked again. From inside, a voice was heard.

'Go away.'

The detectives sighed and Fletcher called. 'It's the police. Open up.'

'No! Go away!'

Frustration dripped on the door mat. 'We only have a few questions about the death of your partner,' called Fletcher conscious a raised voice might be heard by neighbours.

They heard footsteps as she reached the door. 'Is the wire door closed?'

'Yes,' said both detectives together.

'Are you wearing masks?'

'Yes,' said both detectives together.

They waited then heard a lock click and watched the main door open about half way. The girlfriend knew nothing of Queen Victoria's wardrobe choice after her beloved Prince Albert shuffled off this mortal coil, but Liz Delahunty chose the same coloured outfit as Her Majesty. Even Lyn's mask was black.

Both detectives held their ID close to the wire door.

'I won't allow you to arrest me,' she said, and both men found their supply of impatience rising fast.

'We only want to ask a few questions,' said Fletcher, trying to pacify the woman.

'I've been told if I let you into my house, I'll be arrested.'

'Not true,' said the DS.

'Who told you that?' asked Baldwin.

'The same people who told me I tested positive for Covid-19.'

The detectives unconsciously moved back.

'You've been tested?' asked Fletcher.

'No,' replied the woman with a jumbo size serving of sarcasm. 'I read it in the *Herald Sun* Public Notices. Now go away.'

'Well if we stand back here,' said Fletcher stepping back and prompting his partner to follow, 'we should be okay.'

'I have to self-isolate and you are putting me in danger of being fined. If you don't go away, I'll call the police.'

A pregnant pause allowed all three players to ponder the last statement. Baldwin desperately wanted to be the one to say the line.

'Madam, we *are* the police.'

Before the woman could say or do anything else, Fletcher grabbed Baldwin's arm and ushered him away. 'We'll contact you later,' he said.

From the car, Fletcher rang the OIC.

'I hope this is good news,' said Billy. DS Fletcher told her about the Covid infection and the woman's attitude, and Billy's reply would never appear in any Baptist newsletter.

Chapter 9

Jo knocked on the door and spoke to the older man with a pencil in his mouth. 'Mr Ronnie Bumstead?' He stood and grinned.

'Speaking with his voice, and you must be the famous Jo Best.'

She smiled. 'Not so much of the famous, thank you. And thanks for agreeing to have me help with your Cold Case.'

'No, it's me who is thanking you, and as you know, Billy Hughes is one persuasive woman.'

'She is.' Jo removed her jacket and bag and pulled up a chair. 'I'm here to help, Ronnie. Anything you want done, say the word.'

He smiled at her. 'There's no line of command here, Jo. We say what we think, and the other points out the mistakes and benefits.'

'Sounds fair; so what's the case?'

'Ah, the case,' he mused. 'There are those who say it shouldn't even be here, and was wrapped up with a coroner's report decades ago.'

He opened a file and showed her a photo of a gorgeous young woman. Jo read aloud the name on the picture. 'Natasha Kaye.'

'Long story short,' said Ronnie. 'She was found, drowned, on the beach at Queenscliff in 1988. How did she die? Was it suicide, accidental death or homicide? The coroner recorded an open finding.'

'But obviously you believe it's a homicide.'

'I do. I worked on the case way back when I was on the Force. I met the Kaye family and they and I believe there is no way Natasha would ever take her own life. And how could it be an accidental death when the young woman was a champion swimmer?'

'So it's a homicide because ...?'

'Because there's no way any of the other possibilities fit.'

Jo pondered her next question. 'What do you think happened?'

'I think she was raped and therefore had to be killed. She was taken out to sea and drowned and dumped. The killer or killers hoped the sharks or the current would have her disappear. She didn't but drifted back to land and was discovered pretty much intact.'

'But without any DNA.'

'True and to me that was the killer's fail-safe plan. With the body in the water for hours, chances of recovering DNA were next to zero, which is another reason to support my homicide theory. There were marks on her neck to suggest strangulation but her lungs were full of water so drowning was listed as the cause of death.'

'Which I guess the PM stated.'

'Yes but she didn't drown, she *was* drowned.' He tossed his pencil on the desk. 'She was murdered.'

Jo sensed his conviction. First impressions were good and she liked him as a person. She reckoned he was late sixties. His healthy weight made him look fit, and his full head of short hair with grey taking charge added to his kind and friendly nature. It looked like his last haircut used scissors and a pudding basin.

Is it a homemade job? Covid has closed barbers so did he persuade the wife to give him a trim? It's pretty basic. Is it a DIY haircut?

'I knew your grandfather but never worked with him. Is he still with us?'

'He was this morning.

'And well I hope?'

'He lost his wife a while back and needs to move home so I've been chauffeuring him around various retirement villages.'

'Good for you.'

'Okay,' said Jo, 'what's your plan of attack and how can I help?'

'I suggest you read the file; the witness statements, police reports, coronial enquiry, the lot. We're not supposed to have suspects any more so I've drawn up a list of ...

Jo joined in and they spoke together ' ... persons of interest.'

They smiled, already starting to enjoy the other's company.

'My plan,' said Ronnie, 'is to revisit technology and witness statements.'

'There's always the deathbed confession,' said Jo.

'I should be so lucky.'

'What does revisiting technology mean?'

'The boffins are learning new ways to examine old evidence.'

'I thought you said we had no DNA.'

'We don't but there might be a smidgeon and the science has improved. What evidence we do have could be studied again using new technology. We have her clothes, jewellery, and photos of marks on her body. With the new smarter and better science, we may get lucky.'

Jo liked his thinking. 'So no DNA was captured on the body?'

'No and in the late 80s, DNA was just beginning to be used in criminal cases.'

'What about anywhere else?'

'Sorry?'

'Was anything found where she was attacked or found?' He shook his head. 'So what makes you think she was raped?

'Her panties were not in perfect position. And why go to the trouble of drowning her unless she'd been attacked? Then there's the fact she drowned while being a top swimmer. Listen, rather than have me influence your thinking, how about you read first and then we discuss?'

'Sounds like a plan. You mentioned technology.'

'What we know about DNA today is way ahead of science in 1988. I'm hoping new technology can bring the old to life.'

She wasn't convinced. *What can you get from nothing?*

He studied her. 'Being in Homicide, you'll know the boffins at Forensics. Any one in particular you can soft soap?'

Jo ached inside, feeling sick. The dreaded boffin, Alastair Dean, was not her first best friend. He thought she fancied him when nothing could have been further from the truth. It was her fault as she turned on the fluttering eyelashes routine to snaffle a faster service. He took the bait but when she told him his affection was not reciprocated, he turned nasty. She came clean with Ronnie.

'Actually I fell out with a scientist which may come back to bite me.'

'Unrequited passion?' asked Ronnie with Jo nodding. 'I'll deal with Forensics. Now what about IT expertise? Do you have a contact?'

'I do,' said Jo thinking of her last meeting with Michael Chan. 'Although we had our first falling out the other day.'

'Not another jilted boyfriend?' asked Ronnie jokingly. He was not too far from the truth. 'My nephew's single. Should I warn him?'

Jo changed the subject. 'Can I ask who you reckon killed Natasha?'

'You can but again, how about you read the file and then we swap suspects?'

'You mean persons of interest,' said Jo and they relaxed.

This homicide wasn't fresh, unlike the victim found in the Moonee Ponds Creek. But this case appealed to Jo as much as it did to the retired cop in the room.

As Jo and Ronnie began to better understand one another, a second team of investigators, Cathy Feng and Michael Chan, headed to the suburb of Box Hill. Both were excited. Cathy couldn't believe she'd be chasing a concrete lead so soon after starting her search for her birth mother. Michael couldn't believe he'd be part of an investigation which didn't involve Detective Jo Best.

'I don't know how to handle this, Michael, said Cathy. 'I'm scared I'll frighten this woman and cause her to never reveal what she knows.'

'Let's take it a step at a time,' he said. 'We check the lie of the land and make decisions in what the politicians call the pragmatic mode.'

She was driving and without taking her eyes off the road, nodded. 'Thanks, Michael. You're my guardian angel.' Up popped his half smile.

They found the nursing home and their heartbeats switched to lively. Michael thought this PI routine too easy.

Cathy is told she's adopted. She bumps into an old friend, me, who agrees to go with her to visit a whacky PI who finds a woman who may solve the puzzle in a second. They find this woman; ask her a single question and she replies. 'My daughter adopted you and your birth mother is So and So.' Mystery solved. No, it can't be that easy.

Cathy's head exploded with thoughts. Michael tingled. He loved cracking cases with Jo Best but this was as exciting, and he was learning the craft of being a Private Investigator; or so he thought.

They parked and walked to the nursing home. It was late afternoon, the time when residents would be preparing for their evening meal. Alison Feng was inside this building, behind the front door. Alison's daughter adopted Cathy Feng. Is Cathy Feng her real name? Does Alison know Cathy's birth mother and, if so, will Alison talk?

As they approached the front gate they heard arguing. A man and a woman were speaking; she was aggressive, he passive. Cathy and Michael entered the front garden and saw the combatants.

Both were Chinese, with the man wearing a nurse's uniform. 'Please, it's not my decision, I'm sorry.'

'But you know my father is not well. Doctor Lee said he may not last the week. Are you refusing to let me see my dying father?'

'I'm not refusing. I'm obeying the law.'

'Fuck the law,' screamed the woman who wouldn't normally swear. Her elderly father was dying, and she was banned from even seeing him let alone touching and saying she loved him.

The man shook his head and pointed to a sign banning anyone other than essential staff. 'It's the government's decision. Please take it up with the DHHS.'

Michael and Cathy arrived interrupting the argument. The woman turned to them. 'Forget it,' she said. 'No visitors allowed.'

'I'm sorry,' said the man to all three. 'It's to stop the spread of the Coronavirus.' He disappeared inside then closed and locked the door.

Cathy and Michael's hopes were dashed. They were within possible touching distance of their goal then had the door closed in their faces.

'I haven't seen you here before,' said the woman. 'Who have you come to see?'

Cathy froze. The tension grabbed her and Michael stepped in. 'We've just heard a relative might be here. Her name is Alison Feng.'

'Oh I know Alison. But she never has visitors. She'll be super pleased to meet her family.'

Michael wanted more information. 'We know her daughter, Gloria.'

The woman showed surprise. 'I didn't know she had a family. Did you say her daughter's name is Gloria?'

'Yes.'

'I've never seen her here. Do you know if she visits?'

'She recently passed away,' said Michael hating being so blunt.'

'Oh God, I'm sorry. Was she ill?'

'Cancer,' said Michael, desperate to change the subject.

Cathy joined in. 'Her death is how we discovered Alison. How is she? Does she keep good health?'

'Good as far as I know. She keeps to herself. You rarely see her out of her room. You being here will give her a real boost, get her out of herself.'

Cathy gasped. The investigators switched to excited. Then another couple arrived as visitors, and the woman explained the locked-out situation. All three were angry even desperate.

'Let's go,' whispered Michael. Cathy hesitated.

She whispered back. 'What if they open the doors later tonight?'

Michael was reluctant to spell out the facts. 'Cathy, you're a nurse. You must know there's a crisis in nursing homes. This virus is spreading and elderly folk in particular are getting sick and dying. They won't let us inside until the spread of the virus is under control.'

Cathy knew those facts but was desperate. 'But what if Alison dies? She might be the only way to find my mother.' Michael sympathised. 'Can we write a note asking Alison to tell us how her daughter came to adopt me?'

Michael lost interest in becoming a PI. If he agreed to Cathy's suggestion and it scared Alison into silence, they were finished. If they did nothing and the Covid-19 virus killed Alison, their hopes were dashed. *I'd rather work on a whodunit with Jo Best.*

More visitors arrived and the crowd turned angry. 'We should go,' said Michael. Afraid, Cathy agreed.

As they drove away, Michael pushed the positive. 'It's a glass half full, Cathy. Your step-grandmother is alive and seems well for her age. We know where she lives and as soon as we can speak to her, we will.'

Cathy nodded and silently cried, tears sliding down her cheeks. But her mind turned busy.

What about Alison's husband or siblings or cousins, her extended family? Can we trace them too? I have to find my birth mother.

'Let's stay positive and that way you'll find your Mum.'

Michael went for his half smile. Cathy was hanging in there; just. He changed his mind about being a PI. He wasn't worried about not finding Cathy's mum. He was worried about finding her in a cemetery.

Chapter 10

Jack Carr worked long hours. Most days he would start early, soldier on with few breaks, and finish up not heading home till his family had eaten, and his kids were in bed. That wasn't every day but he took his profession seriously. His parents thought *too* seriously. They believed it was because he was a widower. He missed his wife and covered up his sadness by throwing his life into his work. He would be in dire trouble without his parents who moved in to care for their grandkids.

He saw his last patient, chatted to a colleague, and then to the cleaner before heading home. He made a detour calling in on the Cedar Avenue Nursing Home. It was in lockdown. Several elderly patients with symptoms of the new virus were tested and found to be Covid 19 positive. They were transferred to hospital.

He wanted an update, added his mask and knocked on the locked door. The nurse on night duty, Bradley Pearson, unlocked the door. He was dressed for war with a complete PPE uniform.

'Good evening, Doctor. Were we expecting you?'

Jack's relationship with Marion the main day nurse was bright and breezy. His relationship with Bradley was perfunctory at best.

'G'day Bradley. Have we any more possible cases?'

'Not in the last few hours.'

They walked to visit various residents. 'It's a joke,' said Bradley. 'This government wouldn't know its arse from its elbow. First it's a partial lockdown, then complete lockdown. Then they want infected patients sent to hospitals. Now I have relatives threatening the home with legal action and me with testicle removal. It's a nightmare.'

They stopped outside a patient's room. Jack used his best bedside-manner smile, part hidden. 'I'll take it from here, Bradley.'

Behind his PPE, the nurse slipped on a lip-curling, snooty face and squeaked away. The well waxed floors and his shoes didn't like one another.

Jack produced gloves, knocked and entered to start his rounds. He saw several patients. Three were holding their own. One had breathing difficulties and needed immediate transfer to hospital and likely a ventilator. The fifth, Tommy, the oldest jockey in the world, breathed his last as Jack examined him.

Despite constantly dealing with life-threatening illnesses, having a patient die in front of you, was always tough for Jack. He spoke to the now deceased old man.

'It's been lovely knowing you, Tommy. And thanks for all those tips.' He closed Tommy's eyes and lifted the sheet. But Jack wasn't a priest and needed to attend to the living.

He found Bradley reading, and with his eyes gave a look to rankle the nurse. Bradley closed the paper. 'All done, are we, Doctor?'

'Not yet, Bradley. Old Tommy Reynolds has died, and Miss Jamieson needs a ventilator immediately if not sooner. Ambulance first please, and then the undertaker. I'll contact Tommy's family. I don't think Miss Jamieson has any family.'

'She hasn't.'

'I'll sign the death certificate and leave it in your care. I'll do a swift check on a couple of others who are poorly and hope they haven't caught this damn virus. I'll see you before I go.'

He left. He'd wanted to ask when Miss Jamieson was last checked but didn't think a testy exchange right now would do anyone any good. Jack was fired up and ready to complain but his professionalism kept him calm, at least on the outside.

He did his rounds and found what he believed was another possible case of Covid. He reached the front desk.

'Still no ambulance?' he asked, signing the death certificate for the equine-loving Tommy.

'I've called them,' said Bradley now choosing the say-as-little-as-possible approach.

'You may need another. Peter Brain is showing Covid symptoms. How soon can he be tested?'

Bradley sighed. 'I'll get onto it, and also my union.' The men stared at one another. 'Not only are we supposed to work freely in this dangerous environment, we take on extra responsibility, and where is the help from the health department?'

Jack knew he shouldn't but he couldn't help himself. 'Have you been tested, Bradley?'

The nurse added daggers to his eyes. 'Oh, so now I'm the one spreading the virus.'

'I asked if you've been tested.'

'Have you?'

This "chat" was heading towards dangerous territory. Thankfully the ringing doorbell broke up any potential fisticuffs. There were two lots of visitors outside; the ambulance and the undertaker.

Jack waited as the professionals entered. He nodded to the undertakers who were led away by Bradley. Jack spoke to the ambos.

'I know you're busy but how busy?'

'It's the cancer, stroke and heart attack patients I feel for, Doc,' said the driver. 'We're ferrying nursing home residents here, there and everywhere and trying to do the best with the others. People who should be getting medical attention are missing out. It's a nightmare.'

'Of the five patients I've just seen, one has died, another is your pick-up and another is a new case needing an immediate test.'

Bradley returned. 'This way,' he said to the ambos.

Jack stopped them. 'I'll be off, Bradley.' He pointed. 'Death certificate there and Peter Brain needs checking every hour.' He nodded to the ambos and all of them moved.

Driving home, Jack thought about Bradley. *Why do certain people choose to work in medicine dealing face to face with patients when they so obviously hate the job, the patients, themselves or all three?*

That man was born miserable and was like the hotelier who reckoned business would be so much better if they didn't have guests.

I have no symptoms, thought Jack. *But am I asymptomatic? Physician heal thyself.*

As Jack drove home, Jo Best sat on her settee and read the documents she copied from the Cold Case file marked *Natasha Kaye*. A notepad and pen stood ready for any facts, thoughts or questions that popped into her mind. She grasped the basics.

Natasha, 22, fit and healthy, studying to be a vet, spent the weekend on which she disappeared with her boyfriend, Julian Love, in his family's holiday home at Point Lonsdale.

After the party, she and Julian went for a stroll along the beach. Julian claimed they argued, he stormed off, went home and went to bed. He woke in the morning and couldn't find Natasha. He assumed she was back in Melbourne or spent the night with a friend. He rang her flat in Melbourne for no reply. He later saw a TV news report about the body on the beach. He contacted police and discovered it was Natasha.

'Right,' said Jo to herself, 'that tells me everything and nothing.' She made notes. 'Who was at the party? Did anyone see Julian and Natasha on the beach at night? Where and why did they argue? Was the place forensically searched? What new details are revealed by the witness statements, the police reports and the coronial inquest?'

The pile of material stared back at her so she started to examine in detail. Her phone rang. The caller ID meant nothing.

'Jo Best,' she said.

'Good evening, Madam,' said a toffy voice. *This is a wind-up,* thought Jo. 'I wish to speak to the world's wealthiest woman.'

Jo twigged. 'Gabrielle?'

'Yes, darling, reports of my death have been greatly exaggerated.'

'Where are you? I mean *how* are you?'

'Fit as a Mallee bull and twice as dangerous.'

'I tried to visit and call but even your phone calls were blocked.'

'They told me the deranged detective was snooping around.'

'They said you've caught Covid and were in ICU.'

Strange scoffed. 'What would they know? Bloody doctors.'

'So it's not true?'

'I think they call me a false positive; but listen I'm back on a ward and busting to break out of the joint. I'd rather self-isolate and recuperate at home. If I simply walk out they may try and stop me but if my carer comes to collect me, I may be allowed out.'

'Your carer?'

'Have you got a nurse's uniform?'

'No, and when is all this supposed to happen?'

'Let's say 0700 tomorrow at the changeover. The night shift'll be buggered and the new shift'll do anything they think's been approved.'

'You should be in strategic planning.'

The pathologist cackled. 'You're a darling. I'll shout you breakfast. See you first thing tomorrow.' Jo heard her speaking, presumably to a nurse. 'You couldn't get me a block of dark chocolate could you, Love?'

Jo rang off and puffed her cheeks exhaling. It was a huge relief to hear her friend firing and back to her old self.

Did she really have Covid-19?

Jo attacked the cold case notes with a new energy.

Robbo kicked off his shoes then flopped on his bed. His pyjamas slept silently in the chest of drawers—second drawer down. He lacked the energy to grab his jim-jams or even undress. In the last few hours, he'd eaten plenty of the most delicious food, enjoyed two glasses, (or was it three?) of an excellent Cab Sav, and laughed like a loon.

He reminisced. Fanny took him to the in-house dinner. On his table were a retired heart surgeon, his wife a retired dentist, a former barrister he'd seen in court, and a woman he arrested decades ago for prostitution. She'd inherited a small fortune, no longer entertained punters or spoke about them. Both took a while to recognise the other and when they did, a frisson of excitement exploded—or was it fear?

He scored a chauffeured ride home in a new Mercedes driven by the good-looking Fanny who dressed as though she'd just been offered the eponymous role in *The Merry Widow*.

He rolled across the bed, turned off the light and prepared to go to sleep wearing what he left home in apart from his shoes.

Two hours earlier, shortly after dinner, Fanny took Robbo to her room—suite more like—where she phoned the administrator, dragged her out of her room and away from her favourite TV programme, *Would I Lie to You?* in order for Robbo to put down a deposit on a vacant room in this here establishment. Robbo thought he knew what he was doing. Fanny knew exactly what *she* was doing.

Robbo's new room to be was on another floor, and a fair way from Fanny's suite. But hey, what's a brisk shuffle between friends?

The friend even whipped out her cheque book to pay Robbo's deposit. 'I'll fix you up, Fanny,' he muttered wondering how he would tell his granddaughter the news, and what she would say when he did.

Chapter 11

All animals are created equal but some animals are more equal than others. All murders are created equal but some have many leads pointing to rabbit holes filled with herrings coloured red, and which drive homicide detectives around the twist. This one did.

Oh for a suspect holding the smoking gun.

Other than Jo Best, all squad members gathered in the Incident Room brooding and muttering "Bloody hell," or its equivalent. Billy Hughes kick-started the meeting.

'This is what we think we know. John Banks, the former Branko Bankowitz, originally from Serbia, doesn't like fishing, paddling in concrete lined creeks, or visiting Strathmore. But that's where his body was found. There are questions with the first being why Strathmore?

'Dr Laudi tells us his blood contained a large dose of epinephrine, otherwise adrenalin, which the pathologist believes sent Banks' heart into overdrive causing him to fall into the creek, whack his head on the concrete base and die. He did not drown and so far, DNA has given us slightly less than nothing.

'His partner, Lyn Delahunty, seemed pretty cut up about the death, and when approached for a detailed interview, refused point blank on the grounds she's tested positive for Covid, and is required by law to self-isolate.'

DS Fletcher interrupted. 'Yeah but surely she can't refuse point blank. With a medical certificate okay, but without one we could ask questions from outside her home or by phone or even online. People with Covid can remain mentally alert and she sounds with it.'

'We'll look into it,' said Hughes. 'So we think we know *how* he died but what he was doing in Strathmore, and who killed him are the big unknowns, although another unknown involves thugs who called on his business partner, Owen Jones. Justin?'

Fletcher explained. 'This was our second visit. The office was locked and Jones took his time opening up. The guy seemed genuinely scared.'

'He was shitting himself,' added Baldwin.

'He lets us in and tells a tale about two gents he'd never seen before, who barged in and threatened him. Unless they get their money next week, they'll take it out in blood.'

'What money?' asked DS Melody. 'Who owed the money?'

'Jones thought the thugs mistook him for Banks.'

'Well if true, *they* didn't stiff him in Strathmore,' said DI Blunt.

'How much money?' asked Senior Constable Stephen Payne.

'Sixty grand,' said Fletcher.

A hubbub bounced around the room. Fletcher added his theory. 'If Banks was into drugs back in Europe, could he be back in business Down Under? He's run up a debt, fallen behind, and the heavies come the heavy not knowing the bastard's already dead.'

Baldwin threw in his idea. 'Or if he's a gambler, and is in over his head, then the bailiffs called to collect.'

More hubbub as the lines of enquiry kept growing.

'Okay,' called Billy Hughes and members settled. 'It's tough but sadly you ain't heard the half of it. DI Blunt will explain.'

Callum strode centre stage and lapped up the limelight. He'd been given a major role and wanted to tell the world about his success. He always appeared smug and now he flaunted it.

'This is big. Through my national and international contacts, I've done a number on Mr Branko Bankowitz aka John Banks.' Blunt put up a photo of the victim in a paramilitary uniform. 'The United Nations War Crimes Commission was pretty pissed when I told them Bankowitz was brown bread. They've been chasing him for years. There are outstanding warrants for his arrest on charges of genocide.'

The room rocked.

'There are people back in his homeland who would cheerfully cut off matey's bollocks and stuff 'em down his throat. They're the *un*official bounty hunters. Various government departments put him on their Most Wanted list years ago. If anyone found him with his new name in Melbourne, there are any number of political and criminal operatives who would want him dead.' Blunt paused. His snappy report went well, until now. Pity he made a major blue at speech's end.

He assumed colleagues would crave more detail. 'So, questions?' Nobody spoke; not a dickey bird. The silence smacked his smugness as he retreated.

'Thanks Callum,' said Billy. 'So we need to go back to his partners both business and personal. Did he have a gambling problem? Was he dealing drugs? Did he ever mention his life back in Serbia? Was he a womaniser? Yes?' Members agreed. 'Callum, can you check with Border Force to see if any "interesting" visitors from Serbia or Eastern Europeans with political connections have arrived in recent times?'

Blunt nodded and turned grumpy as no-one mentioned his work.

DS Melody raised a touchy subject. 'I have to say I'd like Dr Strange to have a look at the body. When Charley and I called on Dr Laudi, we suggested he ask for an extra test which he'd forgotten to order.'

DI Rose took over. 'Okay, let's keep it professional. The good news is Dr Strange has made a remarkable recovery and goes home today.'

'But not back to work?' asked Melody.

'Certainly not today and possibly not ever. She planned a gradual retirement which might be brought forward because of Covid.' No reaction from the troops. 'And in other news, Jo Best has returned to work but not here. She's investigating a cold case.'

'Pity,' said Baldwin. Others turned to him. Pressure built for an explanation. 'I mean it's a pity she's not here to help us with this case.'

'I'll leave Acting Senior Sergeant Hughes to assign new tasks and please remember to carry PPE with you at all times.'

Jo parked at the back of the hospital. Heading to the door, she was stopped as soon as she tried to enter. Wearing appropriate protective gear, she produced her police ID hoping it might carry weight. It didn't but the magic words, "I'm here to collect a patient being discharged" helped her move deeper inside the Kremlin.

Jo's temperature was taken and a series of questions asked before she got to enter reception on Gabrielle's floor. The pathologist was escorted to her chauffeur, and the women correctly refused to engage in their usual embrace.

Jo took Gabrielle's bag and they made it to the car and home. Gabrielle couldn't stop chatting—nothing new there—as she rabbited on about the new virus.

They made it inside and Gabrielle celebrated. 'Thank God,' she exclaimed, 'sleep in my own bed and no more hospital food.'

'Do medicos treat one of their own any differently?' asked Jo.

'Yes, worse.' She opened her fridge. 'Now breakfast, girly. Let's have a fry up.'

What could Jo say? She was so glad to see her friend home and firing although worried about her health with the proposed breakfast.

'Is that wise in your condition?'

'What, famished?' Jo smiled. Arguing with Dr Strange never worked. 'So what's happened, Detective?' asked Gabrielle wanting all the facts, the gossip and fake news. 'Are you back at Homicide?'

'I'm back at work but not at Homicide.'

That grabbed Gabrielle's attention. 'What? Explain.'

'I'm working on a cold case, a young woman washed up on a beach in Queenscliff in 1988. I didn't see your name on the PM.'

Gabrielle shook her head. 'No, it wasn't one of mine. But why work on a cold case? I saw a bloke was murdered in a creek the other day.'

'I'm not sure if I'll ever go back, Gabrielle.'

She twigged immediately. 'Gotcha. So how have you been?'

'It's not only the shock of things, Pierre's recovery, the engagement, and then his sudden collapse and death, it's what came after. He's more or less left me everything. I can't wrap my head around it.'

'Bacon and sausage?' Jo wasn't thinking food.

'I need financial advice, Gabrielle. Do you know anyone?'

'I know everyone, Detective. Leave it with me. So what's happened about this latest homicide?'

Jo hesitated. Charley Baldwin rang her yesterday to complain about Dr Laudi but for Jo to report said conversation to Gabrielle would be unprofessional. Several detectives wanted Dr Strange to conduct another post mortem. Jo said nothing.

'I'm right out of it, Gabrielle. Sorry.'

'Liar; you're never out of it.' She changed tack. 'So where are you living now? East Melbourne in Oz and Paris in the Spring?'

'I'm happy in good old Clifton Hill.'

'You do know your body is no longer your most important asset.' Jo didn't understand. 'Men will covet your financial appeal. You need investment advice and an anti-money-grubber spray.'

'Thanks. Now I need some help with my cold case. What are the changes in DNA technology since 1988?'

'Eat first.'

Fletcher and Baldwin made their third visit to *Advanced Security*. The office was locked and empty. ''Let's give it half an hour,' said the DS. 'Why don't you get me a coffee and an iced doughnut?'

'Why don't you give me the money upfront?'

Fletcher feigned horror. 'We can't handle cash in Covid, Senior Constable.' He grinned. 'I'll fix you up online.'

They'd finished their sustenance break when Jones arrived.

'There he is,' said Baldwin. 'I think we need to stir him up, Sarge.'

'Good,' said Fletcher. 'You're the attack dog, I'll be his mate.'

They let Jones get inside then followed. He was in the reception area when they appeared. He was sprung and reluctantly let them in.

'This is a joke. I've told you all I know.'

'We beg to differ, Mr Jones,' said Fletcher, 'and the sooner you answer our questions, the sooner we're out of your hair.'

He grumbled. Baldwin was set to start.

'Tell us about your encounter with the thugs.'

'I've already told you.'

'Describe their appearance. Were they masked?'

'What a stupid question.' He pointed at the masked Baldwin. 'You're masked, I'm masked, and they were masked.'

Baldwin accepted the rebuke. 'Accent? Did both of them speak?'

'Only one and he sounded local. It was hard to understand because of his mask.'

'And who owed them money? Was it you, Mr Jones?'

If the business owner was upset before, now he was furious. 'What the hell! I've lost my business partner, and been threatened by gangsters. *I'm* the victim here.'

'Bit convenient though,' said Baldwin going for the kill. Jones swung between astonishment and apoplexy. 'You're in debt and when threatened, tell us it was your mate they were after. He's dead so can't explain. Or *were* there any thugs? Did you invent them to make you the victim?'

'I *am* the victim,' screamed Jones.

'So where were you the night your partner died?'

'What?'

'How's business, Mr Jones? Did you catch your partner with his hand in the till? Did you argue and push him into the Moonee Ponds creek.' He paused. 'Well?'

Jones grabbed his phone. 'I'm calling my lawyer.'

Fletcher stepped forward placing a hand on the suspect's arm. 'No need, Mr Jones. Give us a few facts and we're out of your hair.'

Jones seethed but settled slowly. 'Is this how cops always behave?'

Fletcher's tone was gentle and his movements relaxed. Baldwin backed off. 'The facts, Owen, please.'

Jones sat. 'John had money and women worries. I never asked for details. He said he'd lost money gambling, and was juggling two women. Don't know anything about the other bird except she's married and lives I think in Essendon. Isn't that near Strathmore?'

The detectives sensed progress was being made.

'No name?' asked Fletcher. Jones shook his head.

Baldwin joined in with the same calm approach as his superior. 'Does his girlfriend know about the gambling and the other woman?'

Jones shook his head. 'Don't know; don't think so.'

'And your alibi for Tuesday night?' asked Fletcher.

'Don't have one. I'm single, going through the divorce from hell.'

'Did you shop, buy petrol, make a call, drive or walk down a main street?'

Jones became a professional head shaker. 'Nah, I'm a social loser.'

Billy Hughes took DS Melody to call on Lyn Delahunty. Billy waited till she heard from DS Fletcher with his news from Jones. At the South Yarra cottage, Lyn spoke from inside refusing to open her door.

'You're fine, Lyn,' said Billy hoping a friendly and female voice would do the trick. 'We only have a few questions. I assume you want us to catch the person who killed John?'

She did. 'Yes. Okay, go ahead.'

'How are you going with the Covid?'

'Not bad. I have to isolate for 14 days and get tested again before I can go out.'

'Any idea how or where you were infected?'

'What's my infection got to do with John being killed?'

'Probably nothing but you'd be surprised how a minor incident can be a real help in solving a case.'

'I'm not sure. How can anyone know? It might have been at the gym. They're closed now but when they were open, there were a lot of people puffing and sweating and touching equipment and surfaces.'

'Did John go to the same gym?'

'Yes.'

'Ever see him have a disagreement with anyone?'

'No but I did. I argued with a guy who was cleaning.'

'You argued?'

'He was acting strange. I asked him what he was doing and he lost it, said he was Covid cleaning. I told the manager who said the guy wasn't a cleaner and was always moody. I told John about the weird guy and John said he'd have a word with him.'

Billy asked for the name and address of the gym then moved on.

'Lyn, do you know if John had money worries? Did he gamble?'

'No, he was always flush. He put a few bucks in the pokies at the pub but no, he was okay for dough.'

'Was there one pub you went to the most?'

Lyn gave the details.

'Are you renting?'

'No, this is my place. John gives me money for rent.'

Billy wanted to ask how much and how often but didn't. Keeping her involved was what mattered.

'Do you know if John was involved with drugs?'

Lyn turned hostile. 'No, no way. He was a fitness freak. Why would he take drugs?'

'I'm sorry I have to ask this, Lyn, but do you think John may have cheated on you?'

She lost it. 'No,' she spat, 'and no more. We're finished. Get lost.'

The detectives glanced at one another.

'Okay,' said Billy. 'Take care and get well soon. Bye.'

Lyn didn't reply and they left.

Chapter 12

Jo survived the greasy breakfast and headed home. Gabrielle told her about recent changes in DNA testing, and Jo hoped this might be a new angle in the cold case. As she prepared for work, she rang her grandfather to check on him and see if he'd decided on his next home.

'Morning, Chief Inspector. Did you make it home all right last night, and did you do anything to shock your daughter?'

He laughed knowing how Jo's mother was always finding fault in his behaviour. 'Yes and no,' he said. 'But now I'm buggered. I didn't get home till after 10.'

'Oh, do tell, and leave in all the saucy bits.'

'I've been packing since dawn.'

Jo gasped. 'Packing? Packing what?'

'Everything. I'm on the move, Detective. And I haven't rung your father back to cancel the sale of my place.'

'Hey, slow down, Pop, start from the beginning. What's happened?'

He sounded flippant. 'I've done what you suggested. I've bought a place in a retirement village.'

'What? When? Which one?'

'That swanky place in Brighton.'

'You're kidding?'

'Do I ever joke about money?'

Jo floundered. 'But you said it was too posh, that if you lived there people would think you were corrupt.'

'Now Jo, I've done what you wanted. Why can't you be pleased?'

'Pleased? Pop, I'm over the moon. I'm going to work but I'll be over tonight to help. And *I'll* bring the grub.'

'No need, Detective. Fanny's coming over with tea and cardboard boxes to help me pack.'

'Oh,' said Jo not knowing if she was thrilled or chilled. 'But why are you cancelling my father as your agent?'

'I got a better offer. Fanny's son-in-law's an estate agent, and he'll be here at 12 with the contract. It's all under control, Officer.'

Jo blew air being stunned by the events and their speed.

'Good for you, Pop. But please ring me if you need me. Promise?'

'I promise to tell the truth, the whole truth and ...'

'Behave,' said Jo laughing. 'See ya, Pop.' The call ended. She spoke to herself. 'Well Joanna, I think that's what you call a result.'

She rang her father and gave him the bad news. 'But you said the old bloke wanted me to sell the place.'

'I know Dad but he's got a friend who's helping him move.'

'A friend? What sort of a friend?'

'Now Dad, I know friendship is a foreign concept to you, but they're the facts.'

'And how come I can't trust the word of a police officer, *two* police officers?'

'I'll make it up to you, Dad.'

'Promises, promises,' he growled and hung up.

'And Merry Christmas to you too,' said his daughter.

She headed for work and Ronnie Bumstead and their cold case.

As she did, Cathy Feng entered the Michael Chan emporium. As is anyone on their first visit, she was impressed. 'Wow, Michael, what is this place?'

'My humble abode.'

'Humble is not the word I would choose.'

He led her to the nerve centre, his digital playground. 'And this is my office, where I dabble in all things binary.'

She shook her head in wonder. 'And who is this?' she asked as the resident feline stepped forward to receive a pat and deliver a leg rub.

'Cathy meet Alan; Alan, Cathy.'

She knelt and patted him. Her skirt rode up a little and Michael found himself appreciating her thighs and then her legs as a whole.

'Why Alan?' she asked.

'As in Alan Turing, the computer science mastermind.'

'The guy who was hounded because he was gay?'

Michael half-smiled appreciating her knowledge. 'Sadly, yes.'

'Didn't the UK government grant him a posthumous pardon?'

'And named a street after him and put his smiling countenance on a postage stamp.' He smiled at her. 'Better late than never I guess. Now, tea or coffee, and let's plan our tactics.'

They discussed the facts and their options.

'I suggest we go back to the PI,' said Michael, 'and tell her what we found and see if she has any more ideas.'

Cathy turned reluctant. 'You're probably right, Michael although I'm hoping to keep the costs down where possible.'

'Okay, how about I pay for this session?'

'No, this is my family and you've done more than enough already.'

'Okay, fifty-fifty and that's my final offer.'

She smiled. 'Thanks, Michael, you're a real friend.'

Their eyes met and his recent thoughts about her grew stronger.

'I'm enjoying being a PI and I'm hooked on this case, your case. I want to know what happens in the end.'

She nodded wondering if it would all end in tears.

Jo arrived at the Cold Case section. Ronnie had placed a giant homemade map of the Heads, the entrance to Port Phillip Bay, on a wall and was marking the map with Post-it Notes. He spotted her.

'G'day Detective. How ya going?' He was Mr Laidback.

'Good morning, Ronnie.'

'Did you read the notes?'

'Every page,' said Jo.

'And?'

'And what?'

'Who's the killer?' Jo laughed. Ronnie continued. 'I told my wife I have a new partner. She asked who and I said, "You'll never guess". She wouldn't guess so I told her, and have a guess what she said.'

'Ronnie, I deal in homicides not crystal balls.'

He beamed. 'She said Jo Best is the best homicide detective in town, and if anyone can crack this case she can.'

'Terrific,' said Jo, 'so no pressure then.'

'Now you must have a list of suspects. How about you show me yours and I'll show you mine.'

For a moment Jo thought Ronnie was adding a touch of tacky innuendo but he was too busy digging through files to be interested in so-called humour. He rummaged, cursed and searched. Finally he found the page on which he'd listed his suspects, and approached Jo.

'So, where's your list?'

She produced her phone, clicked twice and revealed her names.

'Okay,' he nodded, 'I agree I'm living in the Stone Age.'

They read each other's list.

'Are these in any order?' he asked.

'Yes, most likely at the top working down to least likely.'

'Well, great minds think alike. I've been working on the case for weeks, you 24 hours, and we both reckon Julian, the boyfriend, is our man. Who is this Conrad Van Heflin?'

'He worked on the Drysdale Queenscliff tourist railway.'

'And his connection?'

'He made a statement to police saying he saw Natasha on the night she was killed as he arrived home from work.'

'And how does that make him a suspect?'

'I think they've changed suspect to person of interest for a reason.'

'Sorry, person of interest.'

'Because 32 years later, he may remember something to unlock the case.'

'I can see why you solve Homicides; leave no stone unturned.

She indicated the wall. 'So what's with the map?'

He switched to excited. 'Ah, come and see.' They faced the map. 'My theory is she was murdered or was made unconscious and taken out to sea from Point Lonsdale. The killer thought she'd use her key for Davy Jones' locker, do a Jonah and get swallowed by a whale, or do a Harold Holt and become a fish supper, lemon but hold the vinegar.'

Jo smiled inside. She liked Ronnie's wisecracks.

'But what if,' he said, 'and it's a big if, but what if none of those three things happened? What if she floated back to shore, missed Point Lonsdale, ducked through the Heads, and ended up on the golden sands of Queenscliff?'

'She floated through the Heads?'

'Exactly,' said Ronnie bubbling and set out his case. 'Now we know when she and the boyfriend split up.'

'No, we know when he *said* they split up.'

Ronnie suffered a tinge of anger. 'Okay but we have eye-witnesses from the party who saw Julian arrive back at the house. We know when she was found. So if she was dumped at sea, what were the tide times on the night and what type of tides did we have?'

'What's a type of tides?'

Ronnie beamed. His captive audience of one sat ready. He pointed to the map and its post-it notes.

'There's a thing called the tidal stream which runs through the narrow opening of the Heads. Depending on the level of the water in and outside the bay, the tidal stream runs at about six knots but can be up to twice as fast under certain circumstances.'

Jo watched, listened and wondered if this was a total waste of time.

'If we know the times of the tides and the tidal flow speeds, we can pinpoint how Natasha finished up where she did, and approximately how long she took to get there.'

Jo nodded. 'I'm impressed with the detail and the amount of time you've put into this, Ronnie.'

He knew she wasn't thrilled. 'But?'

'But I reckon re-interviewing witnesses and persons of interest is as good, if not a better way of solving the case.'

'Fair enough.'

'And I spent an hour with a pathologist learning about advances in DNA technique, subjecting old items to new methods of testing, which I know you're keen on.'

'I am.'

She left it hanging. He now knew his dabbling in the moon and tides were unlikely to land the killer, assuming it was a homicide. Jo's ideas were practical and far more likely to solve this cold case.

'Right, so apart from removing my fantastic mural, what else would you suggest I do?'

'Ronnie,' sighed Jo. She hated criticising his work. 'I'm no expert, and because I have a different approach doesn't mean I'm right.'

He started removing the map. 'My missus nailed it. You're the best homicide detective in town. If anyone can crack this case, you can.'

The map disappeared and Jo felt rotten.

Michael and Cathy arrived at *All Round Investigations*. Starlight's office resembled a junkyard.

'Come in,' she said, 'and sit anywhere.'

The chairs were missing, there were cardboard packing boxes everywhere, and only one filing cabinet remained. Michael was thrilled to see the ancient computer still intact.

'What's happened?' he asked.

'I'm done,' said Starlight. 'If I don't retire now, I never will. I'll die on the job. Your case was my last.'

'Was?' asked Cathy. 'But we haven't found my birth mother yet.'

Starlight sniffed. 'Okay, I'll keep going for another week. Take it or leave it.'

The searchers glanced at one another. Their eyes spoke agreement. 'Thank you, Ms Freeman,' said Cathy. 'One more week will be fine.'

'So,' asked Starlight, 'what's happened?' Michael explained. She groaned. 'Bloody Covid,' she said. 'It's another reason why I'm out.'

'So what's your advice on approaching this woman, Alison Feng?' asked Michael.

'And the Covid rules mean no-one is allowed inside her home?'

'Correct,' said Michael, 'other than medical and essential staff.'

'Members of staff are obviously allowed so do you know anyone who works there, even a cook or cleaner?'

Shaking heads from the visitors. 'I think we were so excited to have found a relative who might know about my adoption, we weren't prepared for the Covid problem. It was difficult to think straight, wasn't it Michael?' said Cathy.

'It was crazy. We were a few metres away from the person who may have been part of the exchange, there were relatives screaming because they were locked out of the home, and we didn't know what to do.'

Starlight explained her plan. 'I'd list the ways you could approach Alison to ask her in person. Test every way and pick the best.'

'More than one plan?' asked a surprised Michael.

'The more plans you have, the greater your chance of speaking to the old girl, and finding Clara's family.' She meant Cathy.

Silence set in. 'Do you have any other advice?' asked Cathy.

'Yes, you're from the Chinese community. Have you been to see your people? You don't have to name names. But in that suburb, there may be Chinese people who know the nursing home. My experience is the Chinese are generous people who like to help their fellow Chinese.'

Silence returned until Michael made the farewell speech. 'You've been so helpful, Starlight. If we can find Cathy's birth mother, it will be largely because of you.'

'Exactly,' added Cathy.

'How much do we owe you?' asked Michael.

Starlight waved a hand. 'Forget it, it's on the house.'

'Thank you, you're very generous,' said Michael.

'No I'm not. It'd take a month to find the bloody invoice book.'

Cathy jumped in, grateful and relieved she didn't have to call on Michael's offer of money. 'Thank you Ms Freeman.'

'Not that you'd know, but if you come across anyone interested in buying an ancient but successful PI business, tell them they can have this lot for a song. Well, a song plus the three-piece band.'

She held out a hand and, despite the social distancing and elbow-touching times, the visitors shook it, thanked her again and departed.

Out in the street, Cathy bubbled with happiness. 'We were so lucky, Michael. If we'd come here tomorrow she'd be retired.'

Michael was thinking. 'Yes,' he said not listening to Cathy.

'So what shall we do? Draw up plans as recommended by Starlight?'

'Pardon?'

'Michael?' She waved a hand in front of his face. 'Wakey, wakey.'

He was thinking about talking to his friend, Jo Best. He needed her help with his plan to reach Cathy's step-grandmother.

Chapter 13

Jo and Ronnie reached an agreement. He would continue to work in the office listing questions and issues that needed more work. He would liaise with the forensic boffins to see if new DNA techniques could help. Jo would travel, find and interview people on the Persons of Interest list.

'It has to be face to face, Ronnie,' she said. 'I need to see their eyes, their body language and their attitude.'

'Their attitude? How can you see an attitude?'

'What, you've never interviewed a shifty suspect who tries too hard to be co-operative?'

He nodded. 'You do know one or two on the list may be dead.'

She did know. 'Let's hope the killer hasn't taken his or her secret to the grave.'

'One of the first things I did was ring everyone involved in the case. I told them the police were reviewing outstanding cold cases including the Queenscliff one, and wanted to know if they had anything new to add. None did and I was able to confirm addresses. So unless they've moved in the last few weeks, you should be okay.'

'Thanks, Ronnie, you're a star.'

'Tell me, how long will you be working on cold cases? I bet the heavies at Homicide would prefer to have you finding modern-day murderers rather than an ancient killer.'

She smiled. 'One day at a time, Ronnie. For now I'm here with you determined to crack this case.' He liked her. 'But what about you; haven't you got anything better to do in your retirement?'

'This *is* my retirement. Oh, and working on my pen collection.'

'Pardon?'

'I've been collecting pens since my grandfather gave me my first Mont Blanc when I was a kid.'

'How many have you got?'

'Grandfathers?' She laughed. 'Don't ask. At least a pen is small. Imagine if I collected vintage cars or piano accordions. My wife can't complain about the space I need.'

'So what do you call a person who collects pens?'

'I say pen collector because the alternative is penophile and believe me, you don't want to announce that at a dinner party.'

Jo smiled a la Michael Chan. 'You learn something new every day.'

She and Robbie talked about making an appointment first with each person of interest. Jo preferred no-warning interviews. She liked the idea of catching them unawares, not having had time to prepare their answers.

'You know you run the risk of finding them not at home,' said Ronnie, 'driving all that way for nothing.'

'True but these people are 30 years older, most will be retired, and if in Melbourne, all should be following Covid lockdown rules. I reckon my chances of finding them are good.'

'Good thinking, 99.' And so no-warning interviews it was.

'Keep in touch, Jo. I don't want you charging into a dangerous dungeon, exposing a killer and having him go crazy and doing you a mischief. Understood?' He gave her a serious look.

She liked him. 'I'll keep you informed at all times, Guv'nor.'

'Good luck,' he said and she set out to solve a possible murder committed more than three decades ago.

She set her Sat Nav to find her first interviewee. Her phone rang as she was about to drive away. 'Michael Chan, as I live and breathe. How the devil are you?'

'Well, thank you, Detective, and your good self?'

'I'm fine, thanks, and busy investigating this tricky cold case.'

Michael was not one to engage in small talk. He had news and the sooner he said it the better. 'I have a request.'

Jo was intrigued. 'Just the one? Okay, fire away.'

'I need a doctor to go to a nursing home which, thanks to Covid, is in lockdown, and talk to a resident about an illegal baby swap which happened 30 years ago and which the resident may not remember.'

She spoke Facetious. 'Is that all?'

'I was thinking of Jack Carr, and wondered if you could approach him. Is it possible, and would he volunteer to be the doctor?'

'No problem asking, but he may have an issue with the ethics.'

'I thought that. But he might have an idea about how I could achieve the aim without him being involved.'

'And he might know someone to do what you want. Leave it with me, Michael. I'll contact Jack and get back to you. Ciao.'

'Jack Carr,' said the GP answering his mobile. He'd seen the caller ID and enjoyed a shot of happiness but didn't want to jump the gun.

'Good morning, Doctor Carr, it's Detective Jo Best. How are you and your wonderful family?'

'All fine except me.'

'Oh?'

'I always worry when I hear from my favourite policewoman.'

She laughed. 'I have a strange request, Jack. Michael Chan wants access to a resident in a nursing home but can't speak to the patient because of Covid. Can you speak to him about how he might gain access including the possibility of using you as a stalking horse.'

'Right; an unusual and interesting request.'

'A phone call might be all he needs. Can I have him call you?'

'Of course.'

'Thanks Jack, you're a star. When would be a good time?'

'I'm home tonight; any time after 8. Why don't you bring him over and we can sort out his problem face to face.'

'It's not a police matter, Jack and if we're stopped, it could be tricky.'

'Silly me. Tell him to give me a call.'

'Will do, and thanks again, Jack. Talk soon.'

'Bye,' he said and went to collect his next patient.

Bradley Pearson was in bed at noon; normal behaviour for shift workers. He slept lightly and the door being knocked woke him. He swore. He chose the stay-in-bed-and-ignore-it position. The knocking continued. He swore again and got out of bed.

He peered through the bedroom blinds and saw two official-looking types. *Bugger. If I don't answer they'll be back.*

He slipped on his terry-towelling dressing gown with the brand El Cheapo. His pyjama bottoms were shorts and needed a wash last week. He opened the door and yawned.

'Mr Bradley Pearson?' asked one official.

Bradley nodded and scratched himself. 'Who wants to know?'

Showing their ID, they introduced themselves. They were contact tracing officials following up possible infections of Covid 19.

'We were given your name by your gym. There's been an outbreak there. Have you been tested for Covid?'

'Why haven't you checked your records?'

Bradley's unusual response floored the visitors. The common replies they heard were yes or no, I'm getting tested today, and occasionally "Piss off" or worse.

'Sorry?' said the official doing the talking.

'I've been tested and cleared and would need to be as I'm the nurse working the graveyard shift at Cedar Avenue Nursing Home in Surrey Hills. There's a serious spread of Covid there with residents infected, being transferred, and dying. Now, will that be all? This is 2am for a shift worker like me.'

His manner and language whacked the officials. They scribbled comments, apologised and retreated. Bradley went inside, opened his fridge, removed a bottle of a sugar engorged soft drink and guzzled. It was easy to believe Bradley lived alone. Who else would tolerate sharing with an embittered slob. He replaced the bottle, checked the airtight plastic bags then headed back to slumber.

Most of Jo's prospective interviewees lived in Melbourne, one in Daylesford, one in Geelong, two in Point Lonsdale and one in Portland, Oregon, USA. She planned to drive to each address with one exception; she would use Skype or Zoom to chat with the American witness, Chuck Richter.

As she and Ronnie nominated their most likely person of interest, as Natasha's ex, Julian was her first cab off the rank. He lived in Carlton, a short drive from Jo's office or flat.

The address was an old bluestone house, covered in ivy, with a verandah floor of tiny tiles and a black front door containing exquisite stained glass. The doorbell was a pull model as old as the house.

The door opened and a middle-aged woman with free-range hair and a couldn't-care-less attitude contemplated Jo.

'Hello,' said the detective, lowering her mask to show her face before replacing the protection. 'I'm Detective Senior Constable Joanna Best from Victoria Police.' Her ID was shown. 'May I have a word with Mr Julian Love please?'

'Julian,' yelled the woman, more at Jo than to anyone inside.

'What?' came from inside.

'It's for you.'

'Who is it?'

'The police.'

No reply from inside. The two women gazed at one another. Jo said nothing. The woman waited. The door was pulled back and Julian, 58, a beard attached to a man, stood there intrigued and annoyed; the man, not the beard. Hair was popular in this part of Carlton.

Jo went through her spiel. 'I'm investigating a cold case involving the death of Natasha Kaye.'

Julian groaned. 'Oh for God's sake. It was the last millennium. She drowned. What possible reason could you have to still investigate what was obviously an accident?'

Before Jo could reply, the woman pointed at her and spoke. 'You're Jo Best, the cop who found the little girl in Castlemaine.'

The claim, though true, threw Jo. 'Ah, yes, I am.'

'And those murders with the religious weirdo and the drug dealers from Sydney and the States. You're famous.'

Julian's temper caught fire. He thought his partner was about to invite the detective into their home for coffee and a chat. He wanted her gone.

'I've nothing to say.' He went to close the door but was stopped by the love of his life who now became the pest of his life.

'Yes you have,' she said, re-opening the door. 'We were talking about the case only last month. And this woman is the best detective ...' She stopped and put a hand to her mouth. 'Sorry, terrible pun.'

'It happens a lot,' said Jo seizing on the woman's response hoping the interview would go ahead.

The woman with the free-range hair beckoned. 'I'm Becky. Do come in, Officer. I'll make coffee while you and Julian have a chat.' And they did.

Julian tried to be as unco-operative as possible, and scribbled on a document. Jo noted his mollydooker status, never lost her cool and chipped away at his answers. The coffee and expensive biscuits arrived (all the way from Italy) and Jo kept nagging the suspect.

'This argument, Julian, (she asked if she might call him that), you say it was about nothing.'

'It was.'

'But it caused you and Natasha to separate; you returned and she didn't.'

'I walked away, she went swimming and drowned.'

'Did Natasha have any other boyfriends apart from you?'

'No.'

'Yes she did,' said Becky, now Jo's best friend. 'You said she was keen on Natasha's girlfriend's boyfriend.'

Julian lost it. 'Will you shut up?'

Jo studied her notes. 'Would that be Ralph, Zara's boyfriend?'

'Yes,' said Becky, her face alive, now delighting in helping the detective while seemingly attacking her partner. 'You said Ralph and Natasha were flirting at the party.'

Julian's rage came to the boil. He went for the woman in his life. 'You weren't there and you know nothing. So shut up and let me answer the questions.'

Jo said nothing allowing the anger to simmer. 'Is that what you and Natasha were arguing about, Julian, her flirting with Ralph?'

He wanted this over. 'I can't remember. It was no big deal.'

'Are you still surfing, Julian?'

The sudden change of topic threw him. He looked shocked. 'What?'

'Do you still surf at Point Lonsdale?'

'And how is that even remotely relevant?'

'I saw the surfboards in your garage and was curious.'

'They belong to my son who uses this house as a hotel.'

'Are the boards a gift from his father?' asked Jo.

The partner couldn't help herself. 'They used to belong to Julian but his surfing days are over.' She patted his hair. 'Aren't they darling?'

Julian wasn't a violent man but right now wanted to slap his wife, cop in the room or not.

Jo asked a few more questions before ending Julian's agony. 'Thanks for your help, Julian and, I'm sorry I've forgotten your name. She wanted to build a rapport with the woman.

'Blabbermouth,' said Julian and stormed from the room.

Jo was escorted out by Blabbermouth giving Jo the impression she wanted her husband to be found guilty if only to have gossip to share with her pals.

In her car, Jo made notes. Both she and Ronnie put Julian at the top of the suspect list. In Jo's mind, her latest interview kept him there. Only problem, she was bereft of evidence.

From her list she chose one of the people mentioned in Carlton, Zara, girlfriend of Natasha and possible girlfriend of Ralph the flirt. Zara ran a hairdressing salon in fashionable Yarraville, 9 kays away.

The sign on the salon door said CLOSED due to Covid. Jo walked along the side of the weatherboard shop and knocked on the door of the house behind. Zara, 52, opened the door.

'I'm sorry, love, if I let you in a nosy neighbour will squeal and next thing the police will lob on me doorstep.'

Jo loved these moments. 'Hello Zara, I *am* the police.'

It took explaining but eventually they settled in Zara's trendy home, and after discussing the pandemic's effect on small business, they chatted about Natasha Kaye and the night she died.

Zara remembered her boyfriend Ralph, long since an ex-boyfriend, being drunk and infatuated with Natasha. She remembered Natasha and Julian going outside and having an argument.

'Did you see them arguing?' asked Jo.

'In the back yard but then Julian dragged her off to the beach and that's the last I saw of Natasha.'

'What about Julian?'

'He came back looking shithouse. I thought he'd have a go at Ralph but the silly bugger fell asleep. Most of us crashed on the floor or on settees in the lounge.'

'And?'

'I remember Julian getting up again in the night and going outside. I saw him smoking in the backyard, and then I went back to sleep.'

'And when did he come back?'

'Dunno. I fell asleep. In the morning he was asking if anyone had seen Natasha but didn't seem too worried. I think he said she went back to Melbourne.'

Jo smiled. 'Thanks Zara.'

'No worries, and when this bloody Covid's over, drop in for a quality trim. I could make you even more beautiful.'

Ruth did her weekly shop mid-week once the specials were posted. She went to the closest supermarket in Swan Street. She didn't understand this Covid-19 thing but faithfully wore a mask, and even used the hand sanitizer at the front of the store. She popped her groceries in her two-wheeled trolley and toddled off home to her elderly mother.

'I'm home, Mum,' she called and life carried on.

Ruth's mother fell ill first and then Ruth. She rang the doctor. Tele-health was out for the internet-free mother and daughter, and the GP sent an ambulance to the house. Both women tested positive for Covid.

Matt forgot his wife's birthday—again—and raced into the same supermarket to buy chocolates and a card. He grabbed the first reasonable-looking card, and pondered the rows of confectionery. *I'd better go top shelf* he thought. He grabbed a large selection from Belgium and hurried through the self-serve.

Three days later his wife experienced Covid symptoms as did her mother and neighbour. Matt stayed healthy but two of his workmates went down in a heap. All five people tested positive.

The toughest job of many tough jobs with Covid-19 was tracing. Once a person tested positive, isolation was essential. Seriously ill patients went to hospital. But the key question remained: where did the patient catch Covid, and where have they been in recent times? Who are their contacts?

Ruth and Matt were linked. They shopped in the same supermarket which carried on blissfully ignorant of the danger the store posed to shoppers and staff alike.

Chapter 14

Callum Blunt was beside himself. This was a change as he was usually up himself. He'd contacted his mate, the former head of Homicide at Victoria Police, DI Grant Steele, now employed by the Feds in Canberra.

Steele knew people in the old Australian Customs Service now colloquially known as Border Force. Their main role is to keep out undesirables—goods and people.

Because the murder victim found in the Moonee Ponds Creek had possible links to crime and war in the old Yugoslavia, Callum needed to know if the killer had discovered John Banks, and flown Down Under for a spot of retribution. Was Branko stiffed by a former enemy from his home country, Serbia?

Bingo. A gentleman from that part of the world with suspicious criminal connections was recently granted entry to Australia for a short visit. The reason? To visit his dying father and attend the funeral should the old boy pop his clogs. Callum purred.

'Where did he stay?'

'He gave his parents' address in Melbourne.'

'How come he was let in?'

'No criminal record and compassionate reason to attend dying father would be the factors.'

'And I bet the prick's pissed off.'

'Yep, you've just missed him. He must have been on one of the last flights before your lockdown.'

'Thanks,' said Blunt then, 'Bugger.'

'At least you've cracked the case, mate.'

'You reckon?'

'It's beautiful to put one over the Best bitch for a change.'

'She's not here.'

'What? Don't tell me she's transferred?'

'No, she's wasting her time on a forgotten cold case with a forgotten retired DS.'

Steele scoffed. 'Long may she reign.'

'There's a feeling she won't come back. That rumour about Maurice Chevalier's will looks like being true. She's now the richest cop in the world.'

'Bitch,' said Steele with a mix of envy and hate. 'Let's know how the others take it when you tell them you cracked the Moonee Ponds murder.'

Jo headed back across town. She wanted to break her rule of not warning the interviewee but didn't. In this case it was interviewees as she drove to see the victim's parents, Les and Marie Kaye. Do parents who've lost a child ever get over their sadness?

They were in the back garden and Jo spotted them, waving as she took the short cut along the side path.

'Hello,' she called.

Les was gardening and Marie sitting in the shade. The garden suited the house; big, established and magnificent.

Jo introduced herself and was soon sitting in the garden enjoying a cool drink. The parents were keen to chat. They hated the subject being brought up but appreciated the effort to find a resolution.

'Natasha was our only child. She would be 54 next week,' said Marie. 'She'd probably be a mother making us grandparents.'

Jo couldn't think of a reply. The mood was sombre and still heartbreaking for the parents, and particularly in their final years. Jo reckoned Marie looked unwell.

'Please don't feel you have to answer any of my questions,' said Jo, 'but the team are keen to solve this cold case once and for all.'

'Fire away,' said Les and meant it.

'Do you think Natasha met with foul play?'

'You mean was she murdered?' asked Les.

'She was such a good swimmer,' said Marie. 'Even in the surf she could ride the swells and swim ashore with ease. For the coroner to rule she drowned is too hard for me.'

Jo waited then put forward a theory. 'It could be true she drowned, but equally true that someone helped her to drown.'

The claim shocked the mother and Jo regretted saying it.

'I agree,' said Les who grabbed their attention. 'Marie's right about her swimming ability. And Natasha would never put herself in danger. Yes, she drowned because the killer needed her dead.'

Another long silence followed. Some doves cooed. 'May I ask if you have any thoughts as to who was involved?'

The parents were reluctant. Decades of waves had washed the sand where her body was found. Their thinking was simple. *Our girl is gone. Let her rest in peace.* Jo prepared to leave when Marie spoke.

'I never liked her then boyfriend, Julian.'

Jo waited and observed Les. He took his time. 'I hated him,' he said. *Okay*, thought Jo, *that's four for the boyfriend.*

'And are your suspicions based on any facts or evidence?'

Marie shook her head. 'Call mine female intuition.'

Les was equally as blunt. 'After she died, he would never look you in the eye.'

Jo thanked them, promised to keep in touch and report any, even no progress, and left. She sat in her car and rang Ronnie.

'I wondered what happened to you. How did you go?'

Jo gave details of her three interviews. 'So everyone reckons it's the boyfriend yet no-one has a single shred of evidence.'

'Not so fast,' said Ronnie, 'I may have something. I contacted a Mr Alastair Dean at Forensics and he sounded keen to help.'

Jo performed the old hairs on the back of the neck routine.

Michael worked on a couple of web page design jobs but kept putting them aside as he worked on Cathy Feng's birth mother quest. She'd given him permission to take action on her behalf.

He rang the nursing home in Box Hill. He didn't have to pretend or tell lies. His was a genuine enquiry.

'Hello, my name is Michael Chan, and I'm calling on behalf of a friend, Cathy Feng, who is the granddaughter of one of your residents, Alison Feng.'

'The woman in the nursing home gasped. 'Oh, I'm sorry, Mr Chan. Alison was taken to hospital this morning. She has contracted the Coronavirus.'

Michael nearly dropped the phone. He bounced out of his chair and frightened Alan. 'Is she all right? I mean how bad are her symptoms?'

'I've only just come on duty. Please hold and I'll ask.'

Michael paced his work space, thinking terrible thoughts.

Like her daughter, she's going to die and tell us nothing. Cathy was so near and yet so far. What will I tell Cathy?

'Are you there?' asked the woman.

'Yes, I'm here.'

'Her temperature was elevated and she had a headache and nasty cough. The nurse called the doctor who called the ambulance.'

Michael's chest pain grew sharper, his breathing quicker. 'Thank you, and can you tell me which hospital she's in?'

'She went to Box Hill.'

'Okay, we can contact her there. Thanks for your trouble.'

'You're welcome.'

The call ended and Michael stared at confusion.

Do I ring the hospital or Cathy or what?

The "what" became a call to Jack Carr. Jo Best paved the way for the GP to help and now Michael really did need practical advice.

'Hello, Dr Carr, it's Michael Chan speaking.'

'G'day Michael, Jo said you might call. How are things?'

'Not good I'm afraid. Did Jo explain the situation?'

'In broad terms, she did. You have a friend who was adopted and wants to find her birth mother.'

'Pretty much but the woman who adopted my friend is dead. We tracked her mother to a nursing home in Box Hill have just heard she tested positive for Covid and is in the Box Hill Hospital.'

'Okay. So how can I help?'

'We need access to the elderly woman who may know the identity of my friend's birth mother.'

'Have you checked the birth certificate angle?'

'A Private Investigator did which is how we came up with the grandmother.'

'When you say you need access, I assume you mean you want to speak to this woman in person.'

'Exactly.'

'And she may be your only hope?'

'True, and the nursing home wouldn't let us in and I'm guessing the hospital will do the same.'

'They will, even more so. The lockdowns are pretty severe.'

'Will she die, Doctor Carr?'

'I'd need to know the details first but the main age group with Covid deaths is in the aged care facilities. Many have chronic health conditions anyway with their immune system not strong. Covid seems to be the tipping point.'

Michael hesitated. He needed to ask the big question. 'If a relative, my friend is by adoption this woman's granddaughter, isn't allowed to speak to this patient, could a medical person, a doctor or nurse do so?'

Jack could see where this was heading. 'The short answer is yes but it's not that simple. If for instance you asked a doctor to chat to the woman and she became upset and then had a health issue, and the reason came out, the doctor could be in trouble. He or she, no matter how noble the cause, is there to provide health care, not to do a favour for a friend or colleague.'

Michael knew it. 'I understand.'

'But leave it with me and I'll talk to people. There might be a way around the issue.'

'I hope so,' said Michael with desperation in his voice.

'Here's a hypothetical. The lady recovers but there is concern for her mental wellbeing. If in therapy she was asked about her family, your friend's birth mother's name might be mentioned, and that could prompt a question or two.'

Michael thought it a long shot but was grateful. 'Thank you, Doctor Carr, I appreciate your help and I'm sure my friend does too.'

'It's a pleasure, Michael and please call me Jack.' There was a pause. 'So how is our favourite detective involved in this saga?'

Michael hesitated. 'Actually she isn't. It's not a police matter and I didn't want to bother her.'

'You mean it's Watson without Holmes?'

Michael was relieved Jack went for the joke. He laughed, thanked the GP again and ended the call.

DI Blunt arrived in the street where the parents of the Serbian visitor lived. Callum would have loved nicking the tourist cum murderer but knew he needed facts. The parents were key. The Bankowitz murder was down to their son who used the death of his father as cover for the kill.

Blunt psyched himself up for family grief. The killer's old man was seriously ill if not dead. Asking questions about the son was hardly apt but a man's gotta do what a man's gotta do. He rang the doorbell.

An elderly woman appeared dressed entirely in black.

Steady Callum, this here's the widow.

He introduced himself, and asked about a Mr Malik Duro.'

'He my son,' said the woman. 'Come in.'

The detective stood in the hall with the patterned carpet, and walls covered with photos of family members in traditional costume plus religious icons and one hideous ornate clock.

'Here,' she said indicating the frosted glass doors of the lounge.

'After you,' said Blunt and followed the woman into the room.

She pointed. 'My husband,' she said and Callum stared at the supposedly sick or more likely dead man who recently changed his name to Lazarus. She spoke in her native tongue. The man rose from his chair and extended his hand.

'Hello policeman,' he said and smiled exposing a set of teeth, which you really couldn't call a set, as they were more a junkyard collection. He indicated a chair. 'Please to sit.'

And so using broken English, Callum asked about their son and heir. Clearly he lied on his visa application. What did he do when in Melbourne? What did he do on the night of the murder?

The answers were so vague to be meaningless which suited Callum. Vague meant the son could have been anywhere including a footbridge over the Moonee Ponds Creek. The crim from o/s dropped in pretending to attend the funeral of his healthy old man, and while here, did for his former criminal or war enemy foe. Case closed.

Chapter 15

Many crims will tell you jails are full of criminals who were wrongly convicted. 'I never done it, your Honour. I wasn't even there, m'lud.' But getting a conviction overturned ain't easy. If it was, every Tom, Dick and Harriet would flood the court with requests for their immediate release. They don't because you need serious new evidence, a shed load of money and a ton of time. But if you fancy your chances, obtaining leave to appeal from the Court of Appeal is the way to go.

Annie Cleary was doing time, convicted for mariticide; she knocked off her old man. Annie, or AC as she was known, protested her innocence loud and long using her favourite barrister, Parrish Lamb, known in legal circles as Parrish Counsel. He took the case, a tough case because AC made a clumsy killer.

She started in crime once she left school, stealing and turning tricks. Over the years she built a criminal empire selling sex and drugs while doing favours for people with influence. She called it insurance.

Her little black book, or its digital equivalent, was said to contain enough explosive data to keep police, pollies and do-gooders in perpetual silence. But the silly woman was caught holding the smoking gun over hubby's corpse and even Parrish Counsel couldn't get her off. She appealed, of course, and failed. She hated the slammer and figured even with time off for good behaviour, she'd be non-compos mentis when released or brown bread before release. The walls kept closing in.

Her son, Shane, made regular visits to Mum, but the boy stood at the end of the line when the brains were handed out. AC pumped her son with instructions and finally, after his umpteenth visit to Mr Lamb's chambers, the brief agreed to visit the Queen of Crime. He couldn't think of anything worse. Yes he could. It would be listening to Shane whining about his poor old mum.

It was visiting time. 'Tell me, Parrish, how I get leave to appeal?'

'How many more times, Annie? You need compelling *new* evidence. No court will allow an appeal unless it is compelled to do so.'

'How's this for compelling?' she asked. 'The pathologist who examined my old man was (a) an alcoholic and drunk while on duty and (b) not qualified to assess plant samples and how they related to her report.'

Parrish didn't immediately point out the weaknesses of her argument. 'No court will accept unsubstantiated allegations. Who says she was drunk on duty?'

'I have two sworn statements. One is from an experienced pathologist, and another from an attendant who assisted at many of her post mortems.'

'Sworn affidavits?'

'I'm not wasting your time, Parrish. Both men have firsthand experience and are reliable, rolled-gold witnesses.'

The barrister never took anything Annie said to be gospel. 'What about this other matter with the plants.'

'One of the things the inebriated pathologist stated in her report, and which you didn't challenge, concerned plant material found on Hector's clothing; material found on our property in Kilmore.'

'It was accepted as true evidence.'

'But the pathologist has no expertise in plant material. She never studied or sat for any exams in that subject.'

'Was she defining the material or stating where it was found?'

Annie couldn't see the wood for the trees. 'I've found an expert who read her report and says it's rubbish. I think the word bullshit was used.' She stared at the barrister. He was stuck for a reply. 'Well?'

'I'll check it out.'

'Good and my new solicitor has all the paperwork.'

He gawped. *Not again.* 'You're *new* solicitor?'

'Shane has his details.'

Parrish paused and the chatter from the other visitors filled the silence. Annie leaned forward and spoke softly.

'Now I want you to know Parrish, I don't hold anything against you for failing to discover these matters. You're a busy man. These things happen.' She dropped her voice even more. 'But if you fuck me around and don't win this appeal, your little peccadilloes might accidentally break free and float off into the media ether, or is it the Cloud today?'

He shuddered. Their eyes locked. Breathing rapidly, he spoke.

'Remind me again of the name of this sozzled pathologist.'

'Gabrielle Strange,' she said, her words oozing from a meat mincer.

Jo studied her list of Persons of Interest. Three lived in the area where Natasha died. Three interviews with one visit appealed. Jo rang Ronnie and told him her plan. He was still excited about what Jo told him via Gabrielle Strange of new DNA developments. Another look at old evidence might be the key. But it meant finding the right scientist and Jo had groaned internally when Ronnie told her the name Alastair Dean. Working with Mummy's Boy again did not appeal.

Off she went towards Geelong and the Bellarine Peninsula. Her first interviewee was Maisie Wright who was 12 when she found Natasha on the beach at Queenscliff. Today Maisie, a fulltime Mum, doubled as a teacher with her two youngsters learning online thanks to Covid.

To say Maisie was pleased to meet Jo would be wrong. She was rapt. Jo explained who she was and her mission. Many a parent co-opted into a teaching role reached the stir crazy stage. Maisie hesitated for half a nanosecond before sending her kids out to play.

'I've read your statement, Maisie, but how good is your memory?'

'Pretty good. I thought the lady was sleeping on the beach. My dog went up to her which was unusual. I called him but he stayed sniffing. When I moved closer, I could see she was dead.'

'What can you remember of the area where you found the body?'

She shrugged. 'I was 12 and scared. I got the dog and ran.'

'Did you read about the case in the papers or see it on TV?'

'My family talked about it and reckoned her boyfriend did it.'

'But not you?'

She thought about it. 'I went back later when the police and media and people were there. I saw the boyfriend talking to the TV reporters. To me, he looked sad, like he blamed himself for what happened.'

Their interview was interrupted when one of Maisie's kids came in to report a sibling had allegedly committed a rule infraction of the Backyard Trampoline Usage Act, Section 3, Article 1.5 (iv).

Jo left Queenscliff for Point Lonsdale, about 5 kays away. Conrad Van Heflin still volunteered for the Bellarine Railway. Born with cerebral palsy, Conrad displayed strong communication skills and his mobility was pretty darn good. His grandfather loved trains, helped hook young Conrad, and when the chance came to volunteer for the tourist railway, it was a marriage made in heaven. The company needed helpers and the helper loved trains.

Jo found him at home and the now middle-aged gent welcomed his visitor even more enthusiastically than did Maisie. They chatted.

'So you're not working for the rail company at present?' asked Jo.

'Nobody is thanks to the government and Covid. We're not allowed to operate.'

Jo admired the man. A lifelong disability, no known cure and yet here he was, getting on with life and feeling frustrated he couldn't get out and about.

'Conrad, I want to go over your statement about the young woman found on the beach at Queenscliff more than 30 years ago.'

'I saw her,' he said. 'I saw her on the night she died.'

'You said you were getting out of a car and she went past.'

'She stopped and asked me if I wanted a hand.'

Jo frowned. 'She spoke to you?'

'She was as close to me as you are now.'

'But this is not in your statement.'

'Because they didn't believe me. The policeman thought I was a weirdo. He made me sign the paper and when I struggled to sign ...' Conrad opened his hands indicating his disability. 'I mean duh, what did he expect? He scribbled my name and took off.'

Jo's cheeks puffed. Whoever took Conrad's statement regarded him as an unreliable witness due to his cerebral palsy when in fact his mind was razor sharp and now, 32 years later, it seemed he could remember everything that happened down to the last detail.

'Can you remember what she was wearing?'

'Her red jumper didn't hide her white shirt and it was ripped.' Jo sat stunned. 'And she'd been crying. Her eye make-up was smudged.'

'Where was this?'

'Where was her make-up? On her face of course.'

Jo appreciated his wit and intelligence. 'No, the location.' She indicated the front garden. 'Was it outside in the street?'

'I think you're leading the witness, Officer.' She wanted to kick herself but he grinned. 'No, we lived in Ocean Road then. It's close to the beach, near where she was staying.'

'Can you remember the approximate time?'

'Not approximate, it was exactly ten thirty-seven or rather 2237 hours. I'm a stickler for time. The train was late so I waited for a lift from Jimmy Horne. He's dead now. But I know the times because one of my jobs is to record departure and arrival times and I note my time of arrival at home.'

'So where was the woman coming from, which direction?'

'She was heading towards the Lighthouse.'

Jo struggled with the detail Conrad revealed from so long ago. 'I don't understand why all this information you've given isn't on record.'

'It's because people think I'm stupid. They see me walk and hear me talk and reckon I can't think or observe or remember things. Not everyone mind but some people have no idea.'

'Conrad, I'm a detective and have interviewed many people but I've never met anyone as lucid and helpful. So thank you.'

He wasn't finished. 'Do you know who killed her?'

She gave him a stare. 'Not yet but I'd love you to tell me.'

He laughed for the first time, his body twisting with delight. 'How much is the reward?' he asked with a sparkle in his eye.

She joined in with his joy then took a statement in which he repeated everything he told her. This time he was given an age to add his moniker.

'You're a champion, Conrad, and it's been a pleasure meeting you.'

'Likewise,' he said and stuck out his imperfect hand. Their handshake was as warm and firm as could be imagined.

Jo returned to her car and drove to her final interviewee. This was the now 75 year old Tony Grande who then and still lives next door to the Love beach house at Point Lonsdale. That was the venue of the party Natasha Kaye left and to which she never returned.

Tony was one of those men who improved with age. Grey hair, touch of a tan and a good figure gave him the matinee idol look. *Bloody men have it easy* she thought.

The Stuart Grainger lookalike was up for a chat. Jo was like a visitor bringing joy to people stuck at home thanks to the pandemic.

'I've read your statement, Mr Grande.'

'Please, call me Tony.'

She smiled. 'Can you remember what you said way back then?'

'Pretty much. I was no fan of Julian. His parents were lovely people but when Julian came down for a weekend and his parents stayed in Melbourne, I knew I'd have trouble sleeping.'

'Parties?'

'No problem until say 10 or a bit later but they'd keep going way past midnight. I'd go in and politely ask for the music to be turned down. They were never rude but insisted I join them for a drink. Their parents would come down the next weekend and ask if there were any problems, and I'd lie through my teeth.'

'When did you go to sleep on the night in question?'

He shrugged. 'After midnight; I didn't check. I know my house guest was annoyed. He'd come for peace and quiet.'

She read her notes. 'You said Perry Baker left early that morning.'

He did but you probably know he's no longer Perry Baker.' Tony picked up two books from the coffee table. 'He's now the famous novelist, Perry Batchelor.'

Jo scrutinized the hardback books, both having the face of the novelist on the back of the dust jacket. 'I've heard of him. Wasn't one of these made into a movie?'

'It was and his latest already has an option from the States.'

'Do you still keep in touch?'

'Oh no, he's far too famous for me. He lives up in Melbourne in the Dandenongs with his stunning wife and Afghans.'

'So after all these years, what's your theory on how Natasha died?'

He did have a theory. 'Well if it's true that in the vast majority of murders, the victim knows the killer, the evidence, such as it is in this case, has to point to the boyfriend, he of the loud music.'

'Have you ever thought about that night? Has anything nagged you, an unusual event? Does a thought, an idea, or a question pop up?'

He paused, appeared to start to speak then stopped. 'Nah, nothing, it's all forgotten.'

Chapter 16

'Good evening, madam. How can we help?'

The woman was a looker. The male constable behind the front desk of the cop shop in Mt Alexander Road, Moonee Ponds gave her his full attention; even more so when she spoke.

'I think my husband has killed someone.'

Not a bad opening line. Better than "I've lost my cat" or "me car's been scratched".

The matter was too important for a chat in the front office with a lowly uniformed constable, and there were no forms to fill in headed *Wife Reporting Husband as a Murderer*.

A more senior officer was summoned and the matter continued in a less public space.

The woman recently suffered a disappointment when a date she made with her secret lover didn't happen. Romeo, Romeo wherefore art thou? He stood her up. The reason why was obvious; he showed up on the telly having the big sleep in the local waterway. The missing lover was John Banks aka Branko Bankowitz the chap found face down in the Moonee Ponds Creek. The woman, Sophia Brent, looked scared, terrified more like, believing her husband, Hudson, discovered the affair and ended it by "fixing" the boyfriend.

'If he's killed my boyfriend, he'll kill me. I need protection. I can't go home. Can you find me a place in one of those women's refuges?'

'All in good time, madam. First let's have a few details.'

The interview continued during which time a phone call was made to the Homicide Squad, and DI Rose heard the news. She swore. This simple bloodless homicide now attracted more suspects than customers at a popular coffee shop doing takeaways during Covid.

Detective Sergeant Rick Melody and Detective Senior Constable Stephen Payne were sent to interview the startled member of the public. Detective Inspector Elly Rose gave instructions.

'If she's not a fantasist, you may need to interview hubby. If you think he's likely to spark up, do not attempt any heroics. Yes?'

Melody and Payne acknowledged their boss. 'Ma'am.'

Those two detectives were missing when Homicide met to review the case. DI Blunt sat at the back purring. Not only did he believe he'd cracked the case—okay the killer left town—but it showed how he, Blunt, was able to call on his many national and international contacts. He truly was a man of the world, a detective on the path to promotion and fame.

'Right,' said DI Rose. 'Before I hand over to Billy, I want to tell you about the memorial service for DI Richelieu in the chapel at Glen Waverley on Friday week at 10. It goes without saying all members will attend. If anyone wishes to speak at the service, come and see me later.' Nobody moved. Rose glanced at Hughes who took over.

'Okay, who has the good news?' Callum indicated like a kid putting up his hand at the back of the class with the answer to the question, 2 + 2. 'DI Blunt.'

He strode to the front and gave his spiel. Rose had told Hughes about the frantic wife in the Moonee Ponds police station but, to be fair, they gave Callum first crack. Give the man enough rope.

He explained his wizard investigation with his visit to the home of the parents of the obvious killer. 'His visa was marked For Single Use only. He was never coming back here. His MO was Land, Kill, and Flee.' Blunt concluded his evidence, pushed out a supercilious grin, and, out of kindness, Billy stepped in.

'So we know the ID of the visitor from Eastern Europe, his criminal history but without conviction, that he was here for his father's funeral yet Poppa is alive and well, and the visitor's parents have no alibi for their boy on the night Bankowitz was killed. Yes?'

Callum nodded. He copped a faint inkling of wanting to vomit. 'We ask for the Serbian authorities to hold him pending a visit from us.'

'From you?' asked Billy.

He shrugged. 'I'd be happy to lead the investigation.'

'Okay, thanks, Callum. Anyone else?' The DI left for the naughty corner.

DS Fletcher spoke. 'We still don't know anything about the threat made to Branko's business partner.'

'Did it actually happen?' asked Billy.

'That crossed our minds,' said Charley Baldwin. 'Did Jones invent the threat to cover the fact he stiffed his mate?'

DI Rose interrupted. 'I think we're missing the key point here. Bankowitz wasn't stabbed, shot or strangled. If Dr Laudi is right, he copped a sophisticated heart starter drug, suffered a massive heart attack and fell in the creek whacking his head on the concrete en route. Surely we find the killer by studying the method used. Who would have access to the drug?'

'Drug dealers,' said DS Fletcher.

'Chemists, doctors, pathologists,' added Baldwin.

'Criminals from overseas,' said Blunt, although without conviction.

'Okay, let's explore it,' said Billy. 'Now there's been a development in the last half hour. DI Rose.'

She explained the absence of Melody and Payne. 'If this woman is on the level, our sneaky business partner and international war criminal may both be gazumped by a simple love triangle.' DI Blunt wanted to scream. 'Our victim has been playing away with a married woman in Moonee Ponds which explains the location of the murder. Her old man discovered the affair, and killed Romeo in the local waterway.'

Fletcher shook his head. 'It's not right. Why was Bankowitz's car so far from the murder site? He parks then walks a kay to get killed? I don't think so. And how many cuckolds kill with a serve of upmarket adrenaline?'

'Right,' said Billy, 'we need to follow up with his live-in girlfriend in South Yarra. Did she know about lover boy's affair? We need to sort out Mr Jones and his gangster mates. Do they even exist? And we await news from Melody and Payne and the hysterical mistress.' She omitted Serbia, and Blunt endured a scary experience where incredibly, tears appeared in his eyes. *Is all my work for nothing?*

Melody and Payne arrived at the suburban police station and were introduced to the worried woman, Sophia Brent. She explained to the

Homicide detectives how she and the victim started a relationship only a few weeks ago when they met online. Both were in a relationship but unhappy. The detectives reckoned it might be true for her but Sonny Jim from *Advanced Security* with the wander lust only fancied playing away; understandable as the woman had stunning *Vogue* like features.

Sophia's husband was Hudson Brent, a mean and domineering brute who spent more time looking in the mirror than at his wife, and listed jealously as one of his hobbies.

The night of the murder, Sophia told Hudson she was off to see her ailing parents, her regular excuse, and drove to the lovers' lane meeting-place. He didn't show. No phone message. He ordered her never to contact him as his nosy wife, (his de facto), was always checking his phone. He used two, and the one he left lying around was not the secret model. Damn clever these bastards.

When he didn't show for the rendezvous, she went home via her parents. Hudson wasn't at home. He arrived later and said nothing. The next morning the TV news told the world John Banks was swimming with the fishes.

She watched her husband who seemed unusually quiet as if hiding something. He was especially cruel when asking about her parents.

'Does your husband have a gun, Mrs Brent?' asked DS Melody. She shook her head. 'What about a knife or other weapons? She gave a small nod. 'And where is he now?'

'At work.' They paused. 'He has his own security company. They provide bouncers for hotels and clubs.' She gave the address.

The detectives were not in a hurry to interview Mr Brent. They remembered the words of their boss about no heroics. If a jealous, manipulative bodybuilder kicked off, things might become tasty.

'We'll leave you here with these officers, Mrs Brent. After we've spoken with your husband, we'll be in touch. Okay?'

'Be careful, he has a violent temper.'

They borrowed a couple of uniforms and entered the reception area of the security company run by Hudson Brent. He appeared and seemed amused to find four policemen. He knew one of the constables who didn't want to be recognised. Moonlighting can get you into trouble.

'Good morning, gentlemen. Need any help with security?'

Melody and Payne showed their ID and asked if they could have a word in private. The "murderer" acted surprised and willingly agreed. They squeezed into his office with the uniforms still in Reception. The walls were all cheap bare bricks.

'What's up?' asked Hudson.

'We're investigating a homicide in Moonee Ponds, sir.'

'What, the bloke in the creek?'

'And we'd like to ask you a few questions.'

The penny dropped for Brent. They weren't here for advice or to investigate someone he knew. They were investigating him. It kicked off. He stood with veins flaring.'

'What is this shit?' he spat. Melody stood and Payne cowered. The uniforms came running but the office was so small it took time to even open the door. Chairs blocked the way.

Brent kept threatening daring the cops to have a go. 'You bastards come in here to pin a murder on me. I'll smash your fucking face in!'

Melody tried to calm the man which threw fuel on the fire. The constables were the brave (or foolish) ones and squeezed in with baton and mace at the ready.

As if struck by lightning, Brent surrended. He was brave when the odds were on his side. 'I'm saying nothing without my solicitor.'

It took longer for everyone to vacate the office than for Brent to be arrested and read his rights. He scored a free ride to Homicide. The uniforms reported to Moonee Ponds and Mrs Brent decided to move in with Mum and Dad. It was as much for safety as to assuage her guilt having used her folks as an excuse for her extra-curricular activities.

Chapter 17

Cathy arrived at Michael's warehouse. She'd given him permission to contact the hospital or nursing home for the latest on Alison. His half-smile didn't appear.

'Bad news?' she asked. He nodded. 'She hasn't died?' gasped Cathy.

'No, she's still with us but on a ventilator; not looking good.'

They sat and Alan agreed to take the minutes.

'I think we need to act quickly,' said Michael. 'If we can gain access to Alison, fine, but we're assuming she knows what happened at your adoption, and is willing and able to tell us. We need a Plan B. We need to try and find any of Alison and Gloria's relatives.'

'But even if they exist they may know nothing about my adoption.'

'True, but we'll never know if we do nothing.'

This was a tough assignment. Michael sorely wanted to help his friend but reckoned the missing ingredient was one Jo Best.

This isn't a police matter but I've seen the way she works, the results she achieves. She's working on a cold case right now. This is a sort of cold case. Why can't she lend us a hand?

Michael kept trying to encourage Cathy. 'You remember Starlight suggested we play the Chinese community card; we go to associations, history groups, anywhere Chinese gather and ask them for help.'

'I wouldn't know where to start,' she said.'

'Exploring online is easy. There are plenty of contact details and again, we'll never find your Mum if we do nothing.'

Cathy seemed hesitant and unsure and brushed and tied back her hair. 'I explored those family tree groups. You sign up, pay a sub, and hopefully collect family details.'

'And?' asked Michael.

She sighed. 'I fear my adoption was unofficial, an under the table agreement between two women or two families. If so then the official records either don't exist or are incomplete. It's like looking for a needle in a haystack.'

They paused. He didn't want to talk about a negative but felt it better to have all the possibilities out in the open.

'There is the "don't frighten the horses" problem.'

Her confusion increased. 'Sorry?'

'If we tell people what we're doing, who we're trying to find, the people we need may hear about us and go to ground.'

'You mean we'll scare them off?'

He nodded. 'We might find a person who knows your birth mother and they might tell us in an instant ...'

'But ...'

'But there's always the chance we'll drive them away. "Let sleeping dogs lie" is what they'll say. And an illegitimate baby scares some people. The shame lingers.'

They sat in silence. Alan chewed the end of his pencil.

'If you're right about the adoption being a private agreement, it's a double whammy—there are no records and those in the know may be reluctant to speak.'

Cathy's misery pushed out tears. 'What do *you* think happened?'

'Let's say your birth mother was an unwed teen. She might have had a one-night stand with your father. He might not have wanted you or your Mum. He may not even know he *is* your father. Being a teen, your Mum may not have had a say. Her family and Gloria's family got together and did the deal. They worked out the baby transfer.'

'Could they do that and not be caught?'

'Back in the 70s and 80s, unwed mothers giving up a baby was not unusual.'

'But I wasn't born then.'

'There were situations when an unwed young girl gave her baby to her married sister who had kids. The new baby was raised thinking her aunt was her mother.'

Cathy stood and walked to one of Michael's windows. She couldn't look at him as she spoke with a heavy heart.

'I'm sorry I dragged you into this, Michael. I think it's time we pulled the plug.'

'No, no, you don't mean that and besides there are alternatives.'

She turned to face him, crying. 'Alternatives?'

'First we can tread water. Keep checking on Alison and see what happens, and hope Doctor Carr's scenario comes true.'

He explained the possibility of Alison receiving therapy with a professional asking about her family as part of the treatment.

Cathy managed the smallest smile in Northcote. 'Thank you,' she whispered. If she had hope, it was hiding. Both despaired.

Melody and Payne arrived back at Homicide with their furious visitor. He called his solicitor. The police knew they lacked evidence against the arrested man and expected to get none. Hudson's solicitor advised his client to say nothing, forcing the police to reveal their case; assuming they had one. They didn't.

Rose and Hughes observed from outside the interview room.

'Mr Brent, do you know a man known as John Banks or by his former name of Branko Bankowitz?'

'No comment.'

They showed a recent photo of the victim. 'Do you recognise the person in this photo?'

'No comment.'

'It would help if you actually looked at the photo.'

Brent made a pathetic effort to examine the print, sat back and said, 'No comment.'

'Where were you last Tuesday between the hours of 7pm and 9pm?'

'No comment.'

The detectives realised this was a waste of time, their evidence being the statement of a worried wife. The fish weren't biting. The solicitor's instructions were being followed to the letter, and the sooner this farce ended the better. As a last resort, Melody hit below the belt and played the provocation card.

'Do you know where your wife is at this moment, Mr Brent?' The tactic worked.

Gone was the bland "No comment" and in its place was a snarling, 'You leave her out of it. D'ja hear me?'

The solicitor gave up. *Why do I accept clients like this powder keg?*

Melody tried to couch his taunting in professional terms. 'Are you aware your wife has been having an affair with the man in the photo?'

The short fuse fizzed. Hudson exploded. It wasn't so much his arrest that hurt but rather being branded a cuckold that stung like buggery.

Fletcher and Baldwin knocked on the South Yarra cottage door and identified themselves. They knew the lady inside was self-isolating due to Covid, and knew she was grieving the loss of her boyfriend, and hated being pestered by the police. They were about to make her day even worse by asking about darling John's other girlfriend.

'Go away,' she called. 'You know I have Covid.'

'We do Ms Delahunty but we'll stay outside and you can remain inside,' replied Fletcher'

'Have you caught the man who killed John?'

'We're not sure it was a man.'

Silence. 'What do you mean?'

'Do you know a woman called Sophia Brent?' asked Fletcher.

Baldwin admired the way his DS raised the subject.

'No, why should I? Who is she?'

'You haven't seen her name in a text message on John's phone?'

Oh boy, thought Baldwin glancing at Fletcher. *Such a leading question, Sarge, would never be allowed in court.*

The victim's girlfriend lost control. 'What are you saying? Why are you asking me these questions? Did she kill John?'

Fletcher went for the ubiquitous police response. 'She's helping us with our enquiries.' Baldwin wanted to applaud.

Ms Delahunty could take no more. She threw open the main door meaning only the fly-wire door stood between the three masked combatants. Her mask covered her red cheeks and prevented the spittle she produced from taking flight.

'Have you morons come to ask if I know John's sleeping with some slut? Is that why you're here?'

The detectives retreated because of her aggressive response and knowing she was possibly infectious. Their backward movement was the equivalent of shouting, "Unclean".

Fletcher struggled and Baldwin gave support. 'As my colleague explained, Lyn, we receive lots of information and this woman's name has come up in the course of our enquiries. We're asking people who knew John to see where this woman fits into his life.'

It was a fishing expedition hoping for a detailed explanation. Lyn's reply didn't help.

'Where she fits?' Lyn yelled. 'Where she fits? Well one wild guess would be on the back seat of his Beamer.'

The door slam which followed her reply scared the hell out of a line of ants currently streaming up the front wall.

The detectives spoke to one another with their eyes.

Oops.

Chapter 18

Jo arrived back in town wanting to provide Ronnie with a detailed report on her interviews.

'Home is the sailor, home from the sea,' he said. 'Good trip?'

'I can't decide if it was brilliant and therefore possible case-solving or simply interesting.'

'Well I'll buy one. What are you selling?'

She highlighted 12 year-old Maisie thinking the boyfriend's tears were genuine, the cerebral palsy man's first-hand experiences not being noted, and the next-door neighbour having an unheard of houseguest who is now an international star.

'Wow,' said Ronnie. 'I can see why those Homicide rumours about Jo Super Sleuth Best got started. What's next?'

'I need to line up the last three witnesses in Daylesford, the Dandenongs and the USA.' She opened her laptop and searched. A few clicks later and she hit a brick wall. 'Uh-oh.'

'What's up?' asked Ronnie coming to see the problem.

The flirting boyfriend, Ralph, the party guest who got extra friendly with Natasha, and probably caused the argument between the victim and boyfriend Julian, was no longer available for an interview.

Ralph and hubby ran a B & B near Daylesford. Their web site listed an announcement:

Bookings Cancelled
Due to the sudden and unexpected death
of my beloved husband, Ralph,
Stonehaven is closed until further notice.
Full refunds are available.
Graham Nightingale

Jo turned to Ronnie. He grimaced. 'We have that problem with cold cases; it's not only the victim who dies. Where did he sit in the grand scheme of things?'

'Not sure,' said Jo. 'I think he was the catalyst for the argument between Natasha and Julian.'

'You could get confirmation from Zara and Julian.'

'I doubt Julian will ever speak to me again, and Zara's told me all she knows.'

Ronnie went back to his desk. 'If you find out, let me know.'

Jo returned to her browser, opened up Facebook and searched for the American witness, Chuck Richter. He was popular. She scrolled for his latest post. 'Oh no,' she groaned. 'He's dead too.'

'Who, the American guy?' Jo nodded. 'He wasn't young.'

'91,' she said. 'They're dropping like flies, Ronnie. This cold case is slipping into the deep freeze.'

'He may not have remembered much. And he left before the party ended. If he knew anything, he would have told Julian's parents.'

'Who are both deceased,' said a frustrated Senior Constable.

'Is that the lot?'

'Lucky last is the famous novelist but you've not listed his number.'

'Because he wasn't famous at the time of the party, and I couldn't find him listed as a nobody.'

She found his web site. 'Here's his agent's number.' She rang it.

'Dianne Webster.'

'Oh, hello, Ms Webster; my name is Jo Best and I'm ringing about the possibility of interviewing Mr Batchelor.'

'I thought you cancelled.'

'I'm sorry?'

'Perry is extremely busy and the only time he has this month is tomorrow at 10. Take it or leave it.'

'Ah, thank you, I'll take it. But ...'

'Will you have a photographer with you?'

'No.'

'So it's just the one,' she scribbled. 'What's your number?'

Jo gave it, thinking she should stop the conversation to explain. *I'm not a journalist but a policewoman trying to solve an ancient cold case which I believe to be a murder.* Jo stayed schtum.

'I'll text you the address. Don't be late.'

The call ended and Ronnie turned to Jo. 'Any luck?' he asked.

'What's the jail time for false pretences?'

At home, Jo stressed. Not telling the literary agent the truth might backfire. Many thoughts attacked her brain.

What if the real journalist contacts the agent to arrange the interview? They have my number. I didn't say I was a journalist. But I didn't say I wasn't. Shit. All this hassle and for a person who wasn't even at the party.

She made a call. 'G'day Pop, it's Jo.'

He sparkled. 'Hello, Love. What's news?'

'You sound pretty chipper.'

'Not that one, the other one.'

'Sorry?'

'Not you, Love. I've got a couple of helpers here packing. You wouldn't believe the junk you acquire after 50 years.'

'51,' said a female voice in the background.

'Right,' said Jo wondering who was with her grandfather, and what was happening.

'Fanny has recruited her two grandsons and they're giving me a hand. Lovely lads they are. You should meet them.'

'Right,' said Jo repeating herself and thinking of how she should end the call in order to retain her sanity. 'I'm heading up to the Dandenongs in the morning, Pop. How about I drop in on my way back to town?'

'Not tomorrow, Love. I've got Bridge in the morning and we're going down to Portsea to Fanny's beach house in the afternoon. Another time. You take care now. Bye.'

It took a long time for Jo to start breathing normally.

She made a second call, this time to the pathetic pathologist. She needed to hear a voice of reason, and wanted to know how the former Covid patient was going.

Bugger. Damn answering machine. Gabrielle was not a social butterfly. In fact Jo struggled to name any friends Gabrielle mentioned or met. *She can't be out on the town. She's more or less retired from work. Where are you woman?*

Jo left a brief message saying she'd call tomorrow.

Driving to Kallista brought back memories. Her first homicide occurred in the Dandenongs. She remembered how certain male colleagues went for her big time. The more success she achieved, the harder they attacked. The bastard head of Homicide, DI Steele came to mind. But Gabrielle and Billy stuck by her. Now she was back in the beautiful hills an hour out of Melbourne. If ever she wanted to find an English setting, a drive to the Dandenongs did the trick.

She drove through Belgrave and thought she heard the whistle of Puffing Billy. Ah, memories of murder in the tranquil bush.

Kallista was a quaint village like settlement with tea rooms to match. Mr Batchelor's property was on the edge of the forest. There seemed to be as many trees on his land as there were in the bush. The perimeter fence was Olympic high jump tall and the gates formidable.

She stepped out and pressed a button on the pillar.

'Yes?' said a female voice.

'Good morning. I'm Jo Best and have an appointment with Mr Batchelor.'

No-one responded but the huge gates swung open. Jo drove along the sweeping drive with immaculate lawn either side, and spectacular, huge rhododendrons demanding a wave. Jo drove slower than slow and just as well as a peacock flared its plumage only a few yards from the drive. Jo pulled up in what she hoped was the right place to park. Taking a deep breath and her folder, she hopped out.

Surely I don't lock the car.

There were steps leading up to a patio from which the world was on view. 'Up here,' said a woman who disappeared.

Jo climbed the stairs and saw the woman reclining on an upmarket sun lounge reading a magazine which wasn't *Woman's Whatever*. The front of the house was a wall of glass with brick pillars every once in a while, smothered in ivy.

Nice work if you can get it.

Two dogs relaxed either side of the woman. They were Afghans and their stylist had finished her regular session with both hounds. They surveyed Jo with an expression of, "Look what the cat dragged in".

'Perry will be with you soon,' said the woman from behind her magazine. Not, "Would you like a drink?" or "Please take a seat" just, "Stand there and wait to be summoned".

All this palaver, the grounds, the house, the peacock, the dogs and stunning vista built pressure. Jo was here under false pretences and after this build-up, now knew she should tell the international money-maker she was a fraud. A sinking feeling in her stomach got busy.

One thought concerned her escape. She couldn't open the gates. If forced to flee, it would have to be on foot and over the fence with her vehicle left behind. All would soon be revealed when a voice was heard.

'Are you the journo?' Jo turned and couldn't see anyone. This time the voice was impatient. 'Are you the journo?' Jo looked up. The novelist was above the patio on a balcony.

'Good morning, Mr Batchelor. I'm Jo Best.'

He descended via a spiral staircase on the ivy-covered side wall of the house, walked past Jo and sat on one of the imported outdoor furniture chairs. He gestured and Jo joined him but didn't sit, wanting to be in starting-block position once her true identity was announced.

'What's your angle?' he said lighting a cheroot. The woman on the sun lounge flapped her magazine annoyed at any wayward smoke.

'There may be a misunderstanding, Mr Batchelor. I've come to talk to you about your past.'

'With a view I presume to how I've become a star.'

'Not exactly, sir.'

He contemplated her for the first time. 'Who did you say you were?'

She took the risk and ignored his question. 'It's about a party at Point Lonsdale 32 years ago.' He snapped around and glared at her. 'When you were a guest of a Mr Tony Grande.'

'You're not a proper journalist.'

'I'm not, sir.'

'You're from *60 Minutes*.'

The woman dropped her magazine, and the Afghans flicked their hair as if preparing for another photo shoot.

'Actually I'm from Victoria Police.' She held up her ID.

It took a lot to cause Perry Batchelor to fall silent but gobsmacked was an apt description. It was a double whammy—his past exposed, and a person who sneaked past his agent, the world's best gatekeeper.

'The police!' gasped the woman and the Afghans went "No comment".

In for a penny, Jo was in for a pound. 'I'm interviewing certain people who were in Point Lonsdale on the night a woman called Natasha Kaye died.'

'Certain people!' he exclaimed. 'I'm not certain people. I'm Perry Batchelor.' He omitted to add, "How dare you!"

'Or Perry Baker,' said Jo.

That hurt. Perry buried his old moniker years ago and any mention thereof left a nasty taste in his mouth.

'Mr Grande said you stayed the night at his place.'

Perry fired up and changed his name to Bluster. 'I left before the trouble started.'

'What trouble started, sir?' Jo's heart hit overdrive.

'I wasn't there when the woman died.'

'What time *did* she die, sir?'

His anger bubbled away. 'I don't know.' He screamed sotto voce. 'I wasn't there!'

'Perry,' said the woman trying to calm the frantic novelist.

'What about the party noise and Mr Grande's complaints?'

'What about it?'

'Did you support Mr Grande when he went next door?'

'No, I slept through the whole thing.'

The lie was so obvious and pathetic even Perry experienced nausea. 'Listen, all this is off the record. I've not agreed to any of this being published. Now I want you to leave. What magazine are you from again?'

'Perry,' said the woman, 'she's a cop.'

His nightmare started barking. He blanched, stood and almost ran inside. Jo smiled at the woman. 'I don't suppose you were at the Point Lonsdale party that night?'

'I'll open the gates,' she said and reached for a remote.

Jo forced a grin. 'Thanks.'

The drive back to Melbourne was ... interesting.

Chapter 19

A solicitor entered the Supreme Court in Melbourne to lodge papers. This was part of an attempt to overturn a conviction with an application for Leave to Appeal. It came about because the crime Queen, Annie Cleary, stirred the possum leaving a certain pathologist smack bang in the crosshairs.

As a result of papers being lodged, the court informed interested parties including Victoria Police prosecution services. On the quiet, a friendly administrator sent an email from her phone to Dr Gabrielle Strange's phone. The pathologist opened the file and nearly died.

Driving back to Melbourne after the Afghan and peacock incidents in Kallista, Jo rang Ronnie Bumstead and explained her adventure.

'Hell's bells, Jo, he sounds like a complete prat.'

'If that's what happens when you become successful, I want to remain a Senior Constable.'

'So where does he sit on our list of suspects?'

'Not on top and I've now run out of interviewees.'

'Okay, write up your findings and we'll discuss them later. Now, listen.' He sounded excited. 'I've got great news about new DNA procedures. I'll tell you when I see you. Drive carefully.'

More worry for Jo as DNA and Alastair Dean went hand in hand.

As she approached Clifton Hill to leave her car at home and then catch the train to town, she made a slight detour to Fitzroy North and the Gabrielle Strange abode.

She parked and knocked on the front door. Silence. Birds twittered in this garden rich suburb. A train at Rushall station tooted in the distance but the lady of the house made not a sound.

Jo called. 'Gabrielle, it's Jo.' She adopted a sing-song voice. 'I have chocolate!' The silence remained. She took out her phone and called her. Voicemail. She went into the street and tried peering along the side of the property hoping to see into the backyard. Nothing.

A woman came along and Jo recognised the neighbour.

'Hello. Do you know if Dr Strange is home?'

'I heard her this morning so I assume she's there.'

'She's not answering her phone or the door.'

'Are you the detective she knows, Jo Best?'

'Yes,' said Jo showing her ID.

'Well I guess it's safe to tell a cop. She keeps a spare key outside. It's taped under the garden bench on the verandah.'

'Thanks,' said Jo and opened the front gate. She dropped to her knees and searched. Nothing was obvious. The bench was painted black, top and bottom, and the key was covered with black tape. Jo smiled, recovered the key and stood at the door.

She knocked again and called. Nothing. Afraid, she tried the key and the door opened. She called. 'Gabrielle. It's me, Jo. Hello?'

Heart rate up, blood pressure up, and adrenaline looking like epinephrine was now in full flow. She walked down the hall, her footsteps on the polished boards making a squeaking sound. Her loud heart beat drowned out the squeaks. Passing each room, she checked inside. Bedrooms 1 and 2 were empty; bathroom empty. She called again. She tried telling herself this was a non-event.

She's out shopping. She's asleep in the back garden. Oh God, she's fallen over and died!

The hallway led to the open plan dining room, kitchen and sitting room, all one space at the back of the house. It was empty. The laundry and a second loo were around the corner. She called once again, turned the corner and saw her.

'Gabriel,' cried Jo and rushed to the woman slumped on the floor.

Jo's training kicked in as she checked for signs of life. As she bent over Gabrielle, the smell, more like stench, of alcohol whacked Jo's senses. The groan from the homeowner wasn't the death rattle although she looked like one of the bodies often examined on a metal table in her "office".

Jo moved the Glenfiddich bottle jammed under Gabrielle. Now came the tricky or seemingly impossible bit. How to help the woman up and off the floor? She was vertically challenged but overgrown in the middle third department; a pocket rocket. She'd be an ideal hooker crouched in the front of a rugby scrum.

'It's me, Jo. We need to get you up.' Gabrielle replied speaking Guttural. 'I need you to help me, Gabrielle.' The drunk continued speaking Guttural, two words of which sounded like 'Faaak Ewe'. Jo stepped over her and attacked from behind with a plan to have Gabrielle on her front and hopefully on all fours. Pushing, groaning and grunting followed with Jo making sounds too.

She knelt beside the beached whale and despaired. Her phone rang. She retrieved it and was about to answer. Gabrielle grabbed Jo's arm.

'Don't you dare tell anyone about this,' she spoke in lucid English.

Jo seized the moment, switched off her phone, stuck it in her bag, and took deep breaths. 'I'll tell the world if you don't help me,' said Jo and sounded like she meant it. Gabrielle made unpleasant sounds, not all voluntary, but finished on her hands and knees.

Jo dragged a chair with an extended footrest closer to the patient. She knelt in front of Gabrielle. 'Right, Doctor, kneel, please.'

Jo heaved and lifted under Gabrielle's armpits, and the pathologist knelt. The chair was beside them. 'Use the chair with your right hand and I'll lift on this side.'

They tried. Pushing a boulder uphill was easier.

'Come on Gabrielle, try harder.' She did, they both did until she made it to an upright position only to get the wobbles and fall back. Gravity kicked in. The patient screamed, the unofficial doctor held on fast and guided Gabrielle into the chair. She was lying, half sitting but crooked until Jo grabbed her ankles and swivelled her into position.

Folding her arms, Jo stood and stared at her friend.

Gabrielle waved a hand. 'I'm fine. I was about to get up when you arrived. Would you like a drink?'

Jo went to the kitchen. 'I'd like a coffee.' She made it, keeping an eye on the pathologist. They made small talk ignoring the bleeding obvious until Jo brought two steaming mugs to the steaming woman in the chair.

'Where are the drugs?' asked Gabrielle. 'You can't waltz in here—how did you get in by the way?—and not bring any drugs.'

'Drink your coffee.'

Gabrielle shifted in her chair. 'I need to pee.'

Jo groaned, took Gabrielle's coffee then helped haul her out of the chair. The second powder-room was close, and the pathologist waddled away throwing a hand out to use the wall for support.

'And don't fall in,' barked Jo feeling queasy. It was a terrible scene to witness but the one question was why? Gabrielle was on the wagon well before they met. Why fall off now and why so far and so fast?

The toilet flushed and Jo watched anxiously. The door opened and Gabrielle entered grinning. 'Much better. Now did you put the shot of rum in my coffee as you promised?'

Jo ignored her, waited till she flopped back in her chair before handing back her coffee. Jo sat and they sipped in silence. Finally Jo spoke.

'I'm not leaving, Gabrielle, until you give a detailed explanation of your behaviour.'

'You sound like a bloody detective and my mother.'

'The truth, the whole truth ...'

Gabrielle interrupted. 'Yeah, yeah, yeah and nothing but the truth.' She sniffed and pondered her position.

'Fetch my phone.'

'Please,' said Jo.

Gabrielle snapped. 'Just get my fucking phone.'

A snippet of fear pinched Jo. *This is not going to end well.* She fetched the phone. Gabrielle found what she wanted and handed it back to Jo. 'Read and then ask whatever you like.'

It took a while for Jo to read the attachment. It was the leave to appeal application by Annie Cleary's legal firm. The more Jo read, the more she worried.

Gabrielle being drunk on duty and giving questionable evidence told Jo everything. Now the drunken stupor made sense.

That's why she fell off the wagon.

Forget follow-up questions. Gabrielle's name and reputation were being traduced, and her health was under serious threat.

Jo handed Gabrielle her phone. 'I'm sorry,' said Jo and meant it.

'Me too,' said Gabrielle. 'A drunk is a terrible bore and boor.'

'I meant about the legal case.'

'I didn't.'

They sipped in silence. Jo felt huge sympathy for her friend who breathed easier. A trouble shared and all that, and when the listener offered a friendly face, even better. Jo's next comment was natural and didn't require any thinking or planning.

'So, how can we have this rubbish thrown out?'

Gabrielle wanted to speak but couldn't. The lump in her throat grew and she was left with tears. She made no sound but certainly emptied the reservoir.

She was in the depths of despair and all her young friend could do was to disbelieve the claims, and offer help to quash them. Gabrielle bawled like a baby only without sound. Jo let her cry. A hug would help but Jo reckoned what the woman needed was to let it all out. Bottled up despair is never good.

She fetched a box of tissues, removed the coffee and let time drift by. Eventually Gabrielle recovered. The tears stopped, the eyes were dried, and she complained about her missing coffee.

Jo thought it a good sign and made more. They settled.

Gabrielle spoke. 'Do you want to know my side of the story?'

'Only if you want to tell me and there's no hurry.'

'I have a friend at the court who sent me a copy of the documents. I would have found out eventually but this was a kindness, telling me in private before I found out in public.'

'Is it true?'

Talk about brutal. 'I thought a barrister never asked their client if they're guilty.'

Jo nodded. 'Fair enough,' she said.

'I'm not on trial. If the appeal is granted, it's up to the defence to show there is new evidence. My drinking is new and their evidence is the sworn affidavits of two losers.'

'Oh? Do tell.'

'The mortuary attendant is a problem gambler, and was always chasing money to cover his debts. He will have been paid under the counter to sign whatever they put in front of him.'

'And the pathologist; is he too a gambler?'

Gabrielle wondered if Jo disbelieved her. 'No, only bitter. In two separate cases his PM report was discredited by me pointing out his schoolboy-howler mistakes. He hated me after the first correction and swore vengeance after the second. Here's his chance for payback. Revenge is a dish best served cold.'

Jo cut to the chase. 'But you were drinking at the time?'

'Sometimes, and a member of AA throughout. But I never drank on duty and was never, repeat never affected by alcohol at work.'

Jo went in hard. 'How do you know? I've pulled over drivers who are as lucid and logical as a teetotaller but when they give the one long breath until I say stop, they're over the limit, at times way over.'

Gabrielle stared her down. 'I know when I'm impaired. I wasn't.'

'So are these men who signed affidavits bent?'

'Don't know but they're lying, simple as.'

'And what will happen if this appeal is granted?'

'I'll be ridiculed and whatever good I've done will drown in a vat of cheap whisky.' She reached for another tissue.

'I know Michael Chan will want to help, and I'm sure we can investigate this woman Annie Cleary, and her two star witnesses. We'll expose their farrago of lies.' She paused. 'Do you like that word?'

'I do but you're wasting your time.'

Jo turned sarcastic. 'Oh so this is the feel-sorry-for-myself Gabrielle speaking. Let me wallow in self-pity.'

Gabrielle winced. Jo was dealing with a woman in the pits.

'Thanks for the offer, girlie, but I'll pass.' Neither spoke. 'I'm okay now. You can bugger off and catch a few murderers.'

Jo didn't want to leave. She didn't trust her friend. A thought whispered in her brain. *Leave her now and she'll top herself. I'll come back and find her dead.*

Gabrielle glared at her. 'Are you deaf?'

'I'm not working in Homicide.'

Gabrielle reacted. Jo wanted to switch topics, to have Gabrielle stop thinking about her misery. It worked.

'Oh so it *is* true. You've reviewed your bank account and decided to live the high life. I don't blame you. I'd do the same if I had all that dough.'

'I'm working on a cold case, a 32 year-old murder.'

Gabrielle couldn't help herself. 'Which one?'

'You weren't the pathologist.'

'That's not what I asked.'

'Natasha Kaye, 22, found washed up on the beach at ...'

'Queenscliff; the champion swimmer who drowned.' Gabrielle's face shone. Jo saw the seemingly drunk woman use her mind as if the death happened yesterday. 'I wanted to tackle that case.'

'So drunkenness and senility are not linked?'

Gabrielle ignored her. 'What have you found?'

Jo's excitement meter slipped off the scale. 'I'm working with a retired detective, Ronnie Bumstead.'

'Not the penophile?' shouted Gabrielle.

My God, she knows everyone.

'Lovely bloke and I think he prefers pen collector.'

For the next five, or was it fifteen minutes, Jo told Gabrielle all she and Ronnie discovered. There were questions from Gabrielle whose interest in the case kept growing. The story of the interviews with Maisie and Conrad hooked her. When Jo described her visit to the famous author in the hills, Gabrielle shrieked and tore into the man's pomposity with glee. Forget the application for leave to appeal, Gabrielle wanted in on this cold case.

Jo seized the day. The way to lift the pathologist's spirits, to save her from herself, was to create a challenge. She wanted in. She *was* in.

'Will you come and see Ronnie and give us your advice?'

'Not now,' replied Gabriel. 'I ain't in pristine condition or working order.' She looked terrible; as if a toddler had painted her face in an art class.

'Tomorrow,' said Jo. I'll pick you up at 8.'

'10.'

'9 and that's my final offer.

This time they did hug and Gabrielle put a lot of elbow grease into her response.

'I'll see myself out,' said Jo and left feeling like she'd been through the wringer.

What a day!

Instead of going home and then to work, she rang Ronnie and told him about her new lead, and that she'd be in tomorrow. 'No worries, Jo. Remember there's no hierarchy here.' But when she told him a certain pathologist was keen to be involved, he jumped for joy. 'Not the strange Strange woman?' Jo smiled. 'Bloody fantastic!'

She was doubly pleased because Gabrielle would have insights she and Ronnie lacked, and would possibly be a barrier between Jo and the unrequited love boffin from Forensics.

She rang Michael Chan and asked if she could drop in. He enjoyed most of his work as a PI but seriously missed working with Detective Best. He welcomed her visit.

She arrived and asked about his case with friend Cathy.

Is she jealous I'm working with another woman? Michael quickly dismissed the suggestion as wishful thinking.

Then he returned the favour and asked about Jo's cold case. She mentioned it briefly then raised another topic.

'This is top secret, Michael. Please say nothing to no-one.'

He was fascinated but couldn't resist a dig. 'I assume you mean "say nothing to anyone." The famous half grin appeared.

Jo told him about the court business and Gabrielle's involvement.

'Poor woman,' he said. 'What a terrible way to end your career.'

'I'm helping her fight the bastards, and would love to be able to call on your IT genius to find a way to stop the appeal.'

'You want me to break the law?' said Michael with his amateur histrionics on show. He'd done exactly that before—several times and loved every minute of it. He switched to serious. 'So what's the plan?'

'I have no plan other than to discredit the people who plan to discredit Gabrielle. Can you think of anything else?'

His mind ticked. 'There's always a second way to solve a problem.'

'Ah, an ancient Chinese proverb or are you treading water while you try and come up with a better idea?'

He grinned. He liked the problems she brought and the challenges she provided, and he liked her—a lot. 'What do we know about the lady in prison?'

'I'm not sure lady is the word you associate with Annie Cleary. She was born a criminal but this is her first conviction, and facing 15 years inside, she wants out. Her previous appeal failed so she's turned to dirty tricks, and payment for perjury is crime 101 to Annie.'

'So she's committed other crimes?'

'Many as she started when a teenager.'

'And she's never been charged with these other crimes?'

'No, and that's why she's mad at finally being caught.' Jo stopped. She read his mind. 'Ah, the second way to tackle a problem.'

He was surprised she took so long to catch on. He explained.

'I reckon we concentrate on Annie.'

Jo's face spoke volumes. She loved his mind and this new idea. The penny headed towards the floor and, as it dropped, she saw his plan.

'You're advocating a counter-attack.'

'I am.'

'We check out Annie's past?'

'We do.' He was hot to trot. 'We trawl through her past and find evidence to nail her on one or more of her previous misdeeds. We have her bang to rights then present the evidence to her legal team. We ignore the court and your mob. We tell Annie's legal team there'll be a new prosecution against her unless she drops the appeal.'

'Bloody brilliant,' gasped Jo.

'She can continue with the appeal and even if it's granted and she wins, she'll face an extra 10 or more years inside. However, if she drops the appeal, we drop the new prosecution. What do you reckon?'

'I reckon you're a genius, and I have to admit, Michael Chan, I've missed our case-cracking adventures.'

'Ditto,' he said. In a movie they might have hugged.

'Mind you,' said Jo, 'there are about 50 "ifs" in your scheme and we'll need a jumbo size slice of luck.'

'Thank you for that vote of confidence, officer,' he said in his usual low-temperature form of sarcasm. Alan hopped onto Jo's lap. It was just like old times.

Chapter 20

The only thing worse than an unsolved homicide is an unsolved homicide with a long list of suspects. The violent husband, lying partner, furious girlfriend and the former criminal from overseas were all starters plus, as one politician once said, the known unknowns.

Billy Hughes ran through the list and asked if it was correct. The detectives mumbled their agreement.

No-one was prepared to push their favourite suspect.

Billy tried to tempt them. 'Okay, who wants the reward? Come on, step up, prove your case; bottle of Scotch for the winner.'

'Boiled lollies more like,' said someone quietly.

It was a sombre Incident Room. DI Blunt desperately wanted his claim to be correct but saw the difficulty in speaking.

'Well come on, Sarge,' said Baldwin, 'put your own head on the tipster's block.'

Billy scoffed. 'No thanks, I only look stupid.'

'Have we heard anything more from Dr Laudi?' asked DS Fletcher. 'Surely there must be DNA on the body. It was only his head in the water.'

Rick Melody took the unusual step of supporting DI Blunt. 'What about the Serbian tracked down by DI Blunt? You could say it was the perfect murder. He sneaks in and out before the Covid clampdown. His parents can't give him an alibi. He lied on his visa application. The Serbian authorities confirm he's been a baddie without conviction for years, and he almost certainly knew and clashed with our victim. All we need is DNA or CCTV or a witness statement and we have our man.'

DI Blunt forced himself not to applaud.

Billy stared at Blunt. 'Anything to add, DI Blunt?'

'DS Melody is 100% correct. If Dr Laudi and Forensics can do their job, we'll have proof Sonny from Serbia flew Down Under and did the deed.'

'With a serve of adrenalin?' asked a sceptical DI Rose.

This looked like a major hurdle. Homicide detectives saw any number of murder methods but supercharging a fit man's heart with epinephrine was a first.

'Surely he was taken by surprise,' said Billy. 'The killer couldn't just walk up brandishing a syringe. And where was he stabbed?'

'On the left side of his chest,' said Baldwin.

'There was a full moon,' added Stephen Payne, surprising his colleagues with such a relevant remark. 'Whoever attacked him did so from the front and not under cover of darkness.'

'Okay,' said Billy Hughes trying to ignite the discussion. 'What about his business partner, Owen Jones? What do we know about the thugs who threatened him?'

'It's bullshit,' said Fletcher. 'Once we complete our search of the area for CCTV, we'll prove he's lying.'

'And then what?' asked DI Rose. 'Why make up such a story unless he has something to hide?'

Fletcher tried to sound respectful. 'It's our next step, ma'am.'

Billy kept things moving. 'So what about this angry husband? He gave a No Comment interview until he lost it. Is he angry because his wife cheated on him or because he's a killer or both? We can't hold him. Last time I checked, being a cuckold is not a crime.'

'Ah, but *where* did you check, Sarge?' asked Baldwin, rehearsing his stand-up routine.

Humour didn't cut it and the detectives were reluctant to speak for fear of not being able to substantiate their theory. DI Rose jumped in.

'He's another who has opportunity and motive and no alibi but without DNA, CCTV, eye witnesses, etc, he's only a suspect. But I keep coming back to this, if you're going kill in a fairly isolated spot, why use an unusual drug? The key to me is the method of killing. Who is most likely to use that MO?'

More silence. Billy felt obliged to work through the list.

'The girlfriend apparently went from grief to rage. When DI Rose and I called to tell her the news, she'd already been told by Jones the business partner. She seemed genuinely upset, teary. Then, yesterday,

Justin and Charley drop in, she's got Covid and won't open the door. Then when asked about the woman who's having an affair with the victim, the girlfriend loses it big time and reveals she knows he's a womaniser. So could the girlfriend be a starter all along?'

'It makes sense from the surprise attack angle,' said Baldwin. 'Banks sees his bird coming towards him, thinks, she's following me so I'd better come clean. She says we need to talk so he relaxes. She smiles and sticks in the syringe.'

It was easy for DI Blunt to scoff. 'Why is his girlfriend in the wilds of Strathmore at that time of night?'

DI Rose put him back in his box. 'She suspects he's playing away and follows him to where he's meeting his lover.'

'By parking his car so far away?' asked Melody. 'Why doesn't he park near the footbridge?'

Charlie Baldwin tried another gag. 'He was following social distancing with his vehicle?' Not even a titter.

Everyone could see the case had stalled. Every theory leaked. Discussion was healthy but progress hid under the bed.

'Well speaking of femme fatales,' said Baldwin, 'could the woman who rocked up to the Moonee Ponds nick be doing a double bluff. Banks won't leave his girlfriend or he dumps Sophia so, furious, she agreed to meet him and said thanks for nothing, Johnny, cop this.'

No-one ran with that. 'Where did the killer get the drug?' was a popular question. No-one knew. A sense of frustration increased with Billy uncertain how to proceed. The SIO must be calm and decisive. Right now she was fidgeting and undecided. DI Rose didn't help.

'Through all of this we need to remember the killer may be an unknown, a person not yet labelled a suspect.' Groans arose.

'Okay,' said Billy trying to regain control. 'Anything else?' No response. 'Let's go further with what we have. Get Owen Jones to name the time of the attack. The victim's phone has plenty of texts to the girlfriend. Let's check her phone.'

'What, you mean ask her?' asked Fletcher. 'I thought she was now in the hostile witness column.'

'As well as a suspect,' said Billy getting short. 'DI Blunt, can you do any more with our overseas friend?'

'You mean apart from making a trip to Serbia?'

Billy sniffed. 'I hope that's not necessary. But while you're waiting, why don't you and Senior Constable Payne interview the girlfriend.'

'Which one?' asked Blunt as much from ignorance as spite.

'The one in South Yarra is the girlfriend. The one in Moonee Ponds is the lover.'

'Do we release Mr Brent?' asked DS Melody.

'Yes but you and Stephen check out the story from his wife first.'

'I'm with DI Blunt, Sarge,' said Payne.

Billy boiled inside. She wanted to not only have control but appear to do so. She'd recently won promotion and making simple mistakes in front of the squad was not a good look.

'Sorry, Stephen. You stay with DS Melody.'

'Sarge.'

'DI Blunt, I may tag along with you.' Blunt slipped on his mask of thunder. 'It's a pity Jo Best isn't here.' That made him scowl.

No-one knew if Billy was joking. She couldn't be serious. Blunt's hatred of Best was legendary. Billy let him off the hook.

'How about you interview the girlfriend on your own?' Blunt's relief was palpable. 'DI Rose and I will try Dr Laudi and Forensics leaving DS Fletcher and Mr Comedian to go back to Owen Jones and his gangster tale.'

The squad broke up with no-one excited about their task. If ever a homicide attracted an even field of runners, this was it.

Owen Jones wasn't sure of the time when the thugs arrived.

'Come on, Owen,' said Fletcher losing patience. 'We arrived after 11. Were the hoons here five minutes before us, 20 minutes, half an hour, what?'

He shook his head. 'I don't know. Look, my partner's been murdered, I can't fill orders, Covid is stopping me operate, my business is going down the toilet, criminals have threatened me and you want to know the time!'

'Owen, we want to know if the thugs were actually here.'

He skin colour changed to beetroot. 'Oh so now I'm a liar?'

'You'd be surprised at the stories we hear,' added Baldwin.

'Stories? Why would I tell a story?' He twigged. 'Oh, I get it,' he said sloshing around in sarcasm. 'I made up a story to cover the fact I murdered my mate.'

The detectives glared at him and said nothing.

Gobsmacked suited Owen as he twigged they were serious. 'Piss off.'

They did and went in search of CCTV cameras. A service station down the road covered the main drag and another outside a wine bar overlooked the lane. What they found was telling.

Melody and Payne went searching for Sophia Brent. She'd left home fearing her husband's release would mean terror for her. The detectives tracked her down at her parents' home. She walked outside with the cops not wanting the family to know about her affair.

'Where is my husband?' she asked not faking her anxiety.

'He's still in custody, Mrs Brent, but he hasn't been charged with Mr Banks' murder and should be released soon.'

'He knows I reported him. He'll kill me.'

'Did you take out a family violence intervention order?' asked Melody.

'That won't stop him. He's violent.'

Melody paused, took a deep breath, and attacked. 'Where were you on the night Mr Banks was killed?'

'What?' She knew the nature of the interview was now different.

'It's a simple question, Mrs Brent.'

'I told you. We planned a date. I went to the spot where we meet.'

She flustered. Her parents were watching through the window. She hated giving details of her affair. She panicked thinking she might be a suspect.

'It's behind an industrial estate, a lane, it doesn't have a name.'

'And no-one saw you there?'

She flared. 'No, the whole of Melbourne was there with binoculars.'

Melody kept calm and kept pushing. 'Did John tell you about his girlfriend?'

'The bitch.'

'And?'

Sophia hated her life. 'He told me they were splitting. Once they did, I would leave Hudson and start a new life with John. We were planning on going to Queensland until this bloody Covid stopped our travel.'

'Are you sure he didn't call the whole thing off?'

'No!'

'You were dumped and decided to teach him a lesson?'

She glared at them. Payne grew nervous and edged a little behind Melody. She spat.

'I heard you cops were hopeless. Now I know.'

She stormed inside causing her parents to scurry away from the windows back to their chairs in the lounge.

Payne spoke at last. 'She's gorgeous. I wouldn't dump her.'

Rose and Hughes called on Rowdy Laudi. He appeared surprised. 'Doctor,' said Rose, and Hughes nodded.

'I have no further news, officers,' he said. 'There is a small bruise on the chest, left upper, with a pin prick mark. I believe he was stabbed with a syringe containing the drug epinephrine. His heart exploded, he staggered from the bridge and stumbled into the creek. We found nothing of importance on the bridge or surrounds. His clothes and personal effects were sent to Forensics who've found nothing. Finding the syringe would be helpful. His car has been forensically examined and you'll need to speak to the scientists for any data.' He forced a smile. 'I think that's all although the best news is Dr Strange is in the clear, out of hospital and recovering at home.'

The detectives reacted. 'Brilliant,' said Rose, and Hughes agreed. 'No word of her coming back to work?'

Laudi frowned. 'Hardly; haven't you heard?'

'Heard what?' asked Rose.

Laudi explained the application for leave to appeal from the Queen of Crime. The detectives gawped. They left heading to Forensics and couldn't stop talking about Annie Cleary and Gabrielle Strange.

It didn't matter who they met at Forensics. The work continued, nothing of significance was found thus far, and Homicide would be informed should a break-through occur.'

Callum Blunt fancied his chances with a woman when on or off duty. Being nominated to interview the victim's partner gave him satisfaction. He believed they were saying he could be sensitive. They said no such thing and he wasn't; sensitive that is.

Lyn Delahunty lost her Covid symptoms, was still self-isolating, and shed her anger and grief, a little. With social distancing and masks in place, Callum scored the pass to enter and they sat for a chat.

He was full of bonhomie and she took a strange liking to him. He asked straightforward questions without any sense of suspicion or ulterior motive. When he came to the subject of her phone, she invited him to check it. He flicked through her texts.

'He sent you a lot of texts which seem to be nothing texts – *Hi. How r u. Home soon.* Has he always done that?'

'No, only since he started cheating.' Blunt liked her honesty.

'And what are these about?' he asked showing texts.

'I was talking to a Private Investigator about costs, etc.'

'Why a Private Investigator?'

'I wanted John followed. I wanted to know where he was and what he was doing.'

'And did you?'

'You can see the texts. John was over the other side of town meeting a woman.'

'And were you happy with the PI?'

She shrugged. 'I never met him. I sent the money and he sent the report. No hanky-panky but more watching required,' he said.

Blunt returned her phone. And who is this PI?'

'Starlight Freeman.'

Blunt noted the name.

I think I might pay you a visit, Mr Freeman.

Chapter 21

Jo's diary was full. The cold case was defrosting. Her grandfather was hotting up. The memorial service for Pierre drew closer. The time for the granting of probate for his Will loomed large. And her friend and colleague's public shaming dominated her thinking.

Jo's idea, one of several, involved getting Gabrielle out of her house, out of her self-pity and doing something, anything to keep her busy. Working as a pathologist for Victoria Police was off the agenda but doing so through the back door was a real possibility.

Ronnie Bumstead could hardly wait to see the pathologist again and have her start pontificating on the cold case.

Jo was on time and as she approached Gabrielle's abode, thoughts raced around her brain.

Will the pathetic pathologist be still in bed? Will she be under the bed? Has she climbed back on the water cart?

Jo parked and went to knock on Gabrielle's door. With her hand outstretched, the door opened and there stood the doctor, a darn sight more presentable than when Jo left yesterday.

'Wow,' said Jo. 'You're keen.'

'Don't ask and let's go.'

Happy to follow orders, they set off and Jo wondered which topic to raise. She didn't need to worry as her passenger ran the meeting.

'So have you figured out a way to expose those two lying bastards who claim I was drunk on duty?'

'Don't need to.'

Gabrielle exploded. 'Don't need to? They're pelting me with mud and must be stopped.'

'Fear not, m'Lady, there is a brilliant plan afoot called *Head 'em off at the Pass* or *Cut 'em off at the Knees.*'

'In English please?'

Jo laughed promising to explain everything later. 'Now I need to tell you Ronnie Bumstead has the odd whacky theory which I think is never going to crack this case.' She looked at her passenger. 'By the way, how do you know him?'

'Do you remember the Russell Street bombing?'

'Oh thank you, how old do you think I am?'

'Sorry, I keep forgetting you're still a teenager. Anyway in March 86 I'm a sprightly GP heading to the Windsor for a drink with a pal and kaboom. The explosion was bloody loud. I rush to see if I can help and ended up working with a shocked senior constable.'

'Senior Constable Ronnie Bumstead.'

'We did what we could. He'd hold a victim's hand and I gave first-aid. We only knew each other's first name. An age later I was waiting to give evidence at the coronial inquest and this cheery chap bowls up. We went for a coffee and have exchanged Christmas cards ever since.'

'He's looking forward to seeing you.'

'Likewise,' she said and smiles were on show.

'It's Senior Constable Bumstead,' cried Gabrielle when she spotted Ronnie. Despite Covid restrictions, they hugged and kissed and Jo went all warm and fuzzy remembering the woman she found on the floor yesterday. *The doc is back in a good place.*

They finally settled and Ronnie picked Gabrielle's brain. 'Tell us about DNA, Gabrielle. Have advances in recent years given us a chance to crack this case?'

'Yes and no. If I've got this right, your major problem is a lack of DNA. If the attacker raped the poor girl, any skin, saliva, blood, semen, hair, etc, he deposited on or in her was washed away. How long was she in the ocean; six, eight hours? The pathologist would have been hard pressed to find anything. I assume the victim's clothing and any belongings will still be in storage.'

'They are,' said Jo.

'What are belongings?' asked Ronnie

'Jewellery, combs, watch, footwear, bag, etc,' said Gabrielle.

Ronnie pushed ahead. 'Okay, let's assume we'll never find any DNA; how have things changed forensically since the death?'

'Forensics is a lot more sophisticated now, obviously, and in the last 10 or so years, one significant change concerns databases. They've grown; in both law and order and elsewhere.'

'What's elsewhere?' Ronnie was keen.

'Family history has become popular and people send their DNA to genealogy sites.'

'Which helps how?' asked Ronnie.

'Science is improving by finding DNA from smaller samples and from older material but if the suspect's DNA is not on file, it means bugger all, which is where familial association comes in.'

'You've lost me,' said Ronnie although Jo was on the ball.

'Let's say a cousin of the killer sends their saliva to a Family Tree web site, and you obtain DNA from a crime scene. The DNA the police have doesn't throw up a match but if you do a familial search, you should find siblings, cousins etc from the DNA sent in by the cousin.'

'But hang on,' said Ronnie. 'DNA in a police database is not the same as DNA in a genealogical society database, surely?'

Gabrielle shrugged. 'This is the can of worms time, and a big privacy issue.'

Ronnie pushed out air. 'Bugger me. We have a list of relatives from a person's spit, check out those on the list with opportunity and motive, and there's the cold case solved.'

'Great in theory, Detective Bumstead, but how many suspects do you have?'

He grimaced. 'Spoilsport,' he said then went to make tea.

Jo spoke quietly. 'How are you *really* feeling, Madame Doctor?'

Gabrielle knew this was about yesterday. 'Better since you rocked up. I think I owe you a very big drink, girlie.' Their eyes locked and Jo knew this was a heartfelt thank you, and of course, Gabrielle's offer would not include alcohol. They chatted till Ronnie returned.

'Here we are,' he said carrying a tray with tea and biscuits. 'Help yourself, ladies.' They did.

'So how's the case going, Ronnie,' asked Gabrielle. 'And what do you think I can do?'

'I'd like to know more about databases. But I was thinking you might see something from photos the other experts missed. Jo met a witness the other day who remembered what the victim was wearing, her make-up smudges, and even how her shirt was torn.'

'A witness remembered all that after 30 odd years?'

'He has cerebral palsy,' said Jo, 'and knew everything.'

'Ah,' said Gabrielle thinking about Dustin Hoffman's memory skills in *Rain Man,* and how autism like cerebral palsy has a wide spectrum. For every Conrad there are those who cannot even speak. 'Well okay, where are the pics?'

They were produced and she studied them, picked up a magnifying glass for a closer look. 'Where's the PM report?' It was produced. Jo hung on any comments and Ronnie was positively salivating. He desperately wanted to crack this cold case.

Gabrielle explained. 'The shirt's been torn, a sign of a struggle. See where the bruising is, here on the back of the neck, means the attacker was behind the victim.'

'And the significance?' asked Jo.

Gabrielle shrugged. 'Choking a victim while facing them can be difficult, especially if you know the person. The attacker and victim are staring into one another's eyes. Attacking from behind is a sort of out of sight, out of mind situation.'

'If that's true, Zara's boyfriend Ralph is a contender,' said Ronnie.

'And he's dead,' said Jo.

'But the cerebral palsy witness saw the ripped clothing and bruising which would have come from a front-on attack' said Strange.

'Meaning we have a second, a later attacker,' suggested Jo.

Gabrielle imitated Sherlock Holmes. 'Well done, Watson. You are a reflector of light.'

Both Jo and Ronnie smiled.

'This is brilliant, Gabrielle,' said Ronnie. 'I hope you never retire. Victoria Police don't know how lucky they are to have you.'

The women swallowed. Ronnie knew nothing about the Annie Cleary matter and his enthusiasm bubbled along.

Jo wanted to be clear. 'So the ripped shirt suggests an attack from the front but the neck bruising suggests an attack from behind.'

'Correct,' said Gabrielle, 'and if your cerebral palsy witness is right, there's a gap between attacks. She's in a fight and has her shirt ripped, then she's spotted by the witness. Where?'

Ronnie grabbed an aerial map of Point Lonsdale. 'Here,' he pointed. 'And heading in this direction.'

Gabrielle indicated a general direction. 'So she was in the fight around here, and then moved here where she was attacked again and choked.'

'How do we know she wasn't choked at the same time as the first fight?' asked Ronnie.

'Because those bruises suggest heavy choking even strangulation, and as she was walking normally and able to speak when here, she didn't have those bruises then.'

'Her make-up was badly smudged by crying,' added Jo.

'Which points to boyfriend, Julian,' said Ronnie, getting more excited. 'They argued in the back yard then headed out towards the beach. They've argued again, Julian grabbed her shirt to restrain her, she's pulled away, torn her shirt and they've parted. She's upset and crying, smudging her make-up. She heads down to the beach, meets her killer and drowns.'

'Or is drowned,' said Jo.

'What does the PM say is the cause of death?' asked Gabrielle.

'Drowning,' said both police officers as one.

'But if you're right, Gabrielle,' argued Jo, 'and the victim was choked or strangled, could she drown if unconscious?'

'More likely is the choking subdues her, she's carried into the water and held under so she drowns and is then dumped.'

Jo and Ronnie grinned. 'Great minds, Doc,' said Ronnie.

'Indeed,' said Gabrielle, 'but how does that help you find the killer?'

Ronnie persisted. 'I know this sounds a long shot, but if we drag out Natasha's clothes and belongings, is there any chance you could have a gander?'

'Of course,' said the pathologist but two things, Mr Bumstead; a boffin from Forensics would be a better bet, and I do my best work with bodies, dead bodies.'

He skipped away. 'I'll fetch the evidence bags.'

The women glanced at one another. 'He's keen,' said Jo.

'Does he know I failed Miracles?'

Chapter 22

Michael rang the hospital every day. The nurses got to know the man who asked about Alison, the elderly Chinese lady, a victim of the pandemic. Michael explained to a new nurse he was ringing on behalf of a friend, Cathy Feng, Alison's granddaughter. He made no mention of Cathy having been adopted.

After the nurse gave Michael the latest report, she said something that put the wind right up him.

'As Alison is a little bit better, I'll tell her that granddaughter Cathy is asking after her.'

Michael hung up, worried. Cathy was due at his place. *What will I say?* He opted for the truth.

Cathy arrived and the first thing she always asked was about Alison.

'I have good news,' said Michael. 'Alison is getting better slowly and is no longer on a ventilator. The nurse told me many elderly Covid patients haven't survived this long.'

Cathy sensed something was wrong. 'What are you not telling me, Michael?'

His face betrayed him. 'The nurse said she would tell Alison about her granddaughter Cathy and about Cathy's friend, Michael.'

They looked at one another. Cathy worried. 'It had to happen. We could hardly ask them to not mention my relationship.'

'Even if she does mention our names, we don't know if Alison is mentally well. She may be sedated or senile, and your name may have little or no impact at all.'

Cathy wasn't convinced. 'Or it may bring back unhappy memories of her daughter stealing a child, me.'

'Not stealing, no way,' said Michael trying to keep her calm.

'Michael the one option we don't have is to do nothing. Sitting on our hands won't find my birth mother. Now, here's what I've done.'

Wow, thought Michael, *she's changed her attitude*.

'I've applied for an analysis of my DNA from a genealogy web site and I'll have the results next week.'

'That's brilliant. If you get a hit, you'll be that much closer to finding your Mum.'

'I hope so. Look, I have no ill feelings towards Gloria and Alison but they are not my family, they are not related to me by blood.'

He understood the heavy stress her search was causing. 'Of course.'

'And having my DNA in the genealogical database means if my mother or one or more of her family are also there, I can track them.'

Michael hesitated. 'Is it that easy?'

'Of course it isn't. Privacy laws are all over these things. But I think the company are allowed to tell me if there's a match but not identify the other person without their approval.'

'Wow, you're being so positive, Cathy, and I love that.'

His enthusiasm encouraged her. 'I've applied for Gloria's death certificate and Gloria and Alison's birth certificates.'

'That's brilliant, Cathy, well done.'

'You've been a huge help, Michael, but I feel bad about taking up so much of your time.'

'It's no problem.'

'I don't want to interrupt your life and work anymore.'

He sat stunned. *She's giving me the flick. Why?*

'Cathy, it's no trouble and I *want* to help.'

She gave him the deep stare. 'I'm not sure, Michael. Your problem is you're too nice. All the investigating you did with the police detective was so exciting and challenging makes my little case boring.'

Wow, where is all this coming from? Michael struggled. He badly missed working with you know who but this was a nice sideline. Now, even the Second Division mission was being snatched from his grasp.

'As they have my name, how about I contact the hospital from now on?'

Oh hell, she's angry because I've dobbed her in.

'Sure, if that's what you want.'

'Of course I'll keep you up to date with any progress I make and again, I could never be where I am without your help. You're a star.'

She stepped forward and kissed his cheek. He'd been dumped before and remembered the signs, the sentences and the body language. He followed her to the front door. She waved to the cat and called back to Alan, filling in time until she was able to escape.

They reached the door, she stood back and he was about to step forward when his phone rang.

He opened the door. She made a hasty exit and whispered.

'You take the call and thanks again, Michael.'

She left, he answered, listened then ran outside and called.

'Cathy!' She turned at his gate and saw him beckoning. Not knowing why, she returned, her face a puzzled picture.

Michael spoke into his phone. 'Can I call you back in five?' He listened. 'Okay, thanks, in five. Bye.'

Cathy oozed curiosity. Michael explained.

'That was Doctor Jack Carr, a friend of Jo Best.'

'Yes you told me about him.'

'One of his patients was in a car accident and taken to Box Hill Hospital. Jack's there now. He knows a nurse at the hospital and he asked her about Alison. She's back in a ward and talking. Is there anything we'd like to ask?'

Cathy stood stunned. 'Now? He's there now?'

Michael nodded. 'They're ready to pop the question to Alison. I said I'd call him back.'

Michael was reinstated on the spot. The two re-entered his HQ and Alan appeared confused. *Didn't she just dump you?'* he thought watching his sole employee.

'I don't know what to say,' stuttered Cathy. 'What should I do? What if we ask the wrong question? What if she becomes angry or depressed and clams up?'

In stepped Father Michael. Be calm, sister, all is well. He went for the hoary old chestnut. 'Come on, Cathy, nothing ventured, nothing gained.'

'Okay,' she whispered. 'Please, can you call the doctor now?'

'I can, and Cathy,' he stared at her, 'I want to do this.'

She understood although her nerves kicked in as he rang Jack Carr.

The GP spoke. 'G'day Michael. I'm here with Nurse Susan. Is your friend there?

Chapter 23

Jo drove Gabriel home. Both were pleased but for different reasons. Jo was delighted to see the pathologist upright and active. Gabrielle was delighted to bump into an old friend in Ronnie Bumstead, and to get to use her brain again. She promised Ronnie she'd return and review the cold case. Already she'd helped the detectives make sense of the time line. Two attackers in different parts of Point Lonsdale was now the theory to explore.

'Thanks for today,' said Gabrielle, and meant it.

'Thank *you*,' said Jo. 'You and Ronnie make a good team.'

'I can tell he doesn't know about my reputation being destroyed thanks to the lovely Annie Cleary.'

'And he never will,' said Jo and took her eyes off the road for a second to make eye contact with the pathologist. 'I'm teaming up with Michael Chan to have the appeal withdrawn.'

Gabrielle's heart missed a beat, two in fact but she slipped into her usual sarcastic demeanour. 'Oh yeah, since when, and how?'

'Listen, lady, you service the organ donors and I'll crush the crims.'

The passenger wanted to laugh or make another sarcastic remark but the driver's words overwhelmed her. The pathologist knew the detective was clever and persistent, and if Jo Best hatched a plan and a will to win, things would bloody well happen.

They discussed the cold case and then Jo's career.

'All I know for certain,' said Jo, 'is I have Pierre's memorial service to arrange, his Will and estate to settle, and only then will I make a decision about returning to Homicide or even to the police at all.'

Gabrielle let the matter lie. They reached her home. 'Coffee and drugs?' she asked.

'Thanks but I have a meeting re your proposed court case.' Gabrielle stared at her. 'I told you the appeal won't be rejected so much as withdrawn. Now bugger off and I'll keep you in the loop.'

Gabrielle squeezed Jo's arm applying serious pressure. 'Thanks, girlie,' she said and heaved herself out of the car. It sighed.

Jo drove from Fitzroy North to Northcote. It was a pre-arranged meeting with Michael which he forgot; understandable given recent events with Dr Jack Carr in the hospital where Cathy's adopted grandmother was recovering from Covid-19.

'Damn, it's Jo for our meeting,' said Michael when his state-of-the-art warning system told him the detective had arrived.

Cathy was confused. 'What's happened?'

Michael headed to his front door. 'It's cool. I forgot I have a meeting with Jo Best. Not to worry. It's another case.'

The door opened and the two "investigators" greeted one another. Jo sensed Michael's unease.

'Come in and meet Cathy,' said Michael, and the women were introduced. 'Remember I told you I was helping Cathy find her Mum.'

'Oh yes; how's it going?'

Michael let Cathy answer. 'Not too bad. We've made a sort of a break-through thanks to a Doctor Jack Carr. Michael knows him and asked for his help.'

Both Jo and Michael were embarrassed because in correcting Cathy, she might be offended. Jo took the path of least resistance.

'I know Jack Carr. Was he able to help?'

'Not quite. He knows a nurse at the hospital where my step-grandmother is recovering from Covid, and thanks to Doctor Carr, we got to speak to her.'

'That's brilliant,' said Jo.

'I can't remember the old lady and from our brief phone call, I don't think she remembered me,' said Cathy.

'There must be other avenues to explore and if anyone can find them, young Michael is a whiz.'

He was back on the team. 'The old lady had vague memories of her daughter adopting Cathy with vague the key word. "She was a beautiful baby," was the best she could remember.'

'Keep at it, Cathy,' said Jo. 'Remember "Success is stumbling from failure to failure with no loss of enthusiasm".'

Cathy took up Michael's trick of the half grin. Michael was embarrassed having two women wanting his attention. He didn't wish to offend Cathy as she'd just sacked then re-instated him. But he desperately wanted to be back working with Jo Best whatever the job. Cathy saved his blushes.

'Michael, I'll head off. Can I ring you when I hear back with my DNA analysis and any news on those certificates?'

'Of course,' said Michael and meant it, 'as soon as you know.'

'Nice to meet you, Jo,' said Cathy, and she left with Michael. When he returned, Jo and Alan were deep in discussion.

'Sorry about that,' he said. 'Coffee?'

'Yes please,' she said, 'and Cathy's a great looking girl.'

He replied from the kitchen. 'She said the same about you.'

Jo removed her phone. 'I'll send you the material on Annie Cleary.' She did so. 'I'm glad Jack Carr was able to help.'

He again called from the kitchen. 'All thanks to you, Detective.'

He returned as the coffee percolated and he checked the email attachment she'd just sent. On her phone it was miniscule. On one of his monitors it was gigantic. He flicked through the pages.

'Heavy stuff,' he said. 'Remind me again, what is our plan?'

'We find details of her crimes, choose one with a long prison term, and prepare a watertight case to be used by police. We show Annie's legal team the case and they "encourage" her to withdraw the appeal.'

'I knew that, I was just testing.' He perused the articles. 'So have you found one spectacular crime?'

'Not yet but she sure broke the law with impunity.'

'I hope you're not suggesting police corruption, Detective.'

She tapped on her phone. 'I've thought of a great source; my grandfather.' She put the phone to her ear. 'Did I tell you I've finally got him to move.' The man himself answered.

'Pop, hi, it's Jo.'

'Hello Love, what's happening?'

'Do you remember a woman by the name of Annie Cleary?'

He laughed so loud, Michael heard him as he headed off to pour the coffee. 'Remember Annie? Everyone remembers Annie. She was the best at not getting arrested; until last year.'

'Were there any of her crimes in particular you remember?'

'Plenty but what's your interest? She's inside and will probably die there.'

'Why did she avoid conviction for so long?'

'She was too clever or police too slack. Listen, call me tomorrow. I'm on my way out as Fanny wants me to help her buy a new bed.'

Jo thought of several things to say, none of which would have been acceptable for children's television.

'No worries, Pop. Take care and keep wearing your mask. Bye.'

'Anything?' asked Michael.

'My grandfather's an octogenarian and is off helping a lady friend buy a bed.'

Michael stopped staring at his screen. 'There are 100 *Carry On* innuendos for that statement.'

She pulled up a stool. 'Remember the two criteria; we have to find evidence to convict, and the minimum possible sentence has to be big.'

Michael flicked from page to page. 'She was a suspect in at least two murders. She ran a brothel for the top end of town.'

'That won't help; half of Melbourne's judges were her clients.'

'What about money laundering for high rollers?'

Jo mused. This was one battle she wanted to win. Solve an unsolved crime. Make the case watertight and force the Queen of Crime to back off in her claim against the pathetic pathologist.

Michael threw in a suggestion. 'We could go for the double.'

'Meaning what?'

'We gather evidence for one of Annie's crimes, and as a back-up, we pressure the two blokes who swear Gabrielle was pissed on the job.'

Jo thought about it. 'How would we pressure them?'

He stared at her. 'Are you serious?'

She knew he meant break the law, manufacture evidence, plant evidence, or do whatever it takes to make them withdraw.

'Okay, let's take the first option and if it seems shaky, we take option two as a back-up?'

'Right, pick a crime.'

She studied Annie's history but as most of her crimes were committed years ago, Jo found choosing difficult.

'What we need is an expert in Annie Cleary crime; an old journo or a retired cop who dealt with her for years.'

Michael thought about it. 'What about an old Private Investigator?'

Jo stared at him. 'Not your dinosaur with the manual typewriter?'

'Starlight must have heard of Annie, and would know who could help us find Annie's perfect unpunished misdemeanour.'

Jo kinda liked the suggestion, and as her grandfather was out buying a bed with his bird—*is that really true?*—she agreed. They hopped in Jo's vehicle and set off for Starlight's emporium.

'Is this a Covid approved journey?' he asked. 'If the cops pull us over, what am I doing in this car?'

Jo missed his wisecracks and played along. 'If the cops pull us over they'll see the dude in the passenger seat and ask for his autograph. She mimicked a cop. 'Aren't you the famous sleuth, Michael Chan, crime solver extraordinaire?'

'Ha ha,' said Michael but inside was rapt to be back on the beat with a certain Detective Senior Constable. He changed the subject. 'What's happening with Pierre's memorial?'

'Friday week and I'd love you to be there.'

'Put me down as a definite. Do I have to book?'

They drove across town noting the light traffic and the number of closed businesses.

As they climbed the stairs to *All Round Investigations*, Michael remembered Starlight was retiring. 'Shit,' he said and Jo reacted. Michael rarely swore.

'What's up?'

'I forgot, Starlight's retired. It could be a wasted journey.'

They kept going and reached her floor. The door was open and Starlight's raspy voice decorated the walls.

'You have to be joking. My list of contacts goes back centuries.'

'Half of them are dead, you silly old cow.'

The other voice was male and coarse. He sounded like a bloke with a lock on his wallet. Michael and Jo exchanged glances and headed to the boxing ring.

Starlight couldn't do subtle if she tried. 'I'd rather give it away than sell to you, you lousy bar steward.'

'Language, language,' reprimanded the tightwad.

Before he could continue, the two visitors arrived and Michael mimed knocking.

'Knock, knock,' he said and Starlight smiled.

'Hello son, have you found that birth mother yet?'

Grumblebum didn't like being interrupted. 'Hey, do you mind? I'm trying to do a bit of business here.'

Michael didn't like the geezer, did like Starlight, and made a rash statement. 'Whatever he's offering, Ms Freeman, I'll better it.'

Jo adopted the goldfish stance. *Did Michael just offer to buy this crumbling historical wreck of a business?* Starlight grinned and the would-be buyer growled and stomped out in high dudgeon.

'Thank you, Love and I know you aren't serious.' Michael's heart sank—he *was* serious. 'So last time you were with another young lady. Are you in the business of helping females in distress?'

Michael nearly laughed and Jo liked Starlight.

'One word, Starlight,' said Michael; 'Annie Cleary.'

'That's two words, and what in God's name have you got to do with that conniving crook, tart and evil malefactor?'

Michael realised he'd forgotten Jo. 'Oh I do apologise, ladies. Ms Starlight Freeman; Detective Senior Constable Joanna Best, Victoria Police Homicide Squad.'

'I've heard of you,' said Starlight.

'I've heard of you,' said Jo.

'We need your help, Starlight,' said Michael wanting to crack on. 'We're trying to make sure the Crime Queen gets another ten years on her current sentence. We're hoping you know someone who knows Annie and would like to see her get what's coming.'

Starlight didn't hesitate. 'Razor McGurk.'

'Sorry?' said Michael.

'Nobody knows Annie's shady deals better or wants revenge more than Razor. She screwed him big time. If she wasn't inside, he would've crapped on her from a great height. If you want to whack Annie, then talk to Razor.'

The duo didn't know what to say. They expected they'd have to give a long explanation and then have Starlight check her little black book with its names and numbers inscribed by quill. Not at all. It was "I know the bitch and this man knows her better. Go see Razor".

They thanked Starlight, took Razor's contact details and left. At the door, Michael lingered, perused the historic contents, gave Starlight his half grin and followed Jo down the stairs.

As they stepped into the street, a man opposite panicked and dived into a shop doorway. The business, like so many others, was shut. The ubiquitous sign attached to the door read—*Closed due to Covid.*

Jo and Michael walked to her car not seeing the man hiding. 'Bloody Jo Best,' whispered Detective Inspector Callum Blunt. 'What the hell is she doing with Starlight Freeman? Fuck! She's working on *my* murder without telling Rose. What ... a ... bitch!'

He fumed, poked his head around the shop doorway, and saw the couple disappear. He paused to help his racing heart settle. His boiler needed an immediate release of steam. One word throbbed inside his brain—Bitch! He said and thought it on a loop.

With the coast clear, he crossed the road and climbed the stairs to the office of *All Round Investigations* and its proprietor, Mr Starlight Freeman.

The door was open and Starlight was on her knees packing more of her junk. Blunt saw the char and knocked. She glanced up, ash falling from her 19th fag for the day.

'I'm looking for Starlight Freeman. Is he in?'

'No and the business is closed.'

Blunt produced his ID. 'Police. Now is he in?'

'Are all you rozzers thick? The business is closed—permanently.'

'Listen Grandma, it's closed when I say so. All right?'

Starlight turned on the mock subservience. 'Oh whatever you say, officer. How can I help?'

'Where's Freeman?'

'Who?'

Callum didn't like losing and at present he was two sets and five games to love down. 'Starlight Freeman, where is he?'

'Not here.' Blunt trusted no-one. The old biddy was protecting her boss. She went into her showbiz routine. It was how she got her name. Starlight's mother was a Tivoli girl and her father, Starlight's Pop, ran a theatrical agency with the name *Starlight Productions.*

'Oh Starlight,' sang Starlight. 'Come out, come out, wherever you are.' Nobody appeared.

Blunt glowered. He did a good line is glowering. He changed tack. 'What was that copper doing here?'

'Copper? We don't do coppers. This is a respectable agency.'

'Listen, you crone, your boss is a person of interest in a murder. He needs to answer some tough questions. Now when is he back?'

She shook her head. 'Did you say "witness to a murder"?'

'Yes.'

'So that's why he's been acting strange.'

Callum was hooked. 'Meaning what?'

She gazed at the detective, pleading. 'Please don't tell me he did it, please.'

'When's he coming back? Today, tomorrow, when?'

'Yes.'

'Yes what?'

'Yes sir.'

The DI was being played on a break and the worst thing, from his point of view, was he never knew. Ignorance is bliss. He produced his business card and dropped it on a box packed with hand-written files.

'Here's my card. Get him to call me the second he arrives. Okay?'

She struggled to stand, moved to the box to read the card. Blunt was kept waiting.

Die Callum Blunt,' she said reading.

'It's Dee Eye Callum Blunt,' he seethed at her pretend ignorance not knowing his stupidity was worthy of a Nobel Peace Prize for cretins.

Starlight smiled. 'I knew a Callum once. Mr Mari; bit wet but nice.'

She smiled at him as he stormed out and hit the stairs with his size 12s. His fury was not so much his failure to find the PI but that Jo Best was secretly working on the case—*his* case. Fear burnt a hole in his handmade shirt. Best's track record was way better than his. The cop who wasn't even on the case was about to upstage him again!

Bitch!

Chapter 24

Pandemic was the right word for this Covid-19 thingamabob. It was everywhere. Lyn, the girlfriend of the murder victim Banks, caught it from her gym. Other gym members likewise and the gym closed. When the second wave went gangbusters in Melbourne, the government ordered pretty much everything to close. Essential services, including supermarkets, stayed open.

When local spinster Ruth popped in for her weekly shop and then went home, her elderly mother became ill testing positive for Covid. Her contact was daughter Ruth but where did Ruth get it?

Matt popped into Ruth's supermarket to grab a gift for his wife's birthday. He went home and gave his wife Covid. The virus then passed to his wife's mother and their next door neighbour, Trinny. She belonged to a book club and pretty soon her group of readers became a Covid cluster. The virus was good at spreading.

With the second wave exploding, the three main planks were shutdown, test and trace. The city locked down and more testing venues opened; even pop-up sites. An army of workers were recruited to trace the contacts. Stop the spread.

With Ruth and her Mum it seemed likely the local supermarket was the source. With Matt, could it have been the same supermarket?

The ladies in the book club were asked for their contacts. Trinny was one and her contacts included her next-door neighbour. Matt was quizzed. Where have you been? He went to a certain supermarket.

So apart from the regular wipe downs and hand sanitiser units, it was time for a deep clean.

But who gave it to the supermarket?

Contract tracers discussed the spread. 'We know about accidental spreading,' said one official. 'But what are the chances someone is doing it deliberately?'

People buzzed. 'What, like sticking needles in strawberries?'

'Could someone capture the virus and then attach it to stock on shelves or to shopping trolleys and baskets?'

'The trolleys and baskets are constantly being cleaned.'

'Yes but could a scientist or a person with the relevant knowledge put the virus in a hand-held atomiser or swab stick or container, and discreetly walk around doing their shop while spreading Covid?'

The idea sent shivers up spines.

'So we not only find contacts, but Covid terrorists as well?'

With the stuff-up using security guards to control overseas arrivals turning into a Covid nightmare, jumpy officials jumped higher at the thought of Covid sabotage.

This prompted a lot of CCTV watching. Was there anything on screen to show how the virus made its way into Ruth's supermarket?

Jack Carr was run off his feet. He was always busy but the second wave of Covid hit the elderly hard meaning Jack's hours became 65 minutes each. He wished he'd trained as a firefighter as he ran to put out medical spot fires.

He called into Cedar Avenue Nursing Home to find both Marion and Bradley on duty. They looked as bushed as he was.

'Evening all. What's happening?'

'We're struggling with the virus, Jack, but worse, it's keeping the families away when their loved ones are dying. That's the killer.'

'A couple of family members turned violent,' said Bradley.

'Tell me about it,' said Jack. 'They're begging me to override government regs and let them in.'

'Three staff have caught Covid,' said Marion.

'From here?' Jack's worries multiplied. 'And is this their only workplace?'

'You're kidding,' said Bradley who left when a carer called him.

'Jack, most of our staff work shifts in other homes. They're paid peanuts and have to take whatever's offered. They need the work. If one staff member gets Covid, they not only risk infecting our residents, they risk taking it to other care homes.'

'Who should I see first?'

Marion opened her large book with notes on residents. Jack read the reports, shook his head and left for his first patient.

Management at Ruth's supermarket was contacted by the DHHS to say their building might be a source for Covid. Word spread like the virus. A deep clean took place. A security guard heard a rumour someone might be deliberately spreading the virus, so set up a monitor to watch old footage. Nothing caught his eye until something looked unusual.

The guard replayed the footage. It showed a man not so much stealing goods as returning them. 'What the heck?' spluttered the guard. A colleague heard him and wandered over.

'What's up?'

'What's that bloke doing?'

The other security guard watched and wasn't impressed. 'He's putting back what he doesn't want.'

'But he didn't take anything. He just strolled up, took a can from his trolley and put it on the shelf.'

'In the right place?'

'I think so.'

'Play it again.' They watched. 'If you go back further, I bet he selected that item ten minutes ago, and now decided he didn't want it.'

'But if people decide to put something back, many of them put it anywhere, wherever they found a cheaper alternative.'

'Well he looks like a good citizen, and whatever he's doing, he's not stealing.'

The first guard shrugged and forgot about it.

Chapter 25

'He lives in Northcote,' said Michael as he and Jo headed to meet Razor McGurk. 'So what's the plan, Detective?'

'This is your baby, Michael.' He stared at her. 'You were the one who suggested we attack Annie from another angle.'

He sniffed. She was correct and he came under pressure. 'I say we play it straight. We say we want to nail Annie Cleary, and Starlight gave us your name. If Starlight's right, we'll strike gold. Razor's hatred of Annie and his knowledge of her will give us the good oil.'

'What do we know about him?'

Michael searched online. 'His real name is Fraser McGurk.'

'Fraser not Razor?'

'Born in Scotland in 1950, came to Oz as a wee laddie, and has a list of convictions as long as the arm of a man with a very long arm.'

'Is there any mention of Annie?'

He scrolled. 'Not that I can see.'

'So we're inside his place and chatting and then what?'

'I'm getting used to your manoeuvring, Detective.'

'Sorry, what manoeuvring?'

'You put a person under pressure, in this case me, in order to sort out your tactics.'

'Are you saying I'm sneaky?'

'Absolutely. And I'm never mentioned in the credits.'

'You're getting a bit cheeky in your old age, Michael Chan.'

She grinned and he half grinned. When they reached Northcote, Michael directed the driver. They parked and pushed open a gate which needed new hinges in 1958. The garden was an eclectic mix of common or garden weeds. The weatherboard house needed paint like a condemned man needs a reprieve, and the verandah stored a variety of items which would fill an entire episode of *Bargain Hunt* and *The Antiques Roadshow* combined.

The visitors eyed one another before knocking. Where is the bell or knocker? Michael rapped his knuckles, and strange sounds emanated from within. It could have been an aging Glaswegian being roused from his daytime slumber. It *was* an aging wee Scot being roused.

The door opened and Razor spoke first. 'I'm broke and don't believe in the giant spaghetti monster in the sky. Now fook off.'

He went to close the door but stopped when Jo spoke. 'G'day Razor, Starlight Freeman sent us.'

Talk about a blast from the past. The door froze. 'Starlight Freeman? *The* Starlight Freeman?'

'She didn't send any hugs and kisses but spoke highly of your knowledge of a certain lady.'

He was genuinely interested. 'Who?'

Jo paused to milk the tension. 'Annie Cleary.'

Razor flung wide the door and gestured for the visitors to enter. They did but with difficulty. Razor was a hoarder and traversing the interior required a machete and a Sat Nav.

'In here,' he said leading the way to a sitting-room with nowhere to sit. The oldest Heinz 57 varieties dog hogged the only spare bit of carpet. It was never Axminster and always threadbare.

'Grab a seat,' said Razor enthusiastic to learn more about his arch enemy. He sat on a sofa with an antimacassar which had seeded and was growing out of the furniture; a form of evolution never observed by Darwin.

Jo and Michael tried to move junk then gave up and sat on the junk on the seats. Razor rubbed his hands together.

'So who are you and why are you here?'

'I'm Jo Best and a copper.'

Razor exploded. If he was Covid positive, droplets were launched in style. 'The filth? In my fookin' home!'

Michael jumped in. 'I'm Michael Chan and I *ain't* a copper.'

'Razor stalled and Jo explained their visit. 'We need help to give Annie Cleary a smack.' Razor smiled—not a good look. 'This is not a police case, we're working alone.'

Michael supported Jo. 'Annie is trying to have her conviction chucked out by claiming a friend of ours lied in her evidence.'

'What friend?'

Jo jumped in. 'A pathologist, Gabrielle Strange.'

'The fat bird?'

Jo hesitated. 'Spot on.'

'So what do you want from me?'

Jo tipped Michael the wink. 'We want to build a case against Annie for one of her many crimes and thus force her to drop her appeal.'

There was a pause and silence. The old dog grunted. 'Which crime?' asked the Scot and the visitors sighed a silent sigh of relief.

'Anything with a hefty jail term and for which you can help us supply powerful evidence,' replied Michael.

Razor thought about it then fixed his gaze on Jo. 'How long do you plan on staying a copper?'

It was unexpected and threw her. 'Sorry, I don't understand.'

'If you attack Annie for a murder I know she done, you'll bring down a retired cop, a former Chief Commissioner who was, and still is popular with you bastards. Your name will be mud. Ex-coppers and serving officers will spit on you with pleasure.'

Jo copped a whack. Her guts churned. She thought of the praise she'd won from high-ranking officers, from colleagues and friends. She thought of the celebrations her enemies would enjoy being able to destroy her. Like Gabrielle, her reputation would be trashed if she ruined the reputation of a saint among the boys in blue.

Michael tried to help his friend. 'Is there another crime of Annie's which we could use; one without a former police officer?'

'None with as long a spell inside; and I want her to go down for this one. She burnt me big time and ratted on my mate who's died. To have him reach out from the grave and smash the bitch would give me the greatest pleasure. I'll die happy if you can make this work.'

Jo's guts went feral. Her mind sat bogged in confusion. She glanced at Michael and nodded. They didn't have to go ahead but wanted to hear Razor's evidence.

'Let's hear your story,' said Jo and they did.

Jo dropped Michael home, all of two blocks from Razor's place. She pulled up and switched off the motor. They hardly spoke since leaving Razor's tumbling tumbleweeds. His story about the murder, planned by Annie, was gruesome. The evidence seemed watertight. Annie, if charged, would be inside for the rest of her natural.

But the elephant in the room was the fact a major player in the saga was a retired Chief Commissioner of Victoria Police.

He was well retired when Jo joined the Force. She'd never met him but knew of his deeds. Her grandfather spoke of the man and what a brilliant leader of men (and women) he was. Now she was about to smash his reputation and, if the matter became public, which it would, possibly have the police hero sent down.

'We're only showing our case to Annie's legal team,' said Michael. 'No-one else, and once Annie withdraws her appeal, the information in our case submission will be buried.'

'You're dreaming, Michael.' He seemed afraid. 'Once the facts about the ex-Chief Commissioner are seen, the can of worms is open. Whisper becomes gossip becomes online comment becomes universal knowledge and the police have to act.'

Michael struggled. 'The police will go after their hero?'

'It'll go political. The Opposition will sense blood, portray itself as the law and order party, and the sacrifice will be made.'

Michael expelled a lot of air. 'It's between a rock and a hard place time, Detective. Go with Razor and you lose your job. Don't go with Razor and Gabrielle dies in a ditch.'

Jo's muscles twisted. Her parched mouth ached for water. Before either could say another thing, someone tapped on Michael's window. He and Jo turned and saw an agitated Cathy. Jo hit the button and Michael's window dropped.

'Michael, great news,' she bubbled. 'My DNA has a hit!'

Michael hated farewelling Jo. He knew she faced a horrible choice. Whichever option she took, pain would follow. He knew she loved Gabrielle, and would do anything to help her but if she did, it would bring down a retired cop basking in his outstanding reputation in his well-earned retirement. No cop would want to work with Jo again. Her enemies would dance on her grave. She'd be banished into the outer darkness.

She decided and urged Michael to go with Cathy.

'Let's sleep on it,' said Jo and left.

Michael took Cathy into his airport hangar where he found it tricky to concentrate on her. She, on the other hand, tingled with excitement.

'I have certificates, Michael, and there are names of relatives of Gloria and Alison's family who might still be alive.'

'Great,' said Michael without conviction.

'They may know nothing about me or my birth mother but at least it's another avenue to explore.'

Michael made eye contact but his brain was elsewhere. 'That's terrific,' he said sans emotion. She was so excited she didn't notice his lack of enthusiasm.

Then her joy exploded. 'But this, Michael,' she showed him a document. 'Look!' He took the page. 'My DNA has a match from the genealogy site. I've found a cousin from my birth mother's family.'

Her euphoria dragged him round. He joined the celebration. 'That's fantastic, Cathy. I'm so happy for you.'

'I've asked if I may contact her and I'm waiting for her reply.'

'She'll reply. Why wouldn't she?'

'If she agrees to me making contact, I want to go and meet her. Will you come with me? Please Michael?'

Now the pressure ramped up and he hated his predicament. Two women faced a different but challenging crisis. Saying no to either would cause pain. This situation did not suit a nice guy like Michael Chan. He saw a possible out with Cathy.

'Do you know where your cousin lives? Is she even in Australia?'

Cathy considered such a possibility. 'I'm hoping she's in Melbourne or at least in Victoria.'

'Well the new Covid lockdown rules will make a face to face meeting hard. If she's in the country, you can't meet and even if she's in Melbourne, if she's 5 kays away, again you're stuck.'

Cathy nodded. Her hopes were sky high. 'There's always Zoom or Skype or FaceTime,' she said.

'And I can set up any of those for you,' he said with that smile.

She hugged him with feeling. 'You're the best, Michael, my hero.'

He thought about kissing her. Something stopped him and Alan didn't help by pointing out the hour of the day—tucker time, Jeeves old boy.

Chapter 26

Jo drove home. The humble two-bed flat complete with mortgage was hers. Her ground floor unit sat in a block of six. Like most Melbourne real estate, it grew in value over the years. Now, today, her flat was irrelevant. Thanks to the last Will and testament of her late fiancé, Jo Best would soon be mega rich. Probate on Pierre's Will was yet to be granted but once settled, her Clifton Hill property would be but a small fraction of her significant real estate portfolio.

She made tea and sat and read the screed she produced for Pierre's memorial service. The list of people who were to speak was set. She would speak but still didn't know her approach.

Do I speak about Pierre as a colleague or as the man I planned to marry? The days seemed to fly by and she needed to put her thoughts on paper pretty soon. As she pondered Pierre, her phone rang.

'G'day Mr Pen Collector.'

'Ha ha. How y'going, Jo? What's happening?'

'A lot and nothing. Listen, Ronnie, I'm sorry I've not been a team player of late. There's a bit going on behind the scenes.'

He knew about her recent bereavement; everyone did. 'Hey, I've already told you there are no rules here. You come and go when you can.'

'Thanks, Ronnie. I'll jump on a train and be with you soon. Anything new at your end?'

'I've made a new timeline for Natasha based on the info you and Gabrielle provided. I think you'll like it.'

'I know I will. See ya.'

On the train she worried about the conflict she faced over Gabrielle and the former Chief Commissioner. That worry didn't help her think straight when working with Ronnie. Guilt roared into view. *You can't be in two places at once, Joanna; you can't serve two masters.*

She entered the office and worried. Ronnie had stuck another huge piece of butcher's paper on the wall like he did with his explanation of the tides at the Port Phillip Bay Heads. Now the routine appeared again only as a timeline.

'What is it with you and giant wall charts?'

'G'day,' he said smiling.

'Is it you wanting to use all sorts of pens but on one giant page?'

'Could be. Let me explain.' He pointed as he spoke. 'We know when Natasha went into the backyard at the party and was seen arguing with Julian. We know when they walked off presumably to the beach. We think we know when Julian returned alone.'

'This is impressive, Ronnie,' said Jo and meant it.

'The next sighting we have of Natasha is here in this road when Conrad comes home and she offers to help him. He remembers her smudged make-up and torn shirt. We know the exact time they encountered each other if your trainspotter witness is right.'

'He is.'

'She leaves Conrad and heads along here and disappears.'

'And is killed.'

They paused and fell silent. Ronnie copied Jo. 'And is killed.' He paused then continued. 'She's found on the beach here at Queenscliff at 0720 hours which leaves eight and a half hours unaccounted for.'

'Most of that time she was in the water or lying on the beach, dead.'

Jo wandered along Ronnie's chart. He loved his pens did Ron. The streets were one colour, the stick figures with name tags another, and the times when each sighting or event took place, another colour again.

Jo genuinely praised his work. 'This puts us right in the picture. I feel as if I'm there at the party.' She tapped the chart. 'If only we knew who she met between here and here.'

Ronnie was a glass half full guy. 'We'll make it. Me with my fancy artwork and you with your thinking-outside-the-square routine is the perfect combination.'

Jo wasn't so confident. 'We certainly won't die wondering.' She picked up a book. 'What's this?' She saw the title and author. 'Perry Batchelor. Where did you find this?'

'I told my wife about your trip to Kallista and she gave me the novel. She's in a book club and Mr Batchelor is one of their oft-read authors.'

Jo studied the back cover and saw the photo of the author. The photo didn't match the man she met in the Dandenongs. Perry's pic had been photo-shopped within an inch of its life.

'So tell me about the novel. How much have you read?'

'Ah, not a great deal.'

'It's that bad, hey?'

'I'm a non-fiction man m'self; war diaries, biographies, books on collecting pens—you know.' Jo laughed. 'Why don't you take it and have a read. If you want to, I mean.'

'Sure, thanks, I will. So what's happened about the search for the missing DNA?'

'Not much. I'm going to meet that scientist at Forensics who seems to know a lot but is able to explain things in layman's terms.'

'Forensics for Dummies?'

'You've got it. This scientist, Alastair Dean, sounds so helpful and I'm planning on dropping in tomorrow or on my way home today. You're welcome to come with me, two heads being better and all that.'

Jo searched desperately for an excuse. *Meet Alastair Dean? I'd rather have root canal surgery sans anaesthetic.* 'Sorry, no can do. I have a date with a dentist.'

'Ouch,' said Ronnie and they spent time reviewing their progress and making plans. Ronnie left and Jo made a snap decision. With the Perry Batchelor novel in her bag, she headed for a familiar spot.

'Well bugger me,' said Charley Baldwin. 'The things you see when you haven't got a gun.' He gave Jo a hug and she enjoyed being back in Homicide after a longish break and a traumatic experience.

Billy Hughes appeared. 'Oi! Have you got clearance to be in here?'

Jo grinned. 'It's all right, Sarge. I know the Acting Detective *Senior* Sergeant.'

'Does DI Rose know you're here?'

Jo slipped into serious mode. 'Not yet. I wanted to ask her about DI Richelieu's memorial service.'

The mood turned sombre in an instant.

'I'll tell her you're here,' said Billy and left.

'So what's been happening?' asked Baldwin. 'I heard you're back on a cold case.'

'True and making pretty slow progress. What about you? How's the Moonee Ponds homicide going?'

Baldwin shook his head. 'We have a Melbourne Cup field of runners and not a favourite amongst them.'

Billy appeared and waved to Jo. 'Gotta go, Charley.'

'Good to see you, Senior,' said Baldwin and meant it.

DI Rose was on the phone but beckoned and Jo and Billy entered and sat. The DI finished her call.

'Good to see you, Jo. You're looking well. How are you?'

'I'm okay, thanks ma'am.'

'And the cold case? How come you haven't solved it?'

'We've actually made progress and uncovered new evidence.'

'Billy said you wanted to ask about Pierre's memorial.'

'Just wanted to check to see if everyone's fit and raring to go.'

Jo sounded crass but the senior officers knew this was a unique and difficult time. Jo spoke like so to cover the hurt inside.

'We'll be there. And if there's anything we can do,' said Billy, 'don't come the Miss Independent routine; ask.'

'Thanks, Sarge.'

DI Rose hesitated but wanted to raise a touchy subject. 'I guess you've heard about the Supreme Court appeal application with some nasty things said about Gabrielle Strange.'

'She told me,' said Jo, working hard to control her nerves.

'There's nothing we can do about it and it may not even make it to first base but it must be bloody painful for Gabrielle.'

Jo gave a nonchalant expression. 'She's one tough lady.'

'I hope you're not thinking about getting involved.' Jo's face became concrete. 'I know you admire the woman but this is not a police matter, and interfering in court proceedings is a no-no with a capital N.'

'I'm not sure why you're telling me this, ma'am.'

Rose gave Jo the weakest smile and both senior women knew their junior colleague would definitely try to help the pathologist. They were right.

DI Rose changed tack. 'So how is the great DCI Robertson?'

Jo startled them. 'I'm a bit worried about your former boss.' Rose and Billy thought he was ill. 'He's selling his house, moving into a swanky retirement home in Brighton and, wait for it, I think he has an admirer.'

The mood shifted. Did it ever? 'You're kidding?' said Rose.

'She's a copper's widow, lives in this Brighton pile, has money to burn, and I'm not sure if she wants to marry or mother him.'

Gales of laughter swept down the corridor into the Incident Room, and detectives reacted. Those who were Jo Best fans noted how her return brought laughter and joy to the place. Those who hated the bitch, found their resentment tunnelling ever deeper.

Cathy hopped up then sat then hopped up again. Alan objected. *Make up your mind, woman. Sit still!*

'Michael, I need your advice. Do I follow up on Gloria and Alison's family or go straight to my blood relative?'

He found it hard to concentrate. 'Both because as we discussed, the more leads you have the better your chance of striking gold.'

'Okay but which one first?'

'Your blood relation sounds the more promising. What have you done about contacting her?'

'Nothing, I can't. I mean she has to give her permission. I contact her via the genealogy site and she replies to them saying yes or no.'

'So what are you waiting for?'

She gave a cheeky grin and held out the screed with the DNA result. 'Would you do it please?'

He sat in his technology hub and prepared a note to send to the site. It appeared on a screen. 'Are you happy?'

She read his wording. 'Perfect; you're a star.'

He sent the email. 'Now what about these certificates?' She handed them to him. He read then started a search for family members related to Gloria and Alison. Cathy performed her hopping up and moving around routine. Her heart jogged and her feet itched. Her hopes soared and her excitement took wing.

Something has to come from this.

Chapter 27

The saying that "those who cannot remember the past are condemned to repeat it" was written specifically for DI Callum Blunt. In the past, he worked alone and stuffed up big-time. But instead of learning from that mistake, he charged ahead, repeated it, and screwed up—again.

Blunt's opinion of his own ability was wildly inflated. He reckoned he was smarter than most. Being ambitious and jealous didn't help. He reckoned working alone was the way to go, and when he cracked the case, all the praise, honour and glory would cascade from on high and land on his ever so slightly balding pate.

He fussed about his appearance, and wanted to be not only the best detective but the best dressed.

When interviewing the grieving Lyn Delahunty, he discovered she hired the PI, Starlight Freeman. Callum wanted to meet the PI—alone.

Lyn never met Starlight, dealing with her online. Lyn assumed Starlight was a bloke and Callum made the same mistake. He reckoned the old sheila he met was Starlight's char and set himself up for a fall.

Back at Homicide when asked to report on his findings, he gave his usual smug and mysterious reply.

'The grieving girlfriend in South Yarra hired a Private Investigator to spy on our victim. I went to question the PI who's disappeared. His cleaning lady knew nothing. This PI may well have the evidence we need to find Branko's killer. He may have pictures of the crime scene.'

Billy Hughes challenged him. 'That can't be right. If any PI filmed a murder scene, he'd be in big trouble with us for withholding evidence, while missing out on a fortune by not flogging them to the media.'

Callum hated being proved wrong. 'I'll know for sure as soon as I find the guy.'

'What's his name?' asked DS Melody.

'Freeman, a stupid first name then Freeman. I'll find him today.'

Billy turned to Justin Fletcher. 'What's happening with the thugs who threatened the business partner?'

'All baloney, there were no thugs.' Other detectives reacted. 'Jones refused to pinpoint an approximate time they allegedly burst into his office. Then we got CCTV footage and found nothing. We went back to Jones and he confessed. Banks has big gambling debts and been siphoning money from the business. Jones reckons he'll go bust.'

'So why the bullshit story?' asked Billy. 'All it does is put him in the frame. Motive certainly and what about opportunity?'

'Plenty and he has no alibi,' said Baldwin.

'Then I repeat, why the thug story?'

'We're still working on it. He's nervous to the point of being terrified. Did he help a former Serbian hit man, and has he been threatened to stay schtum? Does he want the business to fail so the payout to his ex in a divorce settlement is much lower than expected? He's definitely in the frame but it feels a bit NQR.'

'NQR?' asked Billy.

'Not Quite Right, Sarge—a bit like me.'

The SIO lost patience. Running a murder investigation without charging anyone made the person in charge develop itchy underwear.

'Who else?' she said.

Melody put Sophia in the frame. 'She's petrified of her husband and even more so now she knows her lover is her old man's twin; macho, body-builder type who uses women. Her alibi is she was supposed to be with the victim. It's messy.'

Nobody smiled and Charley Baldwin didn't help. 'Why don't we ask Jo Best to drop in and give us a hand?' Silence.

DI Rose took over. 'Right we keep on interviewing and eliminating. What have Forensics found in the victim's car? What about CCTV where it was parked? Near Pascoe Vale station wasn't it? Has Dr Laudi found anything new? What about CCTV at Tullamarine when Branko's pal from Serbia left the country?' She clapped her hands in quick succession. 'Come on, come on.'

Talk about a big agenda for Jo. Her *To Do* list included Pierre's memorial service and his Will; Pop's move and house sale; the cold case involving Natasha Kaye, and last but not least, the big Daddy of them all—saving Gabrielle Strange's reputation by destroying a highly respected retired Chief Commissioner. Phew.

Telling her mother Pop was selling up and her former husband, Malcolm X was the agent selling Pop's property would set off an incendiary device. Having then told her mother the sale was ripped from Jo's father's control would set Shirley's feet tapping. But informing Shirley her father had a floozy was way too much information. It was not the thought the old codger might find happiness in his autumnal years, but rather the possibility some bitch would remove Shirley's cash flow when Robbo made his final arrest. Families? Ha—who'd want 'em?

Finding it hard to sleep was understandable.

She read the Perry Batchelor novel Ronnie's wife provided. It kept Jo turning pages. Her brief meeting with the novelist gave off a feeling of a sterile and snobbish man; he didn't think he was a superior being, he knew it. That feeling came out in Perry's writing. She finished the book not keen to read another of his award-winning tomes.

She switched from cold case to Strange case planning her dangerous sortie to kill the Annie Cleary appeal. Razor McGurk spilt the beans on a murder arranged by Annie and for which she was never charged; not even arrested. Why? Did she have a cop in her pocket? Razor knew the murderer and how he was shafted by Annie. All Jo needed to do was make a case for indicting Annie. Easy. Easy my arse.

She knew Michael Chan was essential to the success of her investigation. But he seemed preoccupied with helping a friend find her long-lost family. In the back of her mind, Jo didn't think about the difficulty of her task but rather the impact if she succeeded. She would ruin the reputation of a former top cop.

She rang another former top cop. 'G'day Pop, it's Jo.'

'Hello Love, what's news?'

'Well that's a bit rich coming from the person whose life is one long adventure. What's happened with the move?'

'I'm all packed and ready to go. The house is on the market although with Covid, inspections are off. I'm told you can take a walk around my place online.'

'I'll check it out. Listen Pop, I heard people talking about a retired Chief Commissioner, Lewis Hayward. I remember you talking about him once.'

'Many times; he was my best mate; a brilliant cop and a marvellous man.' Jo's stomach growled. 'We trained together and kept in touch over the years. Not so much since he lost his wife. She was lovely.'

Jo's stomach hit overdrive. 'I heard he made a good Commissioner.'

'He was the best. His reputation serves as a standard for every Commissioner since and to come. Why do you ask?'

Jo batted away his question. 'I heard senior cops singing his praises.'

'As well they might. So what's happening with your cold case?'

'I think the term is "slow and steady". How's Fanny?'

'My God, what a woman,' sighed the former homicide cop. 'All I can say is I've been saved by Covid.'

'What?'

'She booked us on a cruise to Fiji which of course was never going to happen.' He interrupted himself. 'Oops, it's her calling me now. I'll see you later. Bye.'

What has happened to my grandfather?

Despair was not too strong a word. To save her friend Gabrielle Strange from shame and misery, she must expose her grandfather's best mate, a man with the highest of reputations in public service. Okay, he may have been incompetent or possibly corrupt to allow Annie Cleary to get away with murder, but who would thank Jo if she turned a spotlight on the former Chief Commissioner's feet of clay?

I'll be sent to Coventry in the Force, and my grandfather will never speak to me or die of sadness and shame at what I've done.

'Bugger!'

She turned on her laptop and searched for the main players—Razor, Annie and the Chief Commissioner—and made notes. With the facts provided by Razor, she listed topics to explore and people to interview. Her case needed to be watertight and accurate so Annie Cleary would have no choice but to stay in jail rather than face arrest for a murder she ordered all those years ago. And if they could trap her on a major drug importation and distribution operation as well, that would smash her enthusiasm for an appeal and save Gabrielle's bacon.

It was late. She slipped into running gear, lassoed her hair and hit the road. Much of her best thinking came when running. All sorts of people popped into her head—Ronnie Bumstead, Conrad Van Hilfen,

Commissioner Hayward (ret), Perry Batchelor, Pop and Fanny, and then Pierre Richelieu.

It was only weeks ago he proposed; only months ago they kissed near the Eiffel Tower. Now the lovely Frenchman was gone, forever.

Running with tears streaming down your cheeks isn't easy. It's hard to see where you're going and your emotional energy drains your physical energy.

She stopped and put her hands on her knees. A man came running towards her. Neither wore masks. He sweated and raced past her. A thought clicked in his brain. He stopped, turned and leered. Jo, still with hands on knees, looked back. His footsteps didn't continue into the distance.

'You okay?' called the runner.

Jo raised a hand. 'I'm fine, thanks.'

Her tears stopped but their damage was there for all to see. The man walked back to Jo.

'Are you sure? You don't seem okay.'

Jo stood tall. 'No, I'm fine, really.'

He contemplated getting to know her. She was attractive and her running gear enhanced her figure. He stepped forward. 'I'd like to help you,' he said and placed a hand gently on her arm. Wrong.

She pulled back to show her displeasure. Silly man, wouldn't take no for an answer. 'Back off,' said Jo in a way even a pompous prick would understand. But no the pompous prick reckoned he knew an easy mark when he saw one. Fool.

He tried again moving in close with the touching-her-arm routine while whispering a sweet nothing when he received a gift in return. Her short, sharp knee to the contents in his fishing tackle box produced a short, sharp pain with a cry of anguish as a side serving.

He bent double and joined Jo in the crying routine. His tears were involuntary. He glanced up at her, silently asking for an explanation. She gave it. 'Asking's fine, touching's not.'

Jo turned and ran. He tried even to stagger but every movement stimulated more agony. It was a long trip home for the limping jogger.

Jo ran home, showered, threw a so-called quality instant meal in the microwave then sat and ate it while watching the news on TV; no mention of the recent sudden death in Strathmore. Her colleagues were obviously struggling. An itch annoyed her. Scratching wouldn't help. Only being back in Homicide would do the trick.

Off with the news and on with the research. Batchelor's novel sat on her coffee table. She went online to Amazon. All of Perry's books were listed in an impressive catalogue. She clicked on another of his titles and read the screed noting the many positive reviews. At the bottom of the page was a list of other books under a heading, *Customers who bought this item also bought.*

She saw little of interest until the last book in line was written by a Perry Baker. The name rang a bell. She clicked on the title. It was Perry Baker before he became famous as Perry Batchelor.

She clicked again and up came the cover and description. *The Deadly Tease* didn't appear recent or modern or swish and classy like his other works. It was more a novella than a novel, and gave off a whiff of a first work. The homemade cover didn't help.

It was available as an eBook for the princely sum of US$2.99. She became a customer and downloaded her first eBook.

Chapter 28

One benefit of electronic mail is its speed. On Cathy's behalf, Michael sent an email to the genealogy site. The company found a match with Cathy's DNA to another subscriber, a cousin. Her name was Rachel Foster, 19, a young mother who lived in Box Hill.

She was thrilled to hear from the genealogy site and replied immediately giving Cathy permission to make contact.

Michael was working on an unpaid job at the time, trying to help his friend Jo Best save the reputation of Dr Gabrielle Strange. A new email arrived and he checked it. In no time he rang Cathy.

'You're in,' he said and Cathy didn't understand.

'Pardon?'

'The person with a match to your DNA has given permission to be contacted.' Cathy screamed. 'I have her name and email address.'

'What is it?' gasped Cathy.

'Rachel with no surname and a Hotmail address so no location, not even a country.'

'What should I do?'

'What sort of a dumb question is that? Reply of course.'

Cathy tried to settle. 'Okay, can you send me the details and I'll compose a note. Oh,' she moaned, 'I'm not sure what to say.'

Michael sighed. He liked Cathy and would be rapt if she could find her Mum but holding her hand throughout was becoming a pain.

'Well if you'd like to come over, I'll give you a hand.'

'You're a saint, Michael. I'll see you soon.' She went to hang up. 'And I think I love you, Michael Chan.'

She hung up whereas Michael sat there and thought about pinching himself. He stared at Alan sleeping on top of the sofa. 'Wotcha reckon, Alan?' He reckoned it wasn't his problem.

Michael knew Jo would think long and hard before ruining anyone's reputation. To do so to a respected former cop, would mean the end of her career. It wouldn't be a disciplinary matter; no, this was far worse. She was outing a highly respected man meaning Jo would be shunned and have no choice but to resign.

But then, if this cop was involved with Annie Cleary, albeit when he was a junior officer, he must have a bad side.

Damn, this is serious. Can I find a way of saving Gabrielle without smashing the cop?

His mind changed topics because Cathy arrived. Her last sentence bounced around his mind. 'And I think I love you, Michael Chan.'

Bloody hell.

He opened the door trying to remain calm. He liked Cathy, always did. She was pretty rather than beautiful, had a fabulous figure and a smile a hundred times brighter than his. To Michael, Jo Best was stunning, and though their romance was non-existent, he still carried a torch for the detective; a strong torch with an everlasting battery.

'Oh Michael,' gushed Cathy, 'I'm so excited.' She moved in and hugged him with Michael adopting the non-committal position.

He broke free. 'This could be the break you've been hoping for,' he said as they walked to his control panel.

'What *we're* hoping for,' she said squeezing his arm.

He showed her the email from the genealogy site. She read it. 'Rachel. It's a nice name. What's it origin?'

'I think it's in the Old Testament, Hebrew I guess.'

Cathy's face lit up. 'My mother's Jewish? That makes *me* Jewish.'

Alan was the only calm one in the building. 'I think you're getting ahead of yourself, Cathy. Let's take this slowly.'

She nodded. 'You're right. You're always right.' She leant in and kissed his cheek.'

'What do you want to say in your reply?'

'She handed him a piece of paper. There were cross-outs galore in the handwritten note which, when repaired, appeared like this.

Dear Rachel
My name is Cathy Feng. I was adopted as a baby 28 years ago and I have never met my birth mother. I do not even know her name.

Apparently there is a DNA match between us, and I'm hoping you can help me find my birth mother and family. I am single, a nurse, and live in Melbourne in Kew. The woman who adopted me has died and I have only her mother as my family. This grandmother is elderly and sick in hospital with the Covid-19 virus. If you can tell me a little about your family, I will be delighted.
Thank you and I look forward to hearing from you soon.
Your DNA friend
Cathy Feng

Michael was impressed. 'Excellent.'

'Do you think so?'

'It contains all the necessary information and has a kind and friendly tone. I'm sure Rachel will reply. I'll send it as an email. Okay?'

She beamed at him. 'Let's do it.'

He raised his index finger in a theatrical gesture then used the digit to hit Send. He smiled at her and she stared at him. No smile from Cathy, she was on the warpath. She leant in and kissed his lips with an overdose of passion. Michael surrended. *What the heck?*

They moved in a sort of crab-like walk towards the sofa, kissing and hugging en route. They flopped on the sofa and tried several variations on a theme. Alan was unimpressed. Firstly he was trying to nap and second, he'd endured the major snip op, and this type of behaviour was not in his stream of consciousness.

Just as the passion reached the remove the outer garments stage, Michael's computer went ping. He withdrew from the scrimmage much to Cathy's dismay.

'Michael, we can't stop now.'

He pointed to his platform desk. 'It might be Rachel.'

Cathy lost all interest in sex and headed for the control panel. Michael opened the new email. 'It's from her.'

Cathy clasped her hands to her face and shrieked. 'Read it. I can't see a thing.' Michael read.

Hello Cathy
Thank you for your email and I'm so happy we have found each other. My name is Rachel Foster, I'm 19, married with a baby boy and also live in Melbourne in Box Hill.

My mother is Li Ming Foster nee Sòng and I'm not sure but I think she is your auntie, your mother's sister. My mother has not seen her sister, your mother, since my mother was five. She does not know if your mother is alive. Your mother's name is Jia li Sòng.

Cathy gasped and began to cry.

My mother has a brother, An Sòng, but he was a baby when your mother left the family home and he has no memories of her.
Your mother's parents, our paternal grandparents are alive and live in a retirement home in Bendigo.
I think that's enough news for now. If you would like to meet, I have family photos although sadly none of your mother.
Even though the Covid travel restrictions are in place, we might be able to find a place between your suburb and mine. Let me know if you would like that and I will send you my phone number.
It is lovely to finally meet.
Your cousin (I think)
Rachel

Cathy shed tears for everyone.

'There you are, Cathy. You've found your family and I think it's fair to say you're not Jewish.' She laughed and cried simultaneously. He hopped up. 'Now, let's have coffee.' As he walked he called. 'And yes, Alan, I know it's tucker time.'

Chapter 29

Detective Inspector Callum Blunt was like a dog with a bone. He returned to the PI's office determined to meet Starlight Freeman. He bounced up the stairs. The office was locked. He was about to swear when a loo flushed, and the old cleaning lady he met appeared.

'You again,' she said. 'I've nothing more to say.'

'You haven't but it's your boss I've come to see. Where is he?'

She unlocked the door and they entered the office. 'Can't you see the business is closed?' She indicated the boxes. Everything was packed and ready to go. 'It's kaput, finito, comprende?'

'I know a woman called Lyn Delahunty paid Starlight Freeman to follow a bloke, Branko Bankowitz.'

'Who?'

'Otherwise known as John Banks.' Starlight nodded. 'Now he's been murdered and you and your boss will be in serious trouble with police for withholding vital evidence in my investigation.' It wasn't a police investigation but *his* investigation. He mimicked her. 'Comprende?'

She wondered about revealing her identity. But then she enjoyed playing the cop for a fool. 'So what do you want from Mr Freeman?'

'That's better,' he said. 'I want his report, pics, videos, texts, the lot; all the material your boss produced. Now where is he?'

'Oh it's all here.' She again indicated. 'Be my guest. It'll be in one of these boxes. I think this year's cases are over there.' She scratched her whiskery chin. 'Or are they over there?'

He glared at her. 'Listen lady, wasting police time is a serious offence. Now did your boss take any photos or footage?'

She made a song and dance of the situation pretending she now understood. 'Oh, you want the photos? Why didn't you say?' She produced a phone, surprisingly modern for the Luddite she was. 'This is Starlight's phone but I'm hopeless with these bloody things.'

He snatched it. 'Give it here.' He searched and found photos. He flicked through then stopped as if shot. 'It's the bridge. And the creek.' His voice moved up three semi-tones. 'That's Bankowitz.'

'Who?'

He fumed. 'Is this his phone?'

'It belongs to Starlight.'

Callum gawped. 'He was at the murder scene? He saw it?'

'I don't remember anything like a murder scene.'

Blunt ignored her, fascinated with the photos. 'Who's that? It's a woman. It's the girlfriend.'

'Who?' asked Starlight maintaining her role of octogenarian bimbo.

He studied more photos. 'Where's the money shot?'

'Sorry?'

'Where's the photo showing the bloke being stabbed?'

'No idea. Some woman came and went so I left. Never saw no rendezvous with the wife.'

Blunt stared at Starlight. *Who is this woman?* 'What are you talking about? *You* went home? Were you there?'

'Didn't I say that?'

'No,' almost screamed Blunt.

'You've heard of Santa's little helpers. I'm one of Starlight's very old helpers.'

Callum settled for flabbergasted. 'Lyn Delahunty wanted a PI keeping tabs on her boyfriend. Is that what these photos are about?'

'I told you that.'

Callum flicked back and studied the photos again. 'She looks like the bird who found him.' He glared at Starlight. 'Did she stab him and cover her tracks by pretending to find him in the morning?'

'I've no idea what you're talking about' said the PI still in character.

'Where's the homicide shot?'

'There isn't one. The bloke who was murdered was on his Tod. His girlfriend didn't show, just some jogger. It was getting late so I left, *we* left.' She indicated her phone. 'Wizzy Wig.'

Callum exploded. 'What the fuck are you talking about?'

'It's digital-speak; WYSIWYG; what you see is what you get.'

Blunt's brain began to glow. He was an inch from glory when the world went black. He held proof of everything except the actual event.

He still couldn't find Starlight Freeman; this whacky woman grew even more weird, and the word *failure* flashed on the giant scoreboard.

Fairlight took pity on him. 'Listen, the business is closed. All debts are paid. You can have the pics. If I knew how to send them I would.'

Callum struggled when anyone did him a favour. Kindness confused and upset him. He couldn't even spell *reciprocity*. He grabbed his phone and transferred the Strathmore photos to his. He failed Good Manners. Saying thank you and requesting an interview with Mr Freeman was too difficult. He handed Starlight her phone.

'Go on, it's not too hard,' she said.

He was clueless. *What is she on about?*

Starlight made a big show of using her lips. 'Th ... Th ... ank ... you,' she said, grinning. 'There, it's easy when you try.'

She was taking the piss, he knew it and hated her for it. Actually he just hated her. What she gave him was fool's gold.

As he left she called, 'And thank y'mother for the rabbits.'

When the pandemic hit Australia, Melbourne was Covid City with thousands of infections and hundreds of deaths. Health professionals were the front line troops. GPs conducted appointments by phone. Sick people stayed away from medical professionals they most needed to see. GPs were never so needed and especially in aged care.

The situation was dire as the elderly became infected. Isolation became mandatory. Many died. Families were locked out. It was hell not being able to visit a dying loved one. Which was more important— stopping the spread or treating the infected?

Jack Carr grew to dislike his rounds at Cedar Avenue Aged Care facility. He hated the word *facility*. In the last few weeks, he signed several death certificates. Grieving relatives poured out their hearts online and on his mobile. One even came to his home, begging, in tears, for permission to visit their dying parent. He found it hard to be cheerful with his kids. He struggled to make meaningful eye contact with his folks. They worried about him.

'Who will care for the sick if you're sick?' asked his mother.

'Yes Mum, I know the drill.'

'*We* do as we're told,' said his father. 'Who tells you what to do?'

It was a tricky question. Jack's reply was to leave.

'Must fly,' he said and did.

Calling at the nursing home was a chore. The two permanent nurses were often there together these days. Agency nurses came and went.

'Morning all,' said Jack as he reached reception and saw all the staff dressed to the nines in PPE. 'I didn't know it was fancy dress.'

His attempt at lifting the gloom and sorrow didn't work.

'Mrs Rogers died overnight,' said Marion. 'In case you've forgotten she was at Box Hill.' Even the friendly Marion was slipping in the sarcastic comment. Or was it frustration?

'I'll do my rounds,' he said wanting to depart the misery. He saw several patients, feeling good whenever anyone was happy and healthy.

He entered the room of his last patient and found Bradley attending to the elderly Rupert. Bradley stood back when Jack entered.

'Everything okay?' asked Jack, studying the patient.

'Rupert's been having trouble swallowing,' said Bradley.

Jack ignored his fellow professional and spoke to his patient. 'Good morning, Rupert. It's Doctor Carr. You're looking well.'

Rupert struggled to speak. 'Good morning,' he croaked.

Jack wondered if his PPE upset the elderly patients who were used to his smiling face. Now only his voice sounded familiar. The GP peered into Rupert's mouth. 'Open wide,' he said. Nothing appeared abnormal. Jack lifted a plastic cup of water from the small bedside table and helped Rupert lean forward. 'Have a drink for me, Rupert.'

The old man did and appeared relaxed.

'Good man,' said Jack having a listen to his heart. Rupert knew the drill. He sat forward as Jack checked his breathing. 'Excellent. You've passed your MOT, young man. Good for another 10,000 miles.'

Rupert grinned. He was a vintage car enthusiast and called metric measurements an abomination.

Jack adjusted the bedclothes, annoying Bradley, and wished his patient well. 'Keep up the good work, sir, and I'll see you soon.' Jack indicated with his head and Bradley followed him to the corridor.

'What was that about him having trouble swallowing?'

Bradley resumed his defensive position, his default response. 'It's a statement of fact. I was feeding him and he couldn't swallow.'

'I didn't know registered nurses were responsible for feeding. Isn't that a job for the carers?'

'In a pandemic it's all hands on deck. Surely a doctor knows that.'

Jack stared at the nurse. With both wearing all manner of protective gear, it came across as some sort of jousting match in a laboratory. The GP's regular duties called and he left.

Alastair Dean, the scientist, liar and Mummy's boy worked at Forensics conducting all manner of tests on materials relevant to crimes investigated by Victoria Police.

Once he spoke often with Detective Senior Constable Joanna Best when she called to check on a case she was investigating. Naughty Joanna knew about the queue of requests, the backlog of tests to be conducted, and figured if she smiled enough, the cardigan-wearing boffin might be inclined to expedite her case. Dangerous ploy, Jo, especially if the bachelor boy gets his signals mixed. They were more than mixed, simply lost in translation, and boy did things backfire.

After weeks of their friendly chats, Alastair asked for a date citing his dear old mother would so like to meet the beautiful policewoman she'd heard so much about. Jo trapped herself. How many women get invitations they do not want to accept?

She did accept and attended the afternoon tea from hell. She eventually fled not knowing the boffin tailed her on his bike. He saw her with Jack Carr and his family and decided the babe was a bitch. Alastair and Jo were no more. He gave her hell.

So when Ronnie Bumstead, the cold case pen collector pinned his hopes on Alastair Dean, Jo backed off quick smart.

Ronnie arrived at Forensics at the same time as Billy Hughes and Detective Senior Constable Stephen Payne from Homicide.

'Goodness, why am I so popular?' smiled Alastair.

Billy and Ronnie were pals from years ago and the two caught up. Alastair was a spectator as the reunion continued until Billy asked Ronnie a question.

'So how is your assistant, super sleuth Jo Best surviving?'

Alastair's antennae swivelled.

'Still recovering from the death of her fiancé but doing a great job.'

Alastair's reaction was like that of a swan—outwardly calm but paddling like mad beneath the water. *Jo Best was engaged? Her fiancé is dead?* Finally the cops turned to the boffin.

'So is it first come, first served?' he asked the detectives.

Ronnie spoke. 'Oh my case is 32 years old; waiting another few minutes is nothing. Please,' he said indicating Billy Hughes.

'Well,' said Alastair, 'I have good and bad news, Senior Sergeant.' Billy sensed excitement, Payne nothing. 'We've found a small DNA sample on the shirt of the victim.'

'And the bad news?' asked Billy.

'It's small and we have only a partial reading, but,' he said raising a hand, 'enough to assist in a prosecution if you have a suspect.'

'Cart before the horse, Alastair,' said Billy who should have known better, and the scientist stored her remark for future reference.

Alastair turned to the cold case cop. 'So where is your assistant, Detective? Not too busy to attend Forensics I hope?'

'She's at the dentist but is doing a brilliant job in solving this case. Now I'm hoping you can help us with new DNA developments.'

Before Alastair could reply, Billy interrupted. 'We'll get going, Alastair. I'll be in touch. See ya, Ronnie.'

Hughes and Payne left, the latter with his tongue still in storage.

'We've re-examined the clothing and reckon the shirt rip was made by a left-handed person who was about the same height as the victim.'

'Good,' said Ronnie taking notes. 'Anything on DNA developments?'

'We've found ways to read older and smaller samples but when evidence is immersed in water for so long, just finding DNA is tricky, if not impossible. Have you got her shoes, bag, glasses, etc?'

Ronnie shook his head. 'Sorry, just what she was wearing.'

'And the beach and foreshore were searched?'

'Yes but they found nothing.' Silence reigned.

'What about inside the body? Did the PM turn up anything?'

Ronnie shook his head. 'Nothing.'

More silence. 'Have you thought about cracking the case using anything other than DNA?'

'Like what?'

Alastair shrugged. 'You're the detectives, and isn't Jo Best the best in town?'

Ronnie didn't like the tone of Alastair's voice and wondered if Jo's teeth were really in need of a service.

'Thanks for your help,' he said, went to shake hands then remembered the Covid handshake. He offered his elbow and left.

Chapter 30

Cousins Cathy and Rachel spoke on the phone. It was exciting for Rachel who told her mother and uncle about their new family member. It was beyond exciting for Cathy. Having watched Gloria, the woman she believed was her mother fall ill and die was traumatic. But Cathy being told she was adopted plunged her into a world of pain. Now, weeks later, hope. Cathy discovered her birth family. Her mother's whereabouts, and if she was alive, were unknown but Cathy was off and running on a fantastic life-changing adventure.

She dropped in on Michael. He couldn't forget their romantic interlude. Were they thrown together because of emotion? Were his feelings for her the same as hers for him? She arrived.

'Michael,' she beamed when he opened the door. 'Naturally she moved in and kissed his lips. 'I've spoken with Rachel and we're going to meet tomorrow in a place called the Maranoa Gardens.'

'Great,' he said.

'And I want you to be there. I want to introduce you to my family.'

Michael didn't say great a second time. Instead a sliver of panic tapped his shoulder. 'Well, if it's what you want.' To Cathy his reply represented an enthusiastic response.

'Fantastic,' she cried and hugged him.

He lacked her enthusiasm, and she experienced a slight worry he wasn't as keen to tell the world of their new found love.

What new found love?

He wanted to be cool. 'Listen Cathy, I have sad news.' She froze. 'Doctor Carr sent me a text to say his friend, Nurse Susan, at Box Hill Hospital called him with the news Alison has passed away.'

Cathy gasped, putting her hands to her face. She barely knew her adoptive mother's mother but here was another possible link to her birth mother closed and lost forever.

'That's sad,' she said. 'Was it Covid-19?' Michael nodded.

He tried to be positive. 'But you've spoken with your cousin?'

Cathy switched back to smiling. 'She has photos of her family, *my* family, and is super keen to meet us.'

Us? thought Michael.

'She's hoping her mother can be there and I want my boyfriend to be there too.' He swallowed. 'After all, you're the one who brought us together.'

Michael was the kind of person who found it hard to deliver bad news. Romantically, he wasn't as committed to Cathy as she to him but telling her so was a tough call for the ABC from Northcote.

He dodged the issue but agreed to attend the family gathering.

Jo opened the Perry Baker eBook and read. It was a coming of age yarn about a young man as he discovered sex, drugs and rock 'n roll. The story was told in the first person and Jo found it easy to read.

The protagonist, Christian, came from an upper middle-class family. His professional parents divorced. Christian boarded at an expensive private school. On holidays, he lived with either parent both of whom had a new partner. None of these four adults took a genuine interest in Christian who did what he wanted.

Jo related to the teen as he struggled without love and guidance from his parents. Christian found relationships with girls tricky. He hated being teased by those who led him on then told him to drop dead once he made a move.

At university he studied arts and generally found it a waste of time. The only subject he enjoyed was Creative Writing, and mainly because the woman taking the subject was a young man's dream. Her figure captured his attention, and when she praised his writing, he reckoned sex and literature would do for the rest of his life.

His father knew an editor at a Melbourne daily and young Christian landed his first job. In the 1980s, the information super highway was still being built, and leg work, and phone calls using phones attached to chords were all the go. Drinking was frequent and heavy. Christian learnt to write, get drunk and chase women.

On and off again relationships hurt. He'd wake with a woman in his bed not knowing her name. At times the sex was exciting but the lasting satisfaction never appeared. In short, he was lonely.

Jo became bored with the book until Christian found his niche in writing—true crime. If he could experience something dangerous, unusual, even criminal, then writing about real life would supercharge his work. He could turn exciting non-fiction into exciting fiction.

The adventure began. Now Jo couldn't put down the book. It wasn't a paperback but a file on her laptop. She folded her legs and read.

It was late when she finished. She checked the time finding it hard to believe she'd read the book without a break. She boiled the kettle than rang her cold case colleague.

'Good evening, Ronnie. How is your pen cleaning night.'

'I'm regretting telling you about my hobby. So what's new?'

'You go first. My news is likely to make you laugh.'

'Never,' he said. 'Well I went to Forensics and Billy Hughes was there too. The boffin, Alastair Dean, reckons they've found a partial DNA reading on the murder victim at Strathmore.'

'Great,' said Jo, 'and what has he found for our case?'

'No DNA of course but examining Natasha's shirt, they reckon her attacker was about her height and left-handed.'

'That's Julian, the boyfriend,' said Jo.

'Brilliant,' purred Ronnie.

'But Natasha was seen alive *after* her shirt was torn.'

'Meaning we discount Julian. He was back at the house and stayed there. So what's your news?'

She paused. 'It's nothing much. I'll tell you tomorrow.'

Michael sat in his NASA-type office and pondered his problems. The first was his romantic entanglement with friend Cathy Feng. Helping her find her birth mother was a challenge he enjoyed. Helping her into his bed was different. He was not into hurting people and if he and Cathy became lovers, and he then chose to leave—his way of saying dumped—he knew she'd be hurt. Tricky.

His second problem was his promise to support Jo Best. If he helped her prepare a murder case against Annie Cleary, and it scared the Queen of Crime into withdrawing her appeal, Jo would save her pathologist pal but almost certainly wreck her career.

He investigated Annie Cleary and the crime suggested by Razor McGurk. Evidence pointed to Annie. So why wasn't she charged? Michael kept returning to Chief Commissioner Lewis Hayward.

When Hayward became top cop, he revolutionised Victoria Police. He made it easier for females to move up the ranks. He encouraged people from a range of ethnic cultures to join the Force. On his holidays, he dived into the sea and rescued two young girls who'd been swept out on a rip. This cop was a hero.

How can I destroy this man? How can I let Jo destroy her career?

Thinking anywhere but inside the box, he needed a way to save Gabrielle while protecting Jo. An idea pinged. Excitement attacked him. He thought. *If this works, the Senior Constable is sure to be grateful. And if she launches a Cathy-style romantic foray, I'll do an Errol and be in like Flynn.* Ah, dreams.

He started work on Plan B. Genius is an overused word but if Michael's plan worked, Hallelujah would be back in town.

As the crow flies, not even a mile away in the next suburb, Jo Best read the first novel written by the unknown Perry Baker.

Neither Jo nor Michael was visited by an angel that night, but both experienced a Damascene moment. Jo saw the answer to the cold case and Michael saw the end of Annie Cleary's bid for freedom. A killer was found and a pathologist able to retire with her reputation intact.

Hallelujah indeed.

Chapter 31

The Maranoa Gardens in Deepdene were about midway between Cathy in Kew and Rachel in Box Hill. Under the Melbourne lockdown rules, unless your journey was approved, travel was restricted to a maximum of five kilometres. Both Cathy and Rachel were under the limit.

Both women were on edge. In Rachel's car were her infant son James, and her mother Li Ming, whereas Cathy's passenger was the man she considered the love of her life, the reluctant Michael Chan.

The cousins agreed a meeting place beside the gardens. Rachel parked in the empty street and waited.

'Are you sure this is the right street?' asked Li Ming.

'Yes Mum, be patient.'

'What about the Covid rules? How many people are allowed to meet at one time?'

'Oh Mum, stop worrying. This is a wonderful day. For the first time you are meeting your niece, your only niece. She does not know her mother. Please be happy if only for my sake.'

A car turned into the road.

'There they are,' said Li Ming and Rachel's heart ran through the gears. As she went to open the door and step out, baby James began his singing lesson warm-up. Good timing, Jimmy.

Across the road, Cathy parked. 'That's them,' she said. 'Oh Michael, I'm so nervous.'

His famous half grin appeared. 'You'll be fine. After two minutes, you'll be chatting like a couple of besties. Go on, off you go.'

She panicked. 'Michael! You're coming too. I can't do this without you, please.'

Of course he agreed. He was too nice was Michael as he sank further into the role of faithful support officer.

They hopped out and crossed the road. The driver's window on the other car slid down and the baby's aria filled the street.

'Cathy?' asked Rachel knowing it to be her.

'Hi,' said Cathy fighting back tears.

'The noisy one is my son James.'

'This is my friend, Michael.'

The pedestrians bent to see inside the car. Grandma was nursing the bawling babe.

'And this is my Mum and your Auntie, Li Ming.'

'Cathy and Michael and the grandmother said, 'Hello.'

Then nobody knew what to do. The plan was to gather in the Gardens provided they were not under Covid lockdown. Were people allowed to meet there? In the end, Michael suggested he and Cathy get in the back of the car. They did.

What a reunion. It was grandmother, mother and bub in the front with cousin/niece and boyfriend in the back. Charming. Happy families. Michael found himself sitting on a squeaky toy, Jimmy's favourite. Even the slightest move from Mr Digital caused a squeak. Michael chose to freeze, thankful it wasn't a whoopee cushion.

The arrival of new bodies seemed to have a soothing effect on the wee lad. This gave Rachel the chance to twist in her seat, beam at her cousin and become all emotional.

'I can't believe we've met, Cathy.' She choked and tears appeared.

Cathy went to speak but couldn't. It was a tear-a-thon in a VW Passat hatchback. Cathy reached across and grabbed Michael's hand. All he could do was make an involuntary squeaking sound.

Rachel recovered and pointed to a milk crate in the back. 'There are photos in there. Could you grab them please, Martin?'

So the reluctant hero, now with a new name, lifted the crate of photo albums. His turning produced the loudest cushion squeak and little James wondered if someone had nicked his favourite toy.

'There's a family tree in the plastic sleeve.' Martin aka Michael handed it to Cathy. 'Now I'm not certain about everything,' said Rachel, 'but as you can see, my Mum's parents are Benjimen and Jin Sòng. Their three children are my Mum, Li Ming, my uncle An, and your Mum, Jia li. Sadly we don't have any photos of your Mum even as a little girl.' She pointed to the album. 'Look in there.'

Michael handed an album to Cathy who struggled with nerves. Her hands shook.

'Why are there no photos of my mother?' asked Cathy expecting bad news. 'And do you know if she is still alive?'

Silence came from the front seat except James who now switched to the gurgle and coo routine. Li Ming answered. 'I was only five and my brother An was a baby when your mother left our home. We do not remember her. I used to ask my parents about your mother but they said she ran away.'

Cathy groaned. 'Why? Where did she go?'

'Now you've found us,' said Li Ming, 'we will ask our parents again for any details about your mother.'

Cathy nodded and spoke through tears. 'Thank you.'

Michael decided to help. 'Where do your parents live? Are they in Melbourne?'

'No,' said Rachel. 'They are in a retirement village in Bendigo.'

'Are they in good health?' asked Michael wanting to know what chance they had of speaking to at least one lucid adult.

Li Ming replied. 'They are frail but their minds are good. I think your mother is about 10 years older than me and 15 years older than our brother.'

Michael felt good and Cathy's heart rejoiced. She had questions. 'Because we have met, do you think my grandparents will speak about my mother?'

More silence from the front. Rachel glanced at her mother. 'They may not know,' said Li Ming. 'They haven't heard from your mother for years and it's possible she's passed away.'

The silence sounded loud.

'There are more photos,' said Rachel, and Cathy turned the pages. She saw photos of an older couple.

'Are they my grandparents?' Rachel nodded. 'Do they know we have discovered one another?' asked Cathy.

'Not yet,' said Li Ming. 'I was waiting until after this meeting. Do you want me to tell them?'

Cathy pondered her reply. 'I would like to know why my mother ran away, if she did. I would like to know everything about my mother. I would like to know how I came to be adopted by Gloria Teng. I would like ... ' She paused. 'Do you know Gloria Teng?'

The women in the front shook their heads.

It was a tsunami of change. From nothing came everything. Michael wanted to help Cathy now more than ever but worried the grandparents in Bendigo might have no knowledge of Cathy's mother.

Jo too felt trapped, not sure what to make of her latest theory about the death of Natasha Kaye. She told Ronnie she would explain her thinking in person and delayed departing so as to be sure of her facts.

When she arrived, Ronnie was running out of space on his new wall chart. 'Good morning, Detective,' he beamed from his stepladder. 'This one you'll love. I've listed all known persons of interest and graded them in percentage terms as the likely killer. The ones with an asterisk have unknown information still to be determined. The ones with a question mark are only included because of circumstantial evidence.'

Jo wanted to interrupt and tell him they were *all* included because of circumstantial evidence.

He babbled away. 'If we can agree on the percentages, I say we start with the highest scores and work down. Wotcha reckon?' She paused. 'What, you don't like it?'

'Ronnie, I think I've cracked it.'

His mouth opened and the pen behind his ear fell to the floor in shock.

'This case?' She nodded. 'This 32 year old cold case?' She nodded again. She expected him to swear and curse her having done all this graphic presentation work only to find it a waste of time. Instead he hopped down, grinned like a kid on Christmas morning who got more than what he asked Santa to deliver, and hugged Jo.

'Whoa, hold it,' she said.

He backed off thinking he'd broken the harassment rule, written or unwritten. She didn't mean anything like that.

'Ronnie, I said I *think* I've cracked it. Come and sit down.'

He did and suffered from eager anticipation. 'When I told my wife you were working on this case, do you know what she said?'

'No, but I have the feeling you're going to tell me.'

'Case closed,' is what she said, 'with Jo Best on board it'll be case closed.'

Jo wanted to dampen his sky-high expectations. 'Ron, let's test the evidence first, okay?'

He settled a little. 'Okay, what've you got?'

She handed him a piece of paper. He read it. When he finished he stared at her, disbelief on his face. 'Where did you find this?'

'Never mind that for now, what do you think?'

He thrust the paper towards her. 'Why isn't it signed?'

'What?'

'This is a confession to Natasha's murder. Why isn't it signed?'

'I didn't interview the writer of the confession. I found it in a book.'

'A book!'

'In a novel written by Perry Baker.'

'Who's Perry Baker?'

'Keep up, Ronnie. Perry Batchelor was once Perry Baker.'

Ronnie sat stunned. 'Bloody hell. You found this in a novel?'

'It was published decades ago. It would have been an unknown paperback and someone, I bet not Perry from Kallista, has turned it into an eBook in the hope of making a buck now Batchelor is a star. He probably signed a contract with a Vanity publisher and they have the rights. If he knows it exists, he knows his best response is no response.'

'You mean he shuts up hoping no-one notices.'

'Exactly. He changed the names and places but the details could only have been known to the killer. My guess is he was suffering the old writer's block so created a novel based on a real life experience. Write about what you know.'

'He wrote about what he did.' Jo nodded. 'Where's the novel?'

Jo opened her bag, produced a tablet, and opened the file. Ronnie examined the cover. 'It's not exactly an upmarket publication.'

'There are other things which nail him. He must have been up because of the loud party noise. He could see into the Love backyard and saw Natasha and Julian argue then split. He's followed her and there's even a conversation with a bloke in a wheelchair.'

'Conrad?'

'It has to be. He describes the rape and the drowning out at sea.'

'My God, it's his confession disguised in a novel.'

'But the big question now, Detective Sergeant Ronnie Bumstead, retired, is how do we prove Perry turned fact into fiction and killed Natasha Kaye?'

Chapter 32

Cathy drove Michael home from the family reunion. He offered to drive but she resisted. 'I'm fine,' she said.

'You don't look fine. You have your Mum's name, your family name, and now have the chance to discover if your Mum is alive and, if so, where she lives. That's huge, Cathy. Are you sure you want to drive?'

'I'm sure.' Cathy kept driving with a steely determination to see this through. 'I'll find her. I've come this far, and I won't stop till I find her.'

Michael was pleased with Cathy's success, a side benefit being she spent less time planning love and marriage with Mr Squeaky Bum.

'What do you think?' she asked. 'Is she alive? Do you think she will want to see me? And why do you think she run away?'

'Too fast, Cathy, you need to hasten slowly.' She stared at him. He pointed to the road and she concentrated on driving. Her emotional state influenced her thinking. *Watch the road, kiddo.*

He explained. 'Remember people give wrong information. Even if they're sincere and believe it's the truth, they may be wrong.'

'You're confusing me,' she said preparing to cry again.

'You've been told your mother ran away. Okay, she left the family but did she jump or was she pushed? Did she become pregnant with you at a young age making your grandparents ashamed?'

'If that's true I already hate my grandparents.' Michael said nothing and his silence upset her. 'Well how would you feel if you were conceived and your mother was thrown out of her parents' home?'

Michael adopted the quiet conciliatory approach. 'Why don't we wait till we have all the facts and then decide how we feel? You've had enough sadness in your life to accept anger as well. Find the truth and then respond. Okay?'

She nodded. 'You're right, Michael, you're always right, so wise and kind. That's why I've fallen in love with you all over again.'

Again? Sorry? I don't remember the first time.

He whipped out his half-smile and tried the "be still my beating heart" exercise. It raced not so much because of excitement but fear.

They reached his home and his speech was ready to go; it was all about his jam-packed schedule which would prevent him from doing anything with anyone, including the enthusiastic female sitting next to him. Before he spoke, she did.

'I've been thinking, Michael.' He held his breath. 'I should give you a little breathing space.' His hopes sang. 'I know I've been keeping you from your work so I'll back off and let you get on.' She meant for now.

He was momentarily tongue-tied. She gave him what he wanted; his freedom. 'Okay,' he said trying not to appear relieved. Sadly he didn't see the sucker punch until it was too late.

'Just don't forget to pack your overnight bag.' He threw on his quizzical expression. 'We're off to Bendigo to meet my grandparents.'

Oh shit.

Callum Blunt now knew about rocks and hard places. He scurried from one to the other. He found evidence, photos of the murder scene, the murder victim and … and nothing. Why did the PI take off before the end? He was paid to watch the movie. *Watch the credits, dickhead.*

He printed the photos, placed them on his kitchen table, found his trusty magnifying glass from his stamp collecting days—yes, incredible but true—and poured over each pic for clues.

The victim arrived. He checked his watch. He was waiting for someone. Then a woman came jogging towards him. The two looked at one another but that's all. No stopping, no chatting, no exchange of drugs—nothing. She left and he stayed and then the PI left.

Not only did Callum not have the smoking gun, his list of unanswered questions slowly sent him mad.

If I show these pictures to the Squad, they'll ask me why I haven't got the one with Branko being murdered or else, they'll see something in the pictures I can't see, and they'll solve the sodding murder and laugh at me for being so stupid!

He left the rock and moved to the hard place.

Michael was rapt to arrive home alone and unscathed. Alan noted his valet's arrival, pleased the amorous prawn did not re-appear.

'I need a therapist, Alan,' said the staff member making coffee. 'Ten lessons on how to be assertive, especially, no exclusively with females.' Alan shifted and resumed his siesta.

Leaving family reunions aside, the IT whiz set about saving Dr Strange's good name. His Plan B did not support Jo's quest to nail Annie Cleary. Michael wanted Strange rescued and Best preserved.

He re-read the legal document put up by Annie's lawyers.

How much are the Dr Strange critics being paid?

His idea was simple. It was the one he suggested at the beginning. This was another of Michael's strengths. Find another, a better way to win. He liked a challenge. He liked being a private investigator.

Jo and Ronnie made a decision. No matter how hard they studied statements, reports, photos and recordings, they couldn't find anything to link Perry Batchelor with Natasha's murder. Certainly his juvenile novel had real life crime written all over it. But such evidence by itself would never have the Prosecution Service dancing in the aisles. No, they needed to find another way.

'I say we confront him,' argued Ronnie. Jo disagreed. She'd met the man. 'Jo, Natasha's parents are not getting any younger. What will we think if we let this drag on then later find out it's him, and one or both of the parents die before the bastard's charged and convicted?'

'Okay,' said Jo without confidence. 'So we confront him and if he tells us to get stuffed or worse, goes "No Comment", we'll be watching re-runs of *Schitt's Creek* without a paddle or a choc-top.'

'What else do you suggest?'

'I have an idea about writing him an anonymous letter.'

'Saying?'

She produced the screed she worked on last night, and read aloud.

'Dear Mr Batchelor

I know what you did in the summer of 88 on the beach at Point Lonsdale. I know how you killed Natasha, trying to make her death look like an accidental drowning. Did you know she was a champion swimmer?

I know how you disposed of her body and how it got back into the Bay and onto the beach at Queenscliff. You think you got away with

Ronnie sat stunned, impressed, bowled over. 'It's brilliant.'

'You like it?'

'I love it. It's the perfect ploy. It sounds real because it *is* real. If he's not the killer, he'll think it's a troll who hates his books or success or both. If he is the killer, he'll shit himself. When can you send it?'

'I could make it an email and he'll have it in a minute.'

'Do it. But how can you disguise your address? If he gets lawyered up and they trace the email to us, that'll kill the case.'

'I can't disguise it but I know who can.' She used her phone.

'Detective Best, how lovely to hear from you,' said Michael Chan.

'Hello Michael; as always I need a favour.'

'And as always with the magic word, your wish is my command.'

'Please.'

'Go for it.'

She explained the situation. She sent Michael the email. He found Perry's address and sent the letter from an address in Serbia not far from Branko Bankowitz's old home town.

'It's done,' he said and Jo thanked him. 'I'm checking his response and ... yes, it's been opened.'

'You never cease to amaze me, Michael.'

'What are we talking about? My teeth, my charm, my ...'

'All of the above.' She laughed and prepared to end the call.

'Before you go, on the other matter we discussed, I'm developing an alternative strategy which could achieve the desired result but cause no friendly fire to a certain retiree.'

She sat stunned. 'Are you serious?'

'When dealing with you, Detective, I'm always serious.

'Michael, you're a star. I could kiss you.'

'I'm recording this conversation.' A pause lingered. 'Only kidding. But if you want to see the strategy in person, drop in.'

'I will. And thanks. Ciao.'

She ended the call and Ronnie stared at her. 'Well?'

'The email is in Perry's email folder and has been opened.'

Ronnie gasped. What? How? That's too hard for me.'

'And methinks illegal so please, no more questions.'

'My lips are sealed.'

'So what now?'

'I'll drive,' said Ronnie, 'and you rehearse the dialogue.'

'What if he's not home?' asked Jo vaguely watching the scenery as they headed for the hills. 'We'll have driven all this way for nothing.'

'He'll be home.'

'You're guessing.'

'You have heard of the Covid pandemic I presume?' She twigged. 'He can't go more than five kays, and if he has, we hang around till he rocks up.' He watched her. 'Now rehearse your routine.'

He winked, she smiled and jotted notes.

Jo suggested they pull up in the Kallista township for a re-run of their tactics. 'I'm not as confident as you, Ronnie. His ancient novel may read like a crime report but no prosecutor will go to court on a few pages from a book. Perry might even say it's not his.'

'So there are two Perry Baker's writing novels.'

'He's an international success. He lives for awards and book sales. Going inside for murder is not on his bucket list.'

'You're selling yourself short, Detective. How did you crack all those previous homicides; luck, guesswork, or brilliant sleuthing? Well?'

'All the above,' she said scrunching her face. 'Why do I feel you're like a coach trying to rev me up before the game?'

'As I said, if he's our man and has read your email, he's history.'

They pulled up outside the impressive metal gates. They could see in so undoubtedly those inside could see out. The police alighted and Jo rang the bell. The intercom in the pillar crackled.

'Yes?' said the woman Jo met on her previous visit.

'Good morning,' said Jo. 'It's the police. May we speak with Mr Batchelor?'

The woman made a fatal error. Instead of saying the novelist was not there, she want with "he's not well". Big difference.

'This won't take long,' said Jo, 'and the matter is important.'

'What's so important it can't wait till tomorrow or the day after?'

'I'm sorry I wasn't introduced to you when I called before. My name is Detective Senior Constable Joanna Best. With me is my colleague, Detective Sergeant Ronald Bumstead, and we are from Victoria Police Cold Case Team. May I have your name please?'

Ronnie admired Jo's persistence and perfect manners.

'Why do you need my name?' asked the woman sounding more annoyed and agitated. Both police officers were sure the novelist was listening to the call and making gestures or scribbling notes or both. The cops were pleased with the situation—so far.

'We don't but it will be easier for all if we can have a word with Mr Batchelor. No-one knows about this visit. We are alone. We have not been followed and we can take as little of your time as possible.'

Silence. They waited.

'Hello?' asked Jo. More silence. 'I do hope we can have a discussion with Mr Batchelor without having to call upon other officers to assist.'

It wasn't hysteria but the pitch of the woman's voice edged higher.

'Are you threatening me?'

'No, I'm asking politely if you will allow us to interview Mr Batchelor.' Jo offered an alternative which she knew would never be accepted. 'We don't need to enter the property. If Mr Batchelor is willing to come to the gates, we'll conduct the interview out here.'

Not a chance. The woman's voice snapped from the speaker.

'This is a gross invasion of our privacy. We'll be writing to our MP.'

The voice died and the gates swung open. The detectives returned to the car and drove inside. The gates closed.

'People under pressure always make threats,' said Ronnie.

'I'd love to have your confidence.'

'You lead, Jo.'

'Okay but jump in at any time for any reason.'

They climbed the steps to the empty patio and walked to the wall of glass. They saw no-one inside.

'My kingdom for a doorbell,' whispered Ronnie.

The woman appeared and slid the glass panel open, just enough for the police to enter turning sideways. The woman, still without a name, couldn't bring herself to speak. Jo smiled and entered with Ronnie following.

'Wait here,' said the lady of the house and left. Ronnie admired the room knowing the contents were never purchased at the local bric-a-brac store.

The novelist arrived in a state of distress. He wanted to be angry but his nerves kept swatting away his wrath. The contents of a recent email put the wind up him; right up him.

'This is harassment. I told you all I know last time.'

'This is Detective Sergeant Bumstead,' said Jo who again showed her ID and I'm ...'

'Yes, I know who you are. Can we get this complete waste of time over please?'

No-one was offered a seat. The visitors were never going to enjoy mint tea and gluten-free, twice-baked bickies. A flashing sign, incongruous in such an interior, lit up with *Hurry up and Leave*.

Jo spoke. 'I have questions about the death of Natasha Kaye whose body was found at Queenscliff in 1988.'

'I can't help you.'

Jo ignored his protest and plugged away maintaining a polite and calm demeanour. 'We need a clearer understanding of the time when you left Point Lonsdale.'

Batchelor snapped. 'No more. I've told you all I know. I want you to leave.'

Jo played hard ball. 'Are you refusing to answer our questions?'

'Yes,' he thundered and pointed. 'Get out!'

Jo maintained her calm and measured approach. 'Perry Batchelor, I'm arresting you on suspicion of murder.'

Both Perry and his still unnamed first best friend screamed as one. 'What? No!' although it might have been, 'No! What?'

'You do not have to say or do anything unless you wish to do so but whatever you say or do may be recorded and given in evidence. Do you understand me?'

Cue the fireworks.

Chapter 33

The pregnant pause arrived. You needed to be there to fully appreciate the tension. Perry and pal paused; a new experience for both. Having police in their house was a first. Being arrested, and for murder, set the bar at a new and astronomical height.

Perry reacted. He could have extended his hands and uttered, 'It's a fair cop, Guv,' but didn't. He could've threatened Jo and her pal with all manner of retribution from "people I know". He didn't. What he did was remarkable. He ran; yes, he ran.

Ran? Where did he think he would go? Was there a secret tunnel with its entrance and exit known only to the master of fiction? Was there a hidden locale as in *The Secret Garden* where Perry could disappear? Alas, not so, it was neither of the above.

He raced from the room startling the others, screaming in anger and frustration. His partner, Anonymous, screamed in unison then went after him. The Afghans, which were preening in front of their own hand-crafted mirror, watched on in bewilderment.

'I've never seen them do that before,' said one Afghan. The other said, 'Boring.'

Jo and Ronnie glanced at one another. 'I wasn't expecting that,' said Bumstead. 'Fancy a chase while yelling, "Stop, police"!'

She led the way. Not knowing the layout of the house proved tricky. From the massive open-plan living-room, they entered a corridor. Straight ahead was an airport-hangar sized kitchen. The so-called kitchen island was large enough to stage an off-Broadway musical. The exterior wall was another of those all-glass affairs giving uninterrupted views of the landscaped garden and pool. The decking featured its own waterfall cascading over hand-picked pebbles from an uninhabited Grecian island. Perry called them his Elgin baubles.

The police were stunned by the size and opulence of the house but managed to refocus when the banshee without a name appeared holding two expensive, sharp knives.

'Ronnie!' yelled Jo. He turned and ducked as one and then the other knife zoomed in his direction. The only damage they did was to the wall. The woman despaired.

She whined. 'My Roman tiles! What have I done?'

Ronnie overpowered her and, using a Harrods apron, tied her to a pantry shelf. 'Go,' he ordered Jo, who went back into the corridor and then up the stairs. She heard sounds and followed them.

Behind the door of the master bedroom was a bus timetable advising residents when they could next be transported to the four-poster bed. Jo saw a balcony at the far end and set off. The carpet complained.

She stood on the balcony surveying the property and majestic countryside beyond. *Where's Perry?* She couldn't see a human or a Perry anywhere. She heard him.

'Go away,' he spat.

She glanced up and saw him on the roof. 'Mr Batchelor, come down.'

How the hell did he get up there?

'I'll jump,' he threatened, and Jo's stomach automatically tightened. She went back into the bedroom, saw a window partly open and moved to it. Poking her head out and up, she saw the crazy novelist perched on the apex of the roof. His face screamed terror.

She called. 'Mr Batchelor, come down. We can discuss this in your kitchen.' She wished she'd said living-room. In the kitchen, the member of the knife-throwing act yanked at her Harrods apron.

He stared down at Jo and his anger melted. Fear enveloped him and he squeaked. 'Help me,' he pleaded. 'I can't move.'

Ronnie wandered upstairs. 'Jo?' he called.

'In here.'

Ronnie arrived. 'Where is he?'

She pointed. 'Up there.'

Ronnie poked his head out and saw the frozen-with-fear escapee. 'Bloody hell, will he jump?'

'He's too scared to jump. Ring the fire brigade but tell them no siren. If they spook him he probably *will* jump.'

Ronnie grabbed his phone and moved away so his call would not be heard by his nibs. When Ronnie turned back, he nearly died. 'Jo?'

He rushed to the window, and saw his colleague climbing the roof. Ronnie whispered, furious. 'Jo! For Chrissake, come back. Jo!'

She turned her head. 'I'll keep him company till the fireries arrive. You go and let them in.'

Ronnie became as angry as the residents. 'Be careful,' he snapped then headed downstairs.

Where's the remote for the front gates?

Jo flattened herself against the sloping roof. It had a lip of sorts as a salute to Japanese architecture. Perry couldn't have a straight roof.

How the hell did he get up where he is?

She worked on keeping calm and spreading her mood skywards. Edging higher, she spoke quietly. 'Help is coming, Perry. All you need do is sit still and we'll have you down and safe.'

He mumbled. 'I don't want to die.'

'No-one's going to die; remain still and it'll soon be over.'

'How will I get down?'

'The fire brigade is on its way.'

That didn't help. Jo reckoned he'd lost the plot. The fear he harboured for decades was now a reality. He'd been sprung. His mind became unhinged. All his fame and riches were about to disappear.

'I'm going to fall,' he said to God or the birds or anyone within cooee. Jo decided. She needed to make him stay still until help arrived. Slowly she crawled up the roof, reached the apex and sat like Perry with a leg either side. She was about two metres behind him and spoke quietly.

'I'm here, Perry. I'll stay with you until the rescue people arrive.'

Rather than calm him, he became even more agitated. He started a sort of bucking motion. 'No,' he moaned. 'I don't want to die.'

Jo pictured the headlines. *Famous Novelist Leaps from Roof*. She decided the best move would be to hold him. He wasn't a big man and her athletic prowess gave her confidence. She squirmed her way along the roof using the same horse-riding moves exhibited by her prisoner.

It was uncomfortable but aches and pains lost their importance as she closed in on the frightened novelist.

This would make a good climax to his next novel.

Within touching distance, she didn't know if he knew she was right behind him. *If I spook him, he may panic.* She extended a hand ready to grab him then spoke.

'I'm here, Perry.' He jolted as if copping an electric shock. Jo grabbed his shirt collar in her right hand. 'Relax,' she said and he didn't. Now *she* was scared. He seemed out of control. No, forget seemed, he *was* out of control.

She raised her voice and placed her left hand on his left shoulder giving her no control over her own safety. If he fell, she would too. 'Perry, stop! Stop!'

He tried to shake her hands free. Panic took control. It was fall-off-the-roof time. Then they heard another voice. Ronnie was outside, running and calling.

'Jo, they're here. The fireries are here! Jo!'

Hearing another voice distracted both mountaineers but when a firetruck arrived, the balloon went up.

'Not the lawn!' screamed Perry. Even with a *Please Keep Off the Grass* sign, the driver knew getting to the problem area as quickly as possible was the only way to go. Perry's immaculate turf copped a thrashing.

He half-turned back to Jo and tried slapping. Not effectively mind as the only thing Perry knew about the Marquis of Queensberry was how to spell somdomite.

Jo knew she was in trouble. She could overpower him at Ground Zero but two storeys up and balanced precariously on a steep roof, one slip and it would be a painful exit before death or a wheelchair. Falling forward they'd hit the balcony rail before the concrete tiles below.

The more agitated his body language, the more erratic his slapping. He confessed. 'She deserved to die. The bitch was a tease. I enjoyed killing her.'

This was a first for Jo; a prisoner confessing to murder sitting atop a roof with an extension ladder heading in their direction. Things hotted up as the whir of a helicopter, sporting a TV station logo on its side, hove into view. Now the world was watching.

'She was a bitch and so are you,' screamed Perry as he went for one final slap—or was it a scratch? Though facing the wrong way, he wound up in true haymaker fashion and swung from around his body.

Jo ducked and overbalanced. Perry lost his centre of gravity and fell sideways, dragging Jo with him. They rolled back the way they came.

As they fell, he did the screaming, they passed a fireman on his way up. Later, back at the fire station, he filled in a report of the event. He ticked the box against *Rescue Unsuccessful*, and in the space for comments he wrote, *Fireman 0, Gravity 2.*

Jo's prior thinking about coffins and callipers proved misleading as the couple bounced up from the lip of the roof, missed the patio and landed in the deep end of the pool. Ronnie gave Jo a hand getting out, and managed to stand on Perry's fingers as he scrambled to exit.

'Oh, sorry, sir,' said Ronnie pretending to help the homeowner.

The biggest problem was what to wear for the trip home. Jo neglected to have an alternative strip in her kit bag, and finished up borrowing a track suit from the knife thrower in the kitchen.

It wasn't a good day for the novelist and his friend. He was charged with murder, and she copped resisting arrest, attempted murder of a police officer, and failure to provide a name.

Until Perry cracked and named his silent true love, she was charged under the name Jane Doe. Close as her name was Jane Dean.

Ronnie Bumstead's wife was right. "Jo Best is the best homicide detective in town. If anyone can crack this case she can".

It wasn't difficult to tell members of the Homicide Squad about Jo Best and the Sorrento/Point Lonsdale murder being solved after 32 years. The whole thing was on the Six o'clock News together with that dive—a somersault in pike position ending with a belly-whacker so powerful the overflow watered the surrounding lawn, now sadly chopped to bits thanks to the fire truck.

Jo dropped in on Natasha's parents. The media told them the news. Jo explained the details in as sympathetic a way as possible. 'The person arrested has confessed so there may be a very short trial.'

The parents still flinched as if this was a police officer calling to say their child had been killed. But their gratitude shone through. Their doubts about the coronial verdict always remained.

They were lucky. Plenty of parents of a murdered child die before the killer is even arrested let alone found guilty. As Jo left, despite Covid, both parents embraced her, their gratitude overwhelming.

Chapter 34

Michael worried. He knew how to carry out his plan to save Gabrielle. But he knew what he was doing was illegal, immoral and, if discovered, capable of wrecking his life and Gabrielle's reputation.

No pressure then.

He needed to become involved with child pornography and loan sharks. He had no experience in either but working with Jo Best meant a few shady, even evil characters once crossed his path.

His technical expertise was unrivalled. Investigating people by sneaking in via their digital back door was, for him, straightforward.

He worked on the different "clients" one at a time. He discovered details and created situations, and as he plunged deeper into crime, his eyes blinked. Sweat from nerves does that for those with a conscience.

Then his phone rang and he groaned. He'd seen news of Jo Best's spectacular Wright Brothers venture, and hoped she was calling so he could congratulate her. He'd pulled back of late wondering if they would ever work together again. Having a new admirer kept him preoccupied as well.

Speaking of new admirers, there she was on the line.

'Hello, Cathy,' he said in as flat a monotone as he could muster hoping to not sound rude.

'It's on, Michael. Everything's ready for the final act tomorrow.'

He was uncertain and added new worries to his current collection. 'What's on?' he asked.

She sounded peeved. 'Come on, Michael, get with the programme. Tomorrow we're off to Bendigo.'

'Tomorrow? Bendigo?' Before he could explain his dental appointment, job in Bairnsdale, and follow-up appointment with the DHHS to discuss his idea for a new Covid tracing app, none of which was real or true, she hammered home the details.

'I've told the nursing home where my grandparents reside we'll be there at 10.30 which is their morning tea time. We'll need to leave at 8. I'll pick you up and please don't forget your overnight bag.'

Alarm bells rang and kept ringing.

'Alarm bells?' he said meaning to say, "Overnight bag?". With loan sharks and pornographers in his head, an overnighter with Ms Enthusiastic sent his mind into free fall; a bit like Jo and Perry paragliding in the Dandenongs.

Then Michael twigged. 'Cathy we can't go to Bendigo tomorrow or any time soon. We can't leave Melbourne. The Covid lockdown won't let us go anywhere near Bendigo.'

She brushed his comment aside. 'There are exceptions for special circumstances. I've never met my elderly grandparents or my mother. If they die before this lockdown is over, it's cruel and unfair.'

'Did you write those words on your application?'

'No, I told them we're essential workers and have to make the trip.'

'Essential workers?' Michael panicked.

'I'm a nurse, Michael. You're my support staff.' He failed comprehension. 'Oh come on, Michael. Have you never told a little white lie or broken the law?' He glanced at his monitor and the illegal snooping he'd been working on for the past hour.

Not in the last thirty seconds.

'I've booked us into a nice motel,' said Cathy. Michael tried not to panic and saw Alan was awake and eavesdropping.

"I need you here," said Alan in a feline telepathy transfer. "Do not leave me".

Michael lost control of his "Show some guts" sector. He failed to put his foot down when the issue first arose, and now the floodgates of "I'm a doormat" were wide open.

'Sleep well, my knight in shining armour,' she said. 'And speaking of which, make sure you bring your sexiest pyjamas.'

He couldn't sleep. He liked Cathy and loved being involved in the adventure to find her family. But their relationship pricked his conscience. *Am I using her? Is she using me?* They were consenting adults but for him, right now, getting involved with a full-on relationship didn't have overwhelming appeal. He wasn't sure why but reckoned his carrying a torch for Jo Best was the root cause of his problem.

At 0755 hours, he patted Alan and promised to be back as soon as possible. 'There are food bowls, water bowls and litter trays to last a week,' he said but Alan had the hump and refused to even look at him.

Cathy arrived and they set off on the two-hour drive to Bendigo. She bubbled. This was D-Day. Her grandparents would tell her why her mother allowed Cathy to be adopted, if her mother's alive and, if so, where she's living. Cathy was about to find herself.

As with any long journey, the conversation lagged. The only break was for a police check but having slowed, their car was waved on. Both travellers wore masks which may have helped.

'You *have* got the document allowing us through?' asked Michael.

'I have everything.'

They used the Sat Nav to find the nursing home and pulled into the carpark. Michael found himself squirming. Cathy set out a stall with her affections. His overnight bag was in the boot. It wasn't the search for her mother which troubled him, although it did, it was his relationship with a friend. The line between pal and lover was thin and he was about to cross over. Was he being dragged across? Would this change in their relationship cause him to hurt his friend?

She didn't seem excited to finally be in Bendigo. Her grandparents were inside this nursing home. Surely she should be fidgeting and muttering.

'Michael, I have something to tell you.' He swallowed. She opened her wallet and removed a ring. He swallowed again. She slipped the ring on the third finger of her left hand. He ran out of swallows.

'Congratulations,' he said. 'Or is it felicitations?'

'You know I described you as my fiancé. Well this is the outward confirmation of same. And you know why. It's because a single Australian Born Chinese female would not please her grandparents if she travelled the world with a man who was just a friend.'

He nodded and enjoyed a smidgeon of relief.

'And I know too, Michael Chan, I've been behaving in a, shall we say, over-the-top manner.'

Now he was confused. 'Really? I wouldn't say that.' *Yes I would.*

She knew he was joking but didn't smile. This was serious. 'I know you don't share my romantic feelings, Michael, and I think that might be because a girl you liked once broke your heart.' She punched hard. 'So, sir, I have two more statements to make. One, our "engagement" is a pretence to help me please my grandparents, and hopefully persuade them to tell me all they know about my mother.' He went to speak but couldn't as she placed a finger on his lips. 'And two, I will be grateful and honoured if you will allow me to continue to be your friend.'

Wow. He didn't expect that. 'Oh, I see.'

'So, are we cool?'

He whipped out his half smile. 'We are, we're cool.'

She flashed her ring. 'And I picked this up in the $2 shop. It was on special.' He produced a three-quarter smile.

She leant in and planted a soft but snappy kiss on his lips, opened her door and stepped out. 'Come on, Handsome, my family awaits.'

The sign on the door made them remain outside. A nurse arrived and took their temperature. They entered and were quizzed. They passed.

'Use the hand sanitiser and don't remove your masks. No hugging or kissing. We do not want the virus here.'

The visitors were so overwhelmed with the pressure from the locals, they lost focus on the importance of the visit. Finally they were led into a large day room. Now their focus returned.

The residents were seated and being waited on. The nurse led them to a corner. A resident spotted Michael and called.

'Oh Doctor, Doctor, over here.'

Everyone stopped. The woman beckoned to Michael who froze. The nurse moved to the woman doing the calling. 'This is not the doctor, Mollie. He will be here later. Okay?'

Mollie showed her disappointment and the visitors moved to the couple seated in the corner. The grandparents were told by staff their granddaughter and her fiancé would be visiting today.

There they sat, an elderly, small, wiry couple. Benjimen's parents came from China last century with their infant son. Jin was born in Melbourne to immigrant parents. The nurse introduced the visitors.

'This is Cathy and her fiancé Michael.'

'Hello,' said Cathy, her heart doubling as a jungle drum.

'Hello,' said Michael watching the elderly couple, who were not wearing masks, produce a half smile. *My God, I'm related to them.*

'You can sit here,' said the nurse pointing to chairs, 'and please remember the rules.'

The nurse left and Cathy broke the rules without hesitation by dropping her mask so her grandparents could see her face.

'We are pleased to meet you,' she said. 'We met my aunt, Li Ming.'

The grandparents nodded but said nothing. Michael didn't like their muted response. Cathy continued.

'And we met Li Ming's daughter Rachel and her baby boy, James, your little great-grandson.' More nodding from the oldies. 'Rachel is my cousin.'

Michael and Cathy thought as one. *Will they ever speak?*

Cathy indicated Michael. 'We are from Melbourne.'

Both residents produced a tiny smile. Then the heavens opened and Benjimen spoke. 'We are from Melbourne.'

Cathy's eyes filled with tears. Michael wanted to tell her to slow down. *Don't ask about your mother until you win their trust.*

'I am from Kew and Michael lives in Northcote.'

More nodding and Michael wanted to keep the momentum going.

'I have a cat called Alan,' he said and the grandparents stared at him as if he spoke Welsh or Urdu.

Cathy switched back to familiar ground. 'I hope to meet my uncle, your son An.'

That wasn't Welsh. 'Our son,' said Jin speaking for the first time.

They were running out of relatives. The couple's three children with two mentioned in passing, left the third as definitely the elephant in the room.

Michael found it hard to pick the feelings of Cathy's family members. *Were they shy or frightened?* Their expressions were fixed.

Fear gripped Cathy. Her heart pounded and her head caught fire. She knew what she wanted to say but found it impossible to speak. Michael helped.

'We would like to find Cathy's mother. Can you help us please?' If it's possible, their expressionless faces became more expressionless.

Cathy couldn't wait. 'We want to find your daughter, Jia li Sòng.'

She didn't know why she spoke her mother's full name. It might have been to be sure the parents remembered *all* their children. The room buzzed with Mollie complaining about the missing quack, tea cups clinking and the odd resident speaking in a loud voice, 'Pardon?'

The hubbub or background noise was irrelevant. In the corner, Cathy and Michael hung on a response—any response.

Michael repeated the name. 'Your daughter Jia li.'

Benjimen gave a slight shake of his head. 'She not here.'

Both visitors wanted to ask follow-up questions. Both knew to do so might be useless and counter-productive. Cathy stared at Michael and his eyes spoke volumes. Cathy stood and Michael followed.

'It was lovely to meet you Grandfather, Grandmother. I wish you good health and happiness.' She gave a traditional Chinese bow and said, 'zài jiàn'. This brought a whisper of a smile to the elderly faces.

They murmured their reply. Michael echoed Cathy and he too received a muted but friendly response. Cathy lifted her mask, turned and walked out of the room, tears brimming in her eyes. Michael followed with Mollie spotting him and this time yelling.

'Doctor, Doctor, I'm over here.'

Michael escaped and comforted Cathy. The first nurse approached. 'How did you go?'

Cathy couldn't speak, her tears increasing.

Michael explained. 'Her grandparents wouldn't speak about their daughter who is Cathy's mother.'

'I'm not surprised. They keep to themselves and have few visitors.'

'If you get a chance to ask them anything about Cathy's mother, we would really appreciate it.' He handed the nurse his card.

'I will.' She opened the door for the visitors. 'Have a safe journey.'

In the car, Cathy couldn't help but bawl her eyes out. They both removed their masks and Michael struggled. He gave her a handkerchief—his were always spotless—and she made a mess of it with her tears and snot.

It took a few minutes to settle and finally Michael spoke.

'I'm sure they would have said if your Mum was no longer with us.' Cathy nodded. 'And I'm sure they know about Rachel, Li Ming, and An and little James.' More nodding. 'So, how about we do what we can't do in Melbourne and visit an upmarket restaurant?'

'Thanks, Michael, you're a saint but I don't think Covid allows Melburnians to dine in and anyway, I really want to go home.'

This time he did the nodding. 'Sure, whatever you say.'

They sorted themselves and Michael was dreading the next two hours. Seatbelts in place, Cathy started the engine and released the handbrake when a person tapped on her window. They both jumped.

Engine off, window down and they stared at a young Chinese woman dressed as a cook or kitchen hand. When she spoke, the mood of the travellers went from disbelief to more disbelief.

'Excuse me, are you looking for Benjimen and Jin's daughter?'

What a question. What an answer. The woman explained.

'They never have visitors. I saw you from the kitchen and guessed you might be family. Their daughter came here about six months ago. I was on my break and she asked if Mr and Mrs Sòng lived here.'

Cathy and Michael found it hard to breathe.

'To be sure she was looking for the right people, she showed me a photo in the Bendigo newspaper. It was Benjimen and Jin celebrating their 60th wedding anniversary here in this home. I told her those people were living here. She thanked me and went to the front office.'

Cathy wanted to interrupt but stopped as Michael touched her arm.

'A little while later I was working in the kitchen and the lady went past in a hurry. I ran after her. She was crying, like you.'

Cathy didn't care about tears. 'Please tell me what happened.'

'The lady said her parents did not want her to visit them. I said I was sorry and asked if I could contact her if her parents changed their mind. She hesitated so I asked what she did. She pointed at my uniform and said, "I am a cook like you". I asked where she lived and I didn't understand her reply. "In the French town." And then she ran away.' The young woman told all she knew. 'I hope it is a help.'

'You've been much more than a help,' said Cathy. 'You've saved my sanity.'

'You've been wonderful,' added Michael. 'I'm sorry, I don't know your name.'

'Cathy,' said the young woman. Cathy Feng froze. 'When I told the lady my name, she gasped and put her hand to her mouth.'

That was the clincher for Cathy the seeker. She cried again.

'She'll be fine, Cathy,' said Michael, 'and thanks for all your help.'

'I hope you find her,' said Cathy the cook who smiled, waved and went back to her kitchen.

The couple in the car sat stunned. Their rollercoaster kept flying; from hope to despair to hope and now possible ecstasy.

'We've found her,' said Cathy. 'She's alive, Michael, my mother's alive. We can't give up now. Tell me where she is, Michael, please.'

'It has to be nearby because she saw the photo of her parents in the Bendigo newspaper.' He pulled out his phone and searched *Victorian towns, French*. 'It might be a town in France where Australians served in the Great War and their sacrifices are honoured Down Under.'

No joy as up came towns in France with a connection to Australia. Cathy kept replaying the words of her namesake.

'My Mum is a cook.'

Michael switched the search words and hit one result, French Island, light years away and not a likely place for a Bendigo newspaper. He tried again and typed in *Towns in regional Victoria named after a Frenchman*.

Again only one result. 'St Arnaud,' he said and I think it's near here.' He searched again. 'It's 105 kilometres from Bendigo.'

Cathy started the engine. 'Which way do I go?'

Chapter 35

The frustration at Homicide was palpable. Jokes and piss-taking faded. Phones were abused. The only bit of good news is they didn't have another murder on their hands—yet. Detectives met for a briefing.

'I know we're frustrated,' said DI Rose. 'Having any number of leads with nobody charged is a pain. The difficulty is the visitor from Eastern Europe. To me, he's top of the list or very close thereto.' She paused. 'Did I just say thereto?'

A few detectives muttered.

'You'll never know, ma'am,' said DS Melody, 'until we have new forensics, until we interview him, and even then we may have nowhere near enough for an extradition, meaning we're sunk.'

'He's the perfect person of interest,' said DS Fletcher. 'He has links to crime back home, he knew the victim, he came Down Under for a short stay under false pretences, and left the country the day after the murder. There are more red flags there than at Anfield.'

DI Rose didn't follow any sport. 'Where's Anfield?'

Charley Baldwin was an Everton supporter. 'Home ground of Liverpool FC, ma'am. They wear red.'

Rose didn't care about any football. 'I'm being asked questions from those in the big offices. I don't fancy our chances if we ask for a trip to Serbia for two of our finest.'

DI Blunt shifted in his seat. 'Why two?'

Rose didn't understand. 'Sorry, Callum, I missed that.'

'I asked why *two* officers need to go to Serbia. Surely someone with my rank and experience is sufficient. With support from the local police, the suspect could be questioned under caution, and be cleared or charged accordingly.'

DI Blunt possessed a particular skill to offend his colleagues. The atmosphere in the Incident Room, if measured in terms of tension, would show a reading of Extreme.

'Thank you, Callum, I'll bear it in mind. Now, apart from our overseas friend, do we have anything concrete on any of the others?'

They didn't.

'DNA would help,' said Rick Melody. 'Is it possible to have Gabrielle Strange conduct a second PM?'

Rose and Billy Hughes chose not to share the news about the Supreme Court matter in which Dr Strange was savagely criticised.

'I believe Dr Strange has retired or will soon do so. Look, it is what it is. We need to work harder to find the missing key.'

'And if the key is in Belgrade, what then?' asked DI Blunt.

DI Rose hesitated. Charley Baldwin filled the void.

'I reckon the key is to recruit Detective Senior Constable Joanna Best.' Others glared at him. 'I mean has there ever been an arrest of a murder suspect by jumping off a roof into a swimming pool?'

Blunt hissed, 'Bitch!'

Billy Hughes interrupted. 'Speaking of Jo Best, a reminder about Detective Inspector Richelieu's memorial service this Friday, 10am at the Glen Waverley chapel. Proper shoes please which have been cleaned.'

Baldwin wasn't finished. 'Has anyone seen Jo Best's clean-up rate? I mean that cold case was over 30 years old.'

'We take your point, Charley,' said Billy Hughes.

He wasn't finished. 'I mean if we were paid by results, she'd be a millionaire.'

'She *is* a millionaire,' said Stephen Payne, the silent partner.

Detectives buzzed. Rumours of Jo scoring big in Richelieu's Will did the rounds once the DI died. Talk about hot gossip.

And right now the Senior Constable was at home, hiding from the media, again, and trying to finish her speech for the memorial service. Talk about re-writes. She polished her words, found better ones, and re-wrote, and re-wrote again.

Once she reckoned it was as good as could be, she switched to building a case against Annie Cleary. She wouldn't be charged with the crime. The idea was to present such damning evidence to Annie's legal team, that they would persuade her to withdraw her appeal and if so, Gabrielle would be spared.

But Jo had a new concern. If her case was rock solid, what would stop her colleagues at Homicide proceeding against Annie? If that happened, Annie might allow her application for leave to proceed out of spite. She would have nothing to lose; might as well be hung for a sheep as a lamb.

And anyway, why would a lawyer persuade a client to drop their appeal? A lawyer gets paid only for work done. Why cancel the job? Why hop off the gravy train? What lawyer turns down a brief? Whatever Jo did, Gabrielle could still be exposed.

In the next suburb, the pathologist in question flopped on her favourite chair watching her TV without thinking about the pictures or sound. It could have been an announcement of World War Three, or the fact a well-known AFL footballer has switched to coloured bootlaces, and she couldn't have cared less. The text of the Annie Cleary legal document refused to leave her consciousness.

The phrases "drunk while on duty" and "not qualified to assess plant samples" were seared into her brain. She thought about Jo Best entering her house, finding her drunk and disorderly, and rescuing her from a likely case of alcoholic poisoning.

She remembered the young woman's promise to find a way to squash the document, and how Jo invited her to be involved in the latest cold case. If no-one else cared, Jo Best cared.

Gabrielle knew where her favourite tipple was stored. It would take little effort to go to the cupboard or underwear drawer—always have two hiding places—and enjoy a small snifter; just the one.

The misery of the accusations pounded her from all sides. In the distance, not drowning but waving, the tiny figure of Jo Best tried to be seen and heard.

It was a Shakespearean tragedy; to drink or not to drink.

Chapter 36

The drive from Bendigo to St Arnaud takes about an hour. Michael filled the time searching for a history of the town. He'd watched Cathy go through the emotional wringer. Her grandparents gave nothing. A friendly cook at the retirement home gave everything. Yes, the educated guess about the town of St Arnaud may prove a red herring but Cathy wanted to try. She sensed they were so near and yet so far.

'The town is named after a French military figure who never came to Australia.' He scrolled. 'In fact he doesn't seem to have any attachment to Oz at all.'

'He might have just loved sweeping plains,' added Cathy as they drove through sweeping plains.

'Commander St Arnaud played a role in the Crimean War.'

'I've never heard of him or it.'

'Russia invaded Turkey and the Brits and France took offence. And despite Australia only having two men and a dog over there, we have plenty of place names from that war; Sebastopol, Alam, Inkerman, Balaklava and good old St Arnaud.'

Cathy spoke in a low voice. 'But will it be any good for me?'

Michael glanced at her and tried to keep the conversation light. If this trip proved fruitless, he feared for Cathy's soul. If they found her mother, what would be her response?

'Now as far as eateries are concerned, there are several pubs and restaurants and, wait for it, at least two with Chinese menus.'

'We know she's a cook but she might work in a pub with Aussie grub.'

'True and there's only one way to find out.' He glanced at her. 'We're getting close, Cathy; you are allowed to dream.'

Cathy's nerves were planning a strike. 'So what's our plan?'

Michael knew they were flying blind. 'How about we go and ask?'

'What, use my mother's name and see if anyone knows her?'

Michael sensed the tension in his friend's body language.

'We hasten slowly. We have to think of your Mum. We have to assume she knows little if anything about you. Did she name you Cathy?'

'The cook at the retirement village said she was shocked when she told my Mum her name. Why was my Mum shocked?'

'Probably because she named you Cathy or knew the woman who adopted you chose that name. That sounds logical,' he said and tried to maintain a steady tempo in their conversation. 'Put yourself in your Mum's shoes. She doesn't know her daughter is looking for her.'

'Her parents may have told her.'

'I doubt it. Her visit to Bendigo was well before you discovered you were adopted.' Cathy nodded. 'I think we make discreet enquiries. If we find a lead on her whereabouts, I go alone to try and make contact. I explain everything and discover her reaction.'

Cathy lost it and pulled over. Michael worried. Her plaintive cry was harrowing. 'What if she's like her parents? What if she doesn't want anything to do with me? What if she rejects me a second time?'

Michael seemed to have an endless supply of handkerchiefs.

'I know I'm repeating myself, Cathy, but please, hasten slowly. She may not even be in St Arnaud. The French connection may be through French food or wine. I mean what's the connection between France and Chinese prawn crackers?'

She settled and gave Michael's handkerchief a solid workout.

'Would you like me to drive?' he asked.

'No ... thank you.' She sniffed. 'You're right, I need to toughen up.'

He relaxed a little as she slipped a rod of steel down her spine. She took a deep breath, checked for traffic, and pulled onto the road. 'Into the valley of death rode the six hundred.' He laughed. 'What?'

'You know where that comes from?'

'Where what comes from?'

'Your quote is part of a Tennyson poem about the war in Crimea where Monsieur St Arnaud saw action.'

'I had no idea,' she said. 'I remember an old neighbour used to say it when he went to watch Collingwood.'

'It could be an omen.' Then he remembered what happened to the 600 and decided to change the subject.

They reached the outskirts of St Arnaud with its population of about 2500. Before hitting the main drag with its shops, historic buildings and churches, Michael suggested they find a service station and ask a question or two.

'We'll need petrol for the trip home. I'll top it up now,' she said.

They pulled into the first service station they found and while Cathy worked the pump, Michael went indoors hoping the owners were long time St Arnaud residents.

'Hello,' said a woman by the cash register.

'Hello,' said Michael. 'My friend is getting petrol but I'm hoping you can help with some local knowledge.'

'I'll try.'

'Chinese meals in St Arnaud,' he said. 'Do you know if there are any outlets in town?'

'There's at least two; a café in the main street, a few blocks up, and the sports club have a Chinese menu too.'

'What about the pubs?'

The woman shook her head. 'I don't think so.' She called. 'Doug.'

'What?' came from the service bay.

She called again. 'Do any of the pubs in town serve Chinese meals?'

'If I wanted dim sims, I'd get one of them BYO Asian brides.'

The woman shrugged at Michael. 'He's all class, my old man.'

'We're on a family tree hunt trying to find lost relatives.'

'Well there's the Historical Society next door to the old fire station. They have cemetery records and if your family lived here, you'll probably find their details.'

'Thanks for your help,' said Michael as Cathy came in and paid.

'This lady has been very helpful,' said Michael.

'Oh great,' said Cathy.

'What's the family name you're looking for?'

Cathy glanced at Michael. He took over. 'Sòng, Jai li Sòng.'

The woman shook her head as her husband arrived wiping his oily hands on an oily rag. 'Doug, do you know any Songs?'

'Certainly, what key would you like?'

The travellers left smiling but with hearts cold and afraid. In the car, Cathy wanted help. 'What next?'

'Straight ahead, there's a Chinese café a few blocks away.'

Cathy struggled to start her car. Michael worried she'd flood it. He spoke quietly; he'd been speaking like that since he was a kid.

'Why don't I drive and you can relax.'

She snapped. 'No!' Then she stopped and tried taking deep breaths. Without speaking, she undid her seatbelt, hopped out and walked around to Michael's side. He understood and was out in a flash holding the door for her.

He drove, spotted the Chinese café and found a park.

'Okay, here's the plan. I go and ask if your Mum works in there. If she does, I explain to her how I've come from Bendigo where I met her parents, and am a friend of her daughter. She would like to meet you but only if you wish to meet her. And that's about it. If she agrees to a meeting, I suggest we make it later today or whenever she likes. It's all up in the air and I'll make arrangements on the fly.' He watched her. 'Are you happy with that?'

She nodded. Speaking was tough. She whispered. 'Thanks.'

He squeezed her hand, left and walked to the café.

Three minutes later he was back and Cathy's face became a movie with a new scene every few seconds.

He sat in the car, closed his door and half-smiled. 'She's not there but she *is* in St Arnaud.' Cathy gasped. 'She works at the sports club which is not far.' He waited till her eyes met his. 'We haven't talked about how your Mum might react. She's going to get one hell of a shock.'

Cathy nodded. 'I know.'

He saw her fists clench and unclench. She trembled. He desperately wanted a happy ending.

The sports club boasted a large carpark. The modern building sat on acreage at the edge of town. Prawns and pokies pulled patrons. Michael parked by trees 100 metres from the front door, and with the passenger side not facing the building. He produced his phone.

'I may call you. Otherwise I'll see you soon.

She nodded. She was afraid to speak thinking it might trigger a break-down. Again he squeezed her hand and headed for the building.

It was spacious and modern with enough carpet to open an emporium. Michael approached Reception and because of Covid, chose to slip in a white lie.

'Good afternoon,' smiled the woman on the desk.

'Hello. My name's Michael Chan, I've come from Bendigo helping a friend make contact with her family.'

This was a first for the receptionist and the club. His audience was hooked.

'We've been to see my friend's grandparents and believe their daughter works here. Her name is Jia li Sòng. Do you know her?'

The explanation worked a treat and Michael's heart jumped when the woman spoke.

'Yes, Jia li is our chef. But it's the middle of lunchtime and we're fully booked. Could you come back later?'

'Of course,' said Michael. 'What time would be suitable?'

'Say 3. Lunch will be over and tonight's prep will not have started.'

'Thank you. I'll be back at 3.'

'Who shall I say is calling?'

'My name is Michael Chan and I'm a friend of Jia li Sòng's daughter, Cathy.'

His news was a shock. No-one at the club knew Jai li was a mother. 'Oh, okay, I'll tell her. We'll see you at 3.'

His famous half smile flickered and he left. His excitement wanted to break free. This whole adventure, helping Cathy, gave him a buzz. He loved solving cases with Jo Best but this was different. Happy endings paid a deeper, longer-lasting dividend. Satisfaction trumped money. He looked towards the car wondering if Cathy could see him. He wanted to wave to tell her the great news. He gave a little skip.

The car was about 50 metres away when he heard a sound.

'Hello, sir, hello!' he stopped and turned.

A woman wearing an apron ran towards him, waving and calling.

My God! It's Cathy's Mum. He froze. Do I go to her? Can Cathy see me/her? What do I do?

He opted to move towards her. She was not Olympic material and adrenalin powered her progress. Michael tried to think of what he would say. She came closer. Her hands were outstretched and Michael sensed she would embrace him, thinking he too was a family member. *Am I An, her younger brother?*

As he was about to speak he heard a car door slam. He turned and saw Cathy rounding the vehicle, heading towards him. She'd seen Michael returning, then a woman come running after him.

The way the woman behaved, her appearance, and Cathy's heart rate sealed the deal. This was her mother.

Michael stood still and the two women found him invisible as they stopped as if following social distancing rules, stared at one another and then fell into one another's arms. They swapped a lot of tears.

The restaurant manager was peeved at first when his chef simply ran out of the kitchen without so much as a by-your-leave. But when he heard the story and saw the two emotional women, he came round. In fact he insisted Michael and Cathy have lunch on the house, albeit in the corner in case they carried the Melbourne virus.

Jia li kept popping out to see if everything was okay. It was.

Michael discovered Jia Li lived in a small farmhouse on a large property just out of town. He knew Cathy wanted to stay at least overnight with her mother, maybe longer. He was piggy in the middle and told Cathy he would be away.

She protested but relented and poured out her heart in gratitude. He slipped out to Reception, checked the train times from Bendigo to Melbourne, and asked about a taxi to Bendigo. The fee of $200 tickled his funny bone.

'There is a bus for $15 which leaves at around 3.30 although I think Covid may have changed the timetable.'

Michael considered walking.

It's only 250 kays. I'll be home for Christmas.

A group of patrons was leaving when a chap butted in.

'Excuse me, I couldn't help overhearing. We're from Bendigo, well Strathfieldsaye, and you're welcome to hitch a ride with us.'

Michael purred. 'Thank you so much. Are you sure it's no trouble?'

The chap's wife interrupted. 'But only if you give us chapter and verse on those two ladies who took over the dining room.'

Out came the Chan smile and Michael entertained his fellow travellers with aplomb. He caught the Melbourne train and then a spark and walked from Northcote. Alan made a fuss on his return.

'How was your day, Alan? I bet it wasn't half as good as mine.'

Chapter 37

Jo threw down her pen. It would never have found a place in Ronnie Bumstead's collection. She'd finished writing her case to present to Annie Cleary's legal team. They wouldn't like it. Annie would explode.

Her case was built on evidence provided by professional crims recommended by Razor McGurk. Each of these referees hated Annie. They needed no incentive to rat on the rat. Over the years she'd stitched them up, some more than once. Now it was payback time.

Annie was the guilty party in another murder years ago. She did everything except pull the trigger. The murderer not only didn't get paid, he was hung out to dry by the evil Annie.

Jo's legal training and her work as a Homicide cop meant she created the case in correct and damning detail.

Mixed emotions took over. She experienced relief because she could save Gabrielle's reputation, but despair because the reputation of a former Chief Commissioner would be ruined. The fact the retired cop was a good mate of her grandfather's made it so much worse.

She didn't want Pop to hear the bad news through the media or the police grapevine. As hard as it would be, she determined to tell the retired DCI to his face exactly what she planned to do and why.

If Pop knows former Chief Commissioner Hayward wandered from the straight and narrow all those years ago, will he excuse my behaviour and defend his mate? Will I crush my beloved Pop?

There was only one way to find out. It was after 8 when she rang.

'Hello?'

'Good evening DCI Robertson.'

'Hello Love, what's happening?'

'Just checking to see you're okay.'

'Thanks but I'm not.' Jo sat up. *He never complains.* 'I'm a bit sad, a bit nostalgic. This is my last night in the house your Gran and I bought more than 50 years ago.'

Jo understood his sadness. 'Oh Pop, that is sad. How about I drop in for a cuppa?'

He thought for a few seconds finding it hard to speak. Finally he spoke. 'Good-oh, I'd like that.'

He ended the call, his emotions taking control.

Jo drove, her mind debating the plan to save Gabrielle Strange. The collateral damage involving her grandfather's mate screamed the loudest. She kept finding excuses to not tell Pop about Annie Cleary. If he's sad about leaving the home he loved with his loving wife, telling him his good friend is about to be attacked by his favourite copper and granddaughter, would be too much. She drove through misty eyes.

Jack Carr finished his final consultation. The last few months were hell for many people and not least medical professionals. GPs like Jack had patients who needed an operation which were delayed due to Covid. Patients with serious conditions missed appointments due to this damn pandemic. Even regular patients were reluctant to attend the surgery choosing online consultations instead. Were they effective?

He chatted to the receptionist and the cleaner then hit the road. His day was not over, with a visit to aged-care residents still to come. A few of those were former patients now residing in a cemetery.

Jo and Pop sat on what little of the furniture remained. 'I'm not keeping any of this.'

'Why not? This is a lovely sofa.

'I offered it to your mother and sister and they both declined.'

'But why not take it with you?'

'Fanny says it's the wrong colour or fabric or whatever.'

Jo was fast going off Fanny but couldn't deny she was keeping her grandfather busy. Being a lonely widower was not good for the soul.

'So how come you didn't offer it to me?'

'Oh your mother and sister said you've come into money and wouldn't be interested in my old tat.'

Jo shook her head and knew why she spent so little time with some of her kith and kin.

'Now, Pop, I have news.'

'Not bad news. At my age I now have a craving for good news.'

Bugger. Jo's chest pain began. *He's miserable about leaving his old home and now I come along and destroy his good friend.*

'I've made a report on a crime you investigated years ago.'

He was hooked. 'Oh yeah, which one?'

Her phone rang.

Jack arrived at the aged care facility and tapped on the glass door. A carer peered towards the darkened porch, saw him, and hurried to open the door.

'Good evening Dr Carr.'

'Good evening Esha. Are you well?'

'Fine, thank you, sir.'

They walked to reception where Jack signed the attendance book.

'And how is everyone?'

'Very quiet,' she said in her velvety West Indian drawl. 'Mr Bradley is the nurse on duty.'

Jack smiled at the carer and left to do his rounds. He entered a few rooms to check on patients. Two were asleep. Those awake were delighted to see a friendly face albeit behind a mask. Most wanted to chat. Dispensing medicine was a part of Jack's role but sometimes he reckoned his main task involved being a good listener.

He headed along the corridor, tapped then opened the door to Mrs Rankin. She was 92 with a crumbling set of bones but a mind as sharp as a trap.

'No,' she said with gusto. 'I don't want it.'

The room was dimly lit and the light from the corridor flooded in. Jack stood silhouetted in the door. A person stood over the resident with their back to Jack.

'What's happening?' asked Jack moving quickly inside.

The person next to Mrs Rankin turned to face Jack. Nurse Bradley stepped back, surprised at the visit.

'He wants me to take this new medicine, Doctor Carr, and I won't,' said the determined woman.

'What medicine?' asked Jack examining the patient and then the nurse. 'What medicine?' demanded the medico in as threatening yet as quiet a way as possible.

He saw a plastic bag in Bradley's hands and made a grab for it. The nurse pulled it away and as Jack went to make a second grab, Mrs Rankin coughed. She lost control and coughed again.

Jack turned to the woman and bent over her. As he did so, an almighty pain wracked his body. The water jug on the side table smashed against his head. Jack collapsed, Mrs Rankin coughed and Bradley closed the door.

Bradley came back muttering. 'Shouldn't have interfered, Doctor,' he said tidying his materials. 'Now, madam, open wide.'

Mrs Rankin stopped coughing long enough to protest the unwanted treatment. The struggle continued.

Jack came to and suffered. He needed help and reached for his phone. Calling 000 seemed wrong as he would need to be transferred and speak at least twice. He flicked through contacts, saw *Best, Jo* and hit it.

Jo breathed easier as relief arrived. She was about to hurt her beloved Pop by telling him about exposing Chief Commissioner Hayward.

'Excuse me, Pop,' she said seeing the caller ID. 'Good evening, sir.' She heard nothing. 'Jack?' She heard a whisper.

'Cedar Avenue Aged Care Home.' The call ended.

'Hello?' She studied the phone. 'Pop, where is the Cedar Avenue Aged Care Home?'

'Just off Whitehorse Road. Why?'

She rose, kissed him, and fled. 'Emergency, Pop. I'll call you.' He knew all about such calls.

Jo knew nothing other than the voice and brevity of the call meant danger. She flew. Her Sat Nav gave directions and within 90 seconds she knocked on the door.

In Mrs Rankin's room, the resident would not co-operate. Jack lay dazed on the floor, helpless, while Bradley grew frustrated and angry. 'You have to take it,' he demanded as the old woman moved her head and waved her arms. Bradley looked for a cord to tie her hands.

Jo knocked. Esha approached the front door unsure about any visitor. She saw Jo, an unknown person to her, and assumed she was a relative. Esha wagged a finger and pointed to the sign, *No Visitors.*

Jo pressed her ID against the glass. She pulled down her mask so the woman could see her lips and hear her message. 'Emergency,' said Jo. 'Police emergency, open the door.'

Esha worried about doing the wrong thing but believed this was a genuine person. The door opened.

'Dr Jack Carr, where is he?'

'He's treating his patients.'

'I need to find him immediately. Now!'

They set off into the home. Esha knew which patients would be seen by Jack. Room after room was checked with no sign of the doctor.

'No!' called a voice and Jo left Esha, ran ahead and opened a door. Jack was on the floor with Bradley kneeling over him holding a syringe. She didn't consider a polite request or even a "Drop your weapon, this is the police".

Distracted by the door opening, Bradley raised his head as Jo's fist greeted his nose. He screamed and collapsed clutching his face and even cried. Esha attended to Mrs Rankin while Jo checked on the GP.

'Jack, are you okay?'

'My hero,' he groaned, 'or should I say heroine?'

Jo turned to Bradley who tried to reach for the dropped syringe. She stamped on his hand. He screamed. She yanked his hands behind and cuffed him. He complained, a lot. Jo dragged him into the en suite, came out and closed the door. She knelt beside Jack.

He tried to smile which, behind a mask, didn't work.

She spoke. 'We can't go on meeting like this.' He winced. 'Do you need a doctor, Doctor?'

He wanted to grin but his head throbbed. She helped him stand and led him from the room and to a small sitting area. He sat. 'I'll be fine, Jo. You do whatever you have to do with that bastard.'

She returned to Mrs Rankin's room and entered the bathroom. The cowering nurse hated facing punishment.

'What's your name?' she asked.

He ignored her. Esha stood beside Mrs Rankin. 'Bradley Pearson,' she said with venom.

'Bradley Pearson, you're under arrest for assault.' She grabbed his arm to make him stand. It hurt with his hands cuffed behind his back.

'Ow, stop, you're assaulting me. Ow!'

Jo ignored his complaints and dragged him upright. His busted nose turned his white mask a brighter shade of red. Underneath the mask he looked like your average stereotypical gangster.

'Outside,' she said and dragged him to the sitting area where the GP sat rubbing his head. 'Here's a patient for you, Doctor,' said Jo who dumped the nurse in a chair. 'I'll be back. Don't let him leave.'

She went back to Mrs Rankin's room, asked Esha for plastic bags and used them to store items, once the property of the lovely Brad. With Mrs Rankin settled, Jo secured her temporary evidence bags and joined the two gents, one with a sore head and the other a boxer's nose.

The two men remained seated. 'Everything okay?' asked Jo.

'Not for him, said Jack. 'This bastard's just confessed to spreading the coronavirus all over the nursing home. God knows how many he infected.'

'Is this true?' asked Jo. Bradley declined to answer.

Jack continued. 'I asked about the syringe he was about to inject me with and he said it was the same drug he stuck in the bloke your lot found in the Moonee Ponds Creek.'

'What?' She stared at the nurse. 'Is that true?'

'I want a solicitor.'

'Bloody hell,' said Jo and grabbed her phone.

Billy Hughes lounged in front of the telly nursing a toddy. 'Is this the high-diving champ who cracks cold cases?'

'And current ones too.'

Billy sat up, spilt her drink and scared the cat. Jo explained and Billy repeated many words several of which rhymed with pluck.

While the trio waited for back-up, Dr Carr worked on the nose of the man who recently attempted to do him serious harm; an extraordinary example of the Hippocratic Oath in practice.

Jo needled away at Bradley till he explained the Strathmore murder. Like some criminals, the need to confess, or was it to boast, pushed him to tell all.

Apart from spreading the virus at his place of work, he was doing the same at his gym when fitness-freak Lyn Delahunty saw and challenged him. He said he was cleaning surfaces. She didn't believe him and told her boyfriend. Branko took a punt that Bradley was up to no good, tailed him from the gym, found his address and sent a blackmail note. Bradley panicked. Crime was not his forte. Branko figured Bradley was a wimp and no threat. Branko named the handover location close to where he planned to meet his lover. He could pick up the payment before his no-holds-barred bout in the back of his Beamer.

Bradley arrived with a box purportedly containing the cash. As Branko opened the box, Bradley stuck the syringe with epinephrine into the Serbian's heart. It exploded. He staggered off the bridge and down the bank to the concrete waterway. No money, but a free dip in the creek.

Bradley's other trick was to take swabs from Covid sufferers and wipe small grocery items in supermarkets; like needles in strawberries.

An ambulance arrived, as did Marion the other nurse and local uniformed cops with Billy Hughes, DI Rose and Charley Baldwin hard on their heels. Jack Carr contacted the DHHS and a deep clean of the entire home was set in train.

The reaction of relatives of the residents to the news an employee was not so much caring for their loved ones but attempting to murder them, caused what could only be described as a firestorm. Lawyers hearing the news rubbed their hands with glee. The media ran out of adjectives.

It turned out Bradley was a loser with a capital L. His Hitler complex of brutal father and mollycoddling mother set in train his antipathy to the world. Rejected by medical school, his get-even-with-society mantra slipped effortlessly into operation once the coronavirus turned up. He spread wherever he could. *That'll teach 'em.*

To the Homicide detectives, the real star was a certain Senior Constable. Charley Baldwin said what the others were thinking. 'So not content with solving an ancient cold case, you now solve the current homicide without ever being involved. How the hell do you do it?'

'I was lucky, Johnny on the spot,' said Jo.

'What's your next trick; walking on water?'

'Let's save the celebrations for later,' said DI Rose.

Bradley was removed post haste to avoid lynch mobs and journalists. His new Jimmy Durante nose added to his pathetic persona. Jo Best threw a stinging right hook.

Eventually the circus left town and Jo walked Jack to his car. 'Should you be driving, sir? Concussed while in charge of a vehicle won't look good on the charge sheet.'

'Only a headache, officer; I'll be fine.'

He opened his door and paused. 'You saved my life tonight, Jo Best.' He wanted her to stay. He wanted to hug and hold her. He wanted to kiss her and have her respond in kind.

'All in the line of duty, sir.' She seemed anxious. 'I'd better make a move, Jack. It's Pierre's memorial service tomorrow.'

Then he remembered and his relief was wonderful. What a crass time to try being romantic with the woman he knew he loved, the same woman who recently lost her fiancé.

He gave her a peck and drove home thanking his lucky stars he'd met Jo Best, and even more so that he hadn't embarrassed himself there and then.

Chapter 38

It was a lovely day for a memorial service. Michael Chan drove Jo. He was Mr Thoughtful and she suffered knowing he suffered from unrequited love.

He tooted outside the apartment. She emerged wearing her Senior Constable's uniform complete with hat, tights, shiny shoes and matching blue mask. It was the least she could do for Pierre.

'All set?' he asked'

'All set, and thanks again for the lift.'

They set off for the Police Academy in Glen Waverley. Both harboured news and both were keen to share it.

'So have you recovered from your high-tower dive and arrest? I must admit for someone who is not a big fan of the media, it was a bit OTT even for you.'

'I've forgotten it already, Michael.'

He knew she was lying. 'Liar. You'll remember it for eternity.'

'But it's not my latest case.'

His head spun around. He was hooked. The seriousness of the crimes of a certain nurse meant the police and government controlled the press releases. Michael was ignorant. Jo explained the arrest of the Moonee Ponds Creek murderer and Michael laughed out loud. That was new for him; his reactions were usually under lock and key.

'I bet that went down well with your jealous colleagues.'

Jo smiled and said nothing. She got a text from Billy Hughes to say DI Blunt punched a hole in the wall of the male loo. Okay, he didn't crack the Strathmore homicide but to have it solved by a detective who wasn't even on the investigation, and for that detective to be Joanna Bloody Best was too much, cruelty writ large.

When he discovered Starlight Freeman was the old crone he thought was the cleaner, fortunately he was alone. Humiliation lives.

Michael had news and was glad he kept his powder dry. Jo asked.

'And what's happened with your friend searching for her mother?'

He casually let slip mother and daughter were enjoying the Wimmera together after 28 years apart. He told Jo everything.

'So it was an out of wedlock baby given away to bury the shame.'

'Sadly,' said Michael, 'but with a genuine happy ending.'

'A delighted Jo congratulated him but her happiness died when she mentioned her other mission—the save Gabrielle Strange project.

'I went to tell my grandfather about the case and didn't when Jack Carr rang. I can't bring myself to hurt Pop by damaging his pal.'

'Why don't we discuss it tonight over dinner?'

Jo stalled. *A dinner date with Michael Chan? Is there an unknown motive to this invitation?* She played a straight bat.

'Okay; sounds good and I think it's my turn to pay.'

'But it'll have to be takeaway. I need my control panel.'

She nodded not understanding his motives or news.

The memorial service went well; very well although Covid reduced the attendance. The speakers were sincere and full of praise. Jo's tribute went down a treat. Without trying to be maudlin, her words caused a few to wipe their eyes. Many at the service were unaware of Jo's intimate life with Pierre or only became aware of same in recent days. Now they knew Jo and Pierre were two souls genuinely in love with the world at their feet.

The service ended and people gathered for refreshments.

Jo was touched by the sincerity of people who attended. Most wanted to speak with her including a middle-aged woman with a hat.

Oh my God! It's my mother.

She gave Jo a sterile kiss unlike her Italian gentleman friend who did the right thing. He meant what he said and kissed Jo's hand with passion. Then her sister and brother-in-law appeared.

Bloody hell, is this _my_ funeral?

They too did the performance-for-the-crowd greeting never having learnt how to be sincere and natural. Not so Hugh and Peg Carr who stayed clear until Jo spotted them. She was over in a flash exchanging hugs and kisses, tricky with the wearing of masks.

'It's lovely to see you both.'

'Terrific speech, officer,' said Hugh. 'Have you ever thought about running for parliament?' His wife jabbed his ribs. 'I'll vote for you.'

They knew when to leave and did being replaced by her grandfather dressed as would any retired senior police officer, and proud to do so.

'Pop, it's great to see you,' said Jo her eyes darting to and fro searching for the darling Fanny.

My God, if Fanny and Mum meet, cue the fireworks.

'Fanny couldn't make it,' said Robbo but there's someone I'd like you to meet.' He beckoned to a suited and shiny-shoed gent. 'Detective Senior Constable Joanna Best meet retired Chief Commissioner Lewis Hayward.'

Jo flushed. Her tights became tighter. She shook hands with her grandfather's friend wondering if he had even the remotest idea she'd been investigating him with a view to blackening his name.

'Your grandfather has told me so much about your brilliant career, and I've read reports of your stunning case closures, I can't tell you how proud and pleased I am to meet you, Jo. May I call you Jo?'

She nodded. She might have said 'Yes sir,' but words failed her.

'Your latest cold case knocked me sideways. I worked on that case, I couldn't make head nor tail of it, and you come along and bingo, case solved. I dips me lid to you, Officer, you're a credit to your family and to the Force.'

Pop reckoned the solemn occasion needed a little less excitement and gently steered his friend back to the coffee.

'I'm delighted to meet you, sir,' she said as the retirees departed with Pop turning back to deliver his famous wink.

Jo's emotions went on strike.

As attendees moved away, the last people to say goodbye were certain members of the Homicide Squad. If anyone knew Pierre Richelieu it was his former colleagues. Billy Hughes and DI Rose embraced and congratulated her on her eulogy. Charley Baldwin did likewise whispering, 'For God's sake come back to work. The joint is dead without your wit and pomposity-pricking.'

She playfully squeezed his arm and the detectives left. DI Blunt was ordered to attend but refused. Having the bitch steal his latest case, despite the fact he discovered the wrong suspect, was the straw that broke the camel's back. He was the camel and got the hump.

Coming out of the small chapel, Michael Chan sidled up to her. 'Taxi when ready, madam.'

She nodded and as they walked to his car, she took his arm and found herself thinking about her new wealth, and "crazy" family, and the death of a wonderful, kind and loving Frenchman.

That night, Jo arrived at Michael's bearing food. She thought with Michael having reunited a daughter with a mother who cooked Chinese food, they should dine on a variety of scrumptious Asian dishes. Good choice and Alan was up for anything with chicken.

The news of Bradley's evil deeds was out and they discussed same. As they ate, Michael held back allowing Jo to run the show.

'You know I met the retired Chief Commissioner today?' He nodded. 'Twice I tried to tell my Pop about the case I've prepared and couldn't. Now I've met the man who will suffer terribly because of what I've done, how can I look my grandfather in the face ever again?'

'You don't have to.'

'My love and respect for Gabrielle is so strong I can't ...' She stopped mid-sentence. 'Say that again.'

'You don't have to. The appeal has been withdrawn.'

A pause and the silence lingered. 'Withdrawn? As in ... withdrawn?'

'I only found out an hour ago. I have a friend in the Supreme Court, an admin officer, and he called to say the legal firm working for Annie Cleary withdrew their application for leave to appeal this afternoon.'

Jo didn't know whether to laugh or cry. 'But I haven't shown my case to anyone, not even you. Why would they withdraw?' He worked his chopsticks with ease. 'You did something, Michael Chan. Tell me. What did you do?'

'You're not angry with me I hope?'

'Angry? Apart from letting me slave away for weeks to produce a case which is useless, you've saved Gabrielle from shame and me from probably killing my Pop. But no, I'm not angry just bloody curious.'

He told her.

Using Gabrielle's intelligence on the two men who signed affidavits claiming she was drunk on duty, he created situations where both men were offered little choice; withdraw or suffer.

For the mortuary attendant with gambling debts, Michael arranged for him to receive emailed threats from leg-breaking hoons who hated

Annie. 'Do anything to help her out of jail and your debt-collecting chums will take payment in the form of limbs; yours.'

The mortuary attendant withdrew his affidavit. One down.

The embittered pathologist received what looked like official emails from a shadowy organization, *Fighting Injustice*. The pathologist was warned in explicit terms that should he persist in his attempt to have the evil Annie Cleary released, horrific child abuse photos might mysteriously find their way onto the pathologist's home and work computers. The pathologist withdrew his affidavit. Two down.

Annie's legal team exploded. 'They've *both* withdrawn their affidavits?' raged the senior partner. '*Both* of them?' His colleague nodded. 'They've been nobbled. Can we get them back?' His colleague shook his head. He'd seen the fear in their eyes. 'So what the hell do we tell Annie?' When they did, they stood well back. Annie capitulated.

Having discovered Michael's masterpiece, Jo raised her glass. 'To Michael Chan, the IT genius and all-round nice guy,' she said.

He responded and raised his glass. 'To Joanna Best, the best.'

Her phone buzzed, she apologised and moved away to take the call. Two minutes later she returned. 'That was a certain pathologist. She wants to give you a humungous kiss and something else involving chocolate but you being a nice boy, I won't go into details.'

They clinked glasses and fell silent. Both had used their extraordinary skills and logical thinking to solve a cold case, reunite a family, and save a friend from an unjust and cruel punishment.

Michael had been thinking a lot of late about his relationship with Jo. He knew he held the title of Mr Unrequited Love and wondered with Pierre's passing, if life might change in that sphere. It didn't.

Then came their sleuthing partnership; a triumph. Neither could have achieved their success working alone; at least not without great difficulty. No, they were the platonic dream team.

'Can I ask a question?' he said.

'Sure,' she replied thinking this would not be about the weather.

'Are you going back to Homicide?'

'Not sure. If Pierre hadn't died, we would have married and might have started a family. Now he's gone and left me with his great whacking estate. As Steve Jobs said, "Sometimes life is going to hit you in the head with a brick".'

Michael gawped. 'Becoming a millionaire is like getting bashed?'

'You know what I mean.'

'No I don't and you haven't answered my question.'

'Who knows? Seriously Michael, I honestly don't know.' He believed her. 'So what's next for you?'

'Me? Well I don't have a career in a company or a pot of gold on my doorstep.' They were being frank and earnest.

'But you're planning something, Michael Chan. You're hopeless at keeping secrets.'

'Not true; you didn't know I stitched up Annie Cleary.'

He's right, I didn't. 'But there's something else. Come on, spill the beans, I won't tell; promise.' He hesitated and as a result built the tension. She worried. 'Oh God, it's not illegal is it?'

'Well if you're not going back to Homicide, my career as second banana to the top cop is Red Rover.'

'But?'

'But helping Cathy find her mother was … satisfying.'

Jo's stomach became tense. 'And?'

He worried she would laugh. 'I've decided to buy a business.'

She made a face of "That's interesting". 'Great, I'm impressed.' He paused, annoying Jo. 'Oh Michael, cut the unfinished story routine.'

'It's a private investigator business.' Jo's mouth opened. He pointed at her. 'It's rude to eat with your mouth open.'

'Is this an up and running business?'

'No, like the dead parrot, it has expired.'

She gasped. 'Not that whacky woman you took me to meet?'

He defended his purchase. 'Starlight Freeman has a list of contacts to get me started. I'll work from home so my running expenses will be minimal. I'll put up a classy web site and use the sleuthing skills I learnt from a certain Detective Senior Constable.'

Jo hesitated. She wondered if he knew what he was doing. She wondered if a tinge of jealousy pinged in her brain.

He's taken my skills and set up on his own—the cheeky sod.

'Well I admire your guts, Michael. The world needs entrepreneurs.'

'Thanks and can I say I'm on the lookout for a bit of venture capital? That's in case you know anyone with a lazy 25k.'

He knocked her sideways. *He's asking me for money.*

'I'm after a silent partner to invest in my modest operation and, of course, to share in my modest rewards.'

He is asking me for money. 'Don't undersell yourself, Michael.'

Out popped his half smile. 'You wouldn't have to be silent of course. For an equal investment you could be a full partner.'

'You bastard. You've been planning this for ages.'

'What, buying the business or offering you the opportunity of a lifetime?'

'I've discovered the secret side of Michael Chan.'

He shrugged. 'Think about it. You can pick and choose your cases. You can be full or part-time. You can sell your share if you're bored, and best of all, you can be a detective without having to work with jealous and dopey colleagues.'

'Just a jealous and dopey colleague like you.'

Jo was seriously thinking about his offer but finding it hard to say so. Then the clever man struck gold with his winning pitch.

'I'm going to ask Dr Strange if she'll be the Chief Medical Officer.'

That was the clincher. Was it ever? Having Gabrielle involved was a brilliant idea. Both Jo and Michael were now suffering rapid heartbeats. He desperately wanted her on board. She found herself loving the idea.

'I'd like to give you first refusal, Officer.'

Jo laughed. 'Oh, like you have a long line of budding investors?'

'I've chosen a name. *Chan and Best—Private Investigators.*'

She laughed. 'No way, it has to be alphabetical—*Best and Chan.*'

'It's my idea, I thought of it.'

'Okay, I'll toss you for it. Tails I win, heads you lose.'

She stared at him and yes, he produced the cheeky Chan half grin. She smiled and asked. 'Do I get a PI badge?'

'Two,' he said and raised his glass. 'To us, the best PIs in town.'

She raised her glass and they toasted their new venture. 'To us.'

Bored to tears, Alan hopped down and went looking for another bed; anywhere to get away from those two over-excited humans.

Coming soon
The Best & Chan Mysteries

Sherlock Holmes – Playing the Game

The great man is soon to retire. On his last night at Baker Street, the loyal landlady drops a bombshell. Holmes is staggered. Mrs Hudson has done what!? Sherlock Holmes never panics—until now. Dr Watson arrives and is stunned. It's their greatest challenge. Sir Arthur Conan Doyle is furious. A famous author turned WW1 counter-intelligence spy is on the case. *The Strand Magazine* smells a scoop. Inspector Lestrade from Scotland Yard plans revenge, and at stake is the brilliant reputation of the world's most famous consulting detective. His only hope is to 'play the game'.

www.cenfoxbooks.com

'a delightfully imaginative pastiche' **Peter Blau BSI**
a complex, ingenious and deliciously funny story of intersecting realities, and the conclusion is entirely satisfactory. I love it!
Roger Johnson - The Sherlock Holmes Society of London